By the same author

Spencer Marlowe series:
Spencer's War: The First Journey

Co-author of:
Oh How We Rocked

THE HAWAIIAN INTERVENTION

KELVIN WHITE

Printed by:
Ingram Spark
https://www.ingramspark.com/

(PB) ISBN: 978-0-6489109-3-0
(EB) ISBN: 978-0-6489109-4-7

Interior design by: Red Room Editing
Cover design by: Red Room Editing

This book is dedicated to Jenny, my extraordinarily patient wife, who has painstakingly spent countless hours supporting me in this project.

CONTENTS

PROLOGUE	1
CHAPTER ONE	3
CHAPTER TWO	8
CHAPTER THREE	11
CHAPTER FOUR	24
CHAPTER FIVE	31
CHAPTER SIX	36
CHAPTER SEVEN	42
CHAPTER EIGHT	48
CHAPTER NINE	53
CHAPTER TEN	54
CHAPTER ELEVEN	64
CHAPTER TWELVE	69
CHAPTER THIRTEEN	73
CHAPTER FOURTEEN	78
CHAPTER FIFTEEN	80
CHAPTER SIXTEEN	85
CHAPTER SEVENTEEN	88

CHAPTER EIGHTEEN   96

CHAPTER NINETEEN   103

CHAPTER TWENTY   106

CHAPTER TWENTY-ONE   114

CHAPTER TWENTY-TWO   121

CHAPTER TWENTY-THREE   125

CHAPTER TWENTY-FOUR   128

CHAPTER TWENTY-FIVE   131

CHAPTER TWENTY-SIX   133

CHAPTER TWENTY-SEVEN   139

CHAPTER TWENTY-EIGHT   143

CHAPTER TWENTY-NINE   152

CHAPTER THIRTY   156

CHAPTER THIRTY-ONE   162

CHAPTER THIRTY-TWO   164

CHAPTER THIRTY-THREE   169

CHAPTER THIRTY-FOUR   171

CHAPTER THIRTY-FIVE   177

CHAPTER THIRTY-SIX   182

CHAPTER THIRTY-SEVEN   186

CHAPTER THIRTY-EIGHT   188

CHAPTER THIRTY-NINE   190

CHAPTER FORTY   193

CHAPTER FORTY-ONE   199

CHAPTER FORTY-TWO   209

CHAPTER FORTY-THREE   212

CHAPTER FORTY-FOUR   216

CHAPTER FORTY-FIVE   221

CHAPTER FORTY-SIX   228

CHAPTER FORTY-SEVEN   232

CHAPTER FORTY-EIGHT   242

CHAPTER FORTY-NINE   252

CHAPTER FIFTY   255

CHAPTER FIFTY-ONE   261

CHAPTER FIFTY-TWO   264

CHAPTER FIFTY-THREE   269

CHAPTER FIFTY-FOUR   272

CHAPTER FIFTY-FIVE   281

MANHATTAN STING

CHAPTER ONE   285

Lord Byron, *The Gladiator*, from the *Childe Harolde* cantos (1820)

PROLOGUE

The two adversaries warily circled each other, looking for an opening, an opportunity to inflict a disabling or fatal blow. There was no verbal interaction, just intense concentration, each combatant acutely aware his opponent was a skilled practitioner capable of delivering that lightning-strike blow that could instantly end a life.

A sudden foot sweep put the older man down. With a grunt he bounded to his feet and administered a front roundhouse kick, catching the younger man by surprise. The younger man grinned, apparently unaffected, and then displaying extraordinary agility, he immediately connected with a front kick. Doubling over in pain, the older man stepped backwards holding a hand to his stomach, gasping for breath.

The room the warriors faced each other in was cavernous, with a floor of wide polished teak boards, aged by time, and white-washed plaster walls that soared to meet a ceiling of carved timber beams. Along one side, ceiling-to-floor windows (made from the same aged teak as the floorboards) opened onto a courtyard garden, the ripples in the old glass panes distorting the view of the grounds and the distant snow-capped Mount Fuji.

The older man grunted as he hit the floor yet again. He rolled and leapt to his feet. His breath came in short, sharp bursts as he again confronted his adversary. Their duel continued. Slowly, the younger man's resilience and his ability to draw on untapped reserves became more evident. The older man was now breathing heavily, favouring one leg. It was a struggle to remain upright.

The contrast between the two men couldn't have been starker. The younger man was tall, with Mediterranean good looks, whereas the older man was of indeterminate age and of slight build, lean and muscled, with weathered skin, and the agility of a black-necked crane. It was clear by the younger man's intense concentration that even at this stage, his opponent was still a lethal force.

Suddenly the young man moved and his opponent was on the floor.

'*Hai!*' he yelled, raising his fist to inflict the death blow. Both knew this was the end of a contest that had lasted more than an hour.

The man drew back his fist.

The older man smiled. 'Spencer-*kun*, you now have the skills to move on to the final stage. Tomorrow morning you will rise at four o'clock and you will begin to learn what few know. You will learn how to focus your inner strength; the power of your mind. When properly focussed, you will be able to achieve extraordinary feats of strength and control. Tomorrow you will learn, *Kokoro*.'

CHAPTER ONE

KOKORO: THE POWER OF THE MIND UNLEASHED

Spencer Marlowe handed his passport and travel documents to the Japan Airlines attendant. She was momentarily taken aback when he queried the departure time in Japanese.

'Yes sir, your flight is on time. The business class lounge is—'

'Thank you, I know it well.'

He smiled and she blushed, realising she'd been staring at the tall, handsome *gaijin*.

Spencer descended the escalator into the Sakura business-class lounge. He breathed a sigh of relief as he loosened his tie and glanced at his gold and stainless-steel Rolex. He had just enough time for an espresso and a quick bite. He headed to a cafe and ordered *dorayaki*, the Japanese pancake stuffed with *anko*, the fragrant bean paste that was his favourite snack.

Returning to the business lounge, he settled back with his coffee and gazed around at the ultra-modern and rather bland lounge, with its blonde timber furniture and its sweeping views of the busy runway.

His ability to speak Japanese and his understanding of Japanese culture meant he was frequently in Japan on business.

He was now a partner in the Perth company Dynamic Marketing, and the business trips to Japan enabled him to take time out to visit his old sensei, Katashi. Spencer took another sip of his coffee. Katashi had been teaching him since his early teens. Spencer smiled at the memory of their first meeting. He'd been a thirteen-year-old accompanying his father, a newcomer to Japan and feeling out of place. His father had dragged him to the dojo. *Trust me son,* he'd said. *This will be the making of you.*

The discipline, meditation techniques, and inherent spirituality Spencer had absorbed through Katashi's tough, but patient training, had transformed him from the directionless teenager he'd been all those years ago, into a man of extraordinary strengths, with the ability to face challenges, physical and mental, with calmness and precision. The bond between them now was as strong and meaningful as the bond between father and son.

He'd been working in Japan now for months and was looking forward to meeting up with the love of his life, Michiyo, in Singapore. God, how he'd missed her.

They'd met a little over two years ago, when he'd been in Japan on one of his business trips. Their immediate and overwhelming attraction had culminated in Michiyo applying for a visa, moving to Western Australia, and moving into Spencer's rambling Mediterranean-style home in City Beach, a suburb of Perth. There was a tinge of sadness when he reflected that his father had died before Spencer had met Michiyo. *You would have adored her, old man.*

Spencer recalled the Latin phrase often quoted by his late father, a professor who'd specialised in dead languages: *hominus est in domun suam arce* (a man's home is his castle).

Spencer remembered fondly the cold winter nights in their old, cramped, suburban bungalow where his father had endeavoured to instil in him a love of literature and language.

It'd been so different from the spacious dwelling he and Michiyo now enjoyed.

Their home was a cross between Australian modern, traditional Mediterranean and a blend of Spanish, with its red terracotta roof and dark-coloured brick, and with natural stone detail around the broad windows and arches. It now included an eclectic blend of Japanese and European influence, a home both of them loved.

As a tribute to his late father, Spencer had commissioned a wrought iron relief with the words, *Patria est, ubi cor est* (Home is where the heart is). This message greeted visitors as they approached the front doors of the house.

He thought again of Michiyo. The two years she'd been living with him in Australia had been a time of learning and growth. She was intelligent, ambitious, with a mischievous sense of humour. The hard-nosed Japanese businessmen she dealt with in the Perth office of the Matsu Corporation quickly discovered Michiyo was no pushover.

This was the longest time they'd been apart since Michiyo had moved to Australia.

Their plan was to meet in Singapore and fly to Hawaii and the famed Royal Hawaiian Hotel on Waikiki. They'd organised an intimate celebrant wedding on a secluded Hawaiian beach, to be followed by a long, relaxed honeymoon afterwards.

Spencer reflected on this latest trip to Japan. It was the first since he'd been cast back in time to the early 1940s and found himself embroiled in the Second World War.

He'd given up hope of returning to his century, and to Michiyo, when he'd woken one morning to find himself back in his City Beach home. He'd been away for years but incredibly, he found he'd been gone only one night in his own time.

Michiyo had never been able to get her head around his story. As a consequence, it had become a source of tension between them, one they never talked about. At times, this left Spencer questioning his sanity, believing it was impossible to tell his story to doctors or psychiatrists.

A computerised voice interrupted his thoughts. Speaking first in Japanese, then in English, it announced his flight was boarding.

Twenty minutes later he gazed down at the glittering lights of the sprawling city of Tokyo lying thousands of feet below. A smiling attendant offered him a flute of French champagne. Spencer thanked her in Japanese and settled back into his seat. The flight to Singapore was a six-hour trip.

His body was still sore from his brutal Kokoro training, and Katashi's kick to his midriff had hurt more than he cared to admit. *It's been a month now and I'm still sore, but for an old guy you're still a bloody lethal weapon.*

Spencer opened his book, a novel written in Japanese and in his favourite genre, a fast-paced action thriller about the Japanese mafia, the Yakuza. Feeling restless he soon put the book down and flicked through the in-flight entertainment before checking out the rest of the cabin. The business-class section had the expected complement of smartly attired executives. There was also a young couple who were having a great deal of difficulty keeping their fondling within legal limits.

On the other side of his aisle, a young man with headphones frenetically beat time with his hands, to a thankfully silent, probably heavy metal band. His heavily tattooed arms and expensive designer, hardcore street-cred-attire, suggested he could be a rock star en-route to his next gig. Spencer smiled to himself. Tattooed man might well be famous, but he wouldn't know who he was.

After being drawn into the maelstrom of the wartime years of the 1940s, Spencer had become involved in operation

Do Not Answer, code-named DNA, a perilous mission into Japanese-occupied Singapore. When he returned to his own time, he'd discovered the big band music of that era. As a consequence, contemporary music no longer appealed to him. Louis Armstrong's cornet and Benny Goodman's clarinet moved him more than the electric guitars and synthesised music of his own time.

He wondered what exactly had sparked his interest in the music of the last century. Was it perhaps the same hand of fate that had chosen him for his time travel jaunt? As always when he started to dwell on his experiences, his mind travelled in circles.

He ultimately arrived at the same conclusion. There was nobody he could discuss it with. Michiyo, he suspected, had long reached the end of her tether regarding his 'episodes' as she labelled them. Exhausted from the past week and Katashi's exhausting training, Spencer drifted into a restless slumber. Dark disturbing images flitted through his subconscious, violent and bloody. He woke with a start.

'Excuse me sir,' said the flight attendant as she offered him a menu.

Since his time travel episodes, awakening suddenly from deep sleep was often a frightening experience. Always at the back of his mind he wondered—could it happen again?

CHAPTER TWO

REFLECTION

Spencer gratefully accepted the fragrant *buri daikon*, a simmered dish of wild yellowtail cooked with daikon radish, and matched with a glass of South African, Boschendale chardonnay.

But his mind strayed again to the past, the war, and the people he'd known. He remembered the volatile and psychopathic Albert Lambert, fearless to the point of lunacy, who'd possessed a deep and abiding hatred for the Japanese. Albert's brother George had died in Changi prison at the hands of his guards. As far as Albert was concerned the entire Japanese race were accountable. Then there was Don Bidstrup, ruthless and mysterious. Bidstrup had overseen operation DNA.

Spencer's thoughts slipped to the time he'd briefly been incarcerated in the brig at the Northam army camp. He vividly remembered the horror of seeing stencilled on the wall of his cell the words:

Wayne Kitchener
executed 18th December 1941

The reason for Kitchener's death sentence remained a mystery to Spencer. What crime had he committed and exactly what part had Bidstrup played in the affair? There was no doubt in Spencer's mind—Bidstrup had been instrumental in having Kitchener executed.

Spencer pulled himself out of the past. Instead, he concentrated on the previous week's events and his intense, even brutal induction into the little-known martial arts discipline, Kokoro. Once again, he was on the mountain with Katashi who'd guided him through the labyrinth of tortuous physical and mental assaults that culminated in what amounted to a revelation. He'd struggled up a mountainside with a wicker pannier filled with rocks slung across his back. The pain had felt like red hot daggers being thrust into his muscles. The only thing that kept him going was Katashi. Once he'd passed the pain threshold, he continued on, knowing he was achieving something mystical.

He remembered thinking with a wry grin of the quote: *if you think you can, or if you think you can't, you're probably right.*

Wearing nothing but a *fundoshi,* he'd stood for hours under a waterfall in the mountains with the pristine water pouring over him. The feeling of tranquillity and peace as the icy water thundered down, was like nothing he'd ever experienced. Katashi's method was a little of the carrot and stick. First the unimaginable pain of clambering up the mountain, followed by the relief of the waterfall … then the experience was repeated … again … and again.

The days he'd spent under Katashi's watchful tutelage seemed like years. Another life within a life. The training had driven every thought and emotion from his mind, leaving a blank canvas for Katashi to imprint indelibly on Spencer's subconscious. The opening of the mind that Katashi had relentlessly pushed and prodded him towards—until Spencer had literally and figuratively seen the light—the power of Kokoro.

Spencer contemplated the extraordinary power the mind was

capable of developing and then bringing to bear. The physical strength of the Kokoro philosophy that had been bestowed upon him would forever be a part of him.

In his final test, Katashi had handed Spencer a brick, weathered and hardened by centuries of summer heat. 'Take it between your thumb and four fingers and crush it as you would an over-ripe fruit,' he'd commanded.

Spencer had taken the brick, focussing the way he had learned, driving every other thought and emotion from his mind.

'I'm holding a piece of rotten fruit; I'm holding a piece of rotten fruit,' he'd repeated to himself. It was if his soul had left his body. It wasn't a trance-like state, it was as if some power of the universe was transmitted to his hand. The pressure he'd applied could best be described, as an irresistible force.

Crunch! The brick, rough-cast by a long dead artisan, aged by the wind and sun of centuries past, disintegrated into a pile of dust.

Spencer and Katashi had stood in silence. Finally, Katashi had spoken, quiet and unemotional as always. 'Spencer-*kun*, always use the power of Kokoro for good.'

CHAPTER THREE

SINGAPORE

Spencer arrived at Changi Airport an hour before Michiyo's flight from Perth was due. It was early morning in Singapore, but at Changi the all-consuming pace of business never stopped, day or night.

Seven am and it's already going full pelt. He collected his bags and waited impatiently in arrivals. *Thanks, Michiyo for organising the early check in.*

Checking his watch for the umpteenth time and winding it back an hour, Spencer paced past one of the many duty-free outlets.

'At last!' he said, as Michiyo burst through the arrival doors and waved to him.

She threw herself into his arms. 'I've missed you so much, I've been counting the minutes.'

Spencer held her tight, laughing. 'Hi gorgeous. This's going to be amazing. It's so good to see you—you look fantastic.'

After collecting her bags, they trundled through the impressive airport. Changi was a city within a city. The rhythmic beat of the airport that never slept was invigorating. Spencer was still fascinated by the hustle and bustle of thousands of people of all nationalities, wandering around or shopping to kill time, or waiting for flights to spirit them to all corners of the globe.

With their luggage in tow, they exited the terminal, immediately the humidity hit them like a physical blow. They made for a taxi at the head of the line, an immaculate white Chrysler 300 C.

Spencer stood momentarily as if in a trance. *My God, this is Singapore. What if I'm summoned back again? To confront Harada.*

He really had to get over things. This was Singapore now, not in the past. Harada was dead. Good God! They were probably all dead—everyone he'd known during the war.

Michiyo grabbed him by the arm and shook him. 'Spencer, are you ok?' she frowned, her face showing only care, tinged with the worry of their secret. The secret neither could share with the rest of the world.

Spencer snapped out of his thoughts and with a rueful chuckle, apologised. 'Sorry, I just had a moment of déjà vu, but I'm over it now.'

'Really … are you sure? It never really leaves you, does it?' Michiyo's brow puckered. Her concern over Spencer's dreams once again bubbling to the surface.

Spencer held her hand, squeezing it to reassure her everything was ok. Forcing himself to shut out the demons, that threatened to overwhelm him, he bent and kissed her lightly on the lips.

'You bet I'm fine. Never been better.' He grimaced, feeling like an old war veteran with pieces of shrapnel still lodged in his body. Only Spencer's shrapnel were the memories of the death and destruction he'd witnessed and the way that fate could, for no apparent reason, just throw him back to another century. He shuddered.

The smiling driver had placed their bags into the boot. With a bow he opened the rear passenger door, waving a white gloved hand at the interior of the spotless vehicle.

'Where to sir?'

Spencer turned to Michiyo and shrugged.

'The Raffles, where else! Excuse me driver, would you take us on a scenic route. We want to see the sights. There's no hurry.'

Michiyo hadn't been to Singapore before. They spent the journey to the Raffles Hotel wondering at the modern metropolis Singapore had evolved into. It was not as big and bustling as Tokyo, but nevertheless it was spectacular. People flowed like rivers: the crowds had a life of their own, moving like shoals of enchanted fish. On each side of the wide boulevards, gracious buildings towered.

They drove past the spectacular Marina Bay, along the famous shopping street Orchard Road, then through the Indian section of Serangoon Road. Spencer was silent as they drove down this busy road, which he and the other saboteurs had crept down when he was involved in operation DNA. Back then it had been dark and sinister, surrounded by bombed-out ruins.

His gut wrenched as he remembered the terror that had consumed him when the Japanese truck convoy had passed and they had hidden, not knowing if the brutal enemy would discover them. He remembered the beautiful Trilby Lim, and the fear she had overcome to see the mission through. His greatest fear had been getting killed in action in a foreign land and time and never seeing Michiyo again. Perhaps this particular journey down memory lane hadn't been such a good idea.

Beside him, Michiyo was taking in the sights. She linked her arm through his, her fears cast aside.

'I'm sorry we've so little time here,' she said.

'We're only five hours from Perth. We'll come again.'

Spencer had been feeling a little uneasy about this journey back to the scene of his wartime adventure, but Michiyo's enthusiasm dispelled his maudlin thoughts.

'Thanks for bringing me to see it all.' She turned to Spencer, taking his hand. 'Are you ok darling, you look like you've seen a ghost?'

Spencer was reluctant to talk about his experiences. 'I'm fine, really … Driver would you mind taking us on to the Raffles now?'

Michiyo frowned. 'I know that I've difficulty understanding all you say you went through … and try as I might it just seems …' she squeezed his hand harder, 'I feel at times like I'm a five-year-old trying to understand Einstein's theory of relativity. I know how real it all is for you. And when you told me you met Colonel Harada, the spitting image of … God, I'm not going to mention that bastard's name again. And also, I've heard you cry out during your nightmares, when you've called out, "Trilby". In fact …' she looked searchingly at Spencer, 'I wonder, perhaps … should I be jealous?'

Before he could answer Michiyo laughed. 'I actually worry you might have had an affair with someone seventy-five years ago. Then I start to wonder if I'm going mad. You were only gone one night. In fact, as far as I'm concerned, you were never actually gone at all.'

Spencer tried to think of a suitable response, but he could think of nothing to add since he had in fact been thinking of Trilby. He'd also been dwelling upon all sorts of *what if* scenarios. What if he'd not been catapulted back to Michiyo in the next century? What if he'd remained in that time? Would he have travelled back to Singapore after the war ended to be with Trilby?

Frowning, he wondered ruefully whether this equated to being unfaithful to Michiyo. There couldn't be many precedents like his to come up with the answers he was looking for. *I don't think I've come across any time travellers with tips for beginners.*

He put his arm around Michiyo, giving her a reassuring kiss.

'Michiyo, from the first moment I saw you, I knew you would be the only woman in my life.'

The Chrysler pulled up outside the stunning three-story colonial masterpiece that was The Raffles. It wasn't as Spencer remembered it from operation DNA, however, the ambience and old-world charm of the hotel remained.

Once again that clammy feeling of dread descended on him like a thousand-pound weight squashing the breath out of him. Spencer was angry with himself. He saw these emotions as weakness; unwanted thoughts and memories he simply had to dispel.

A Sikh doorman, clad in a scarlet three-quarter length coat and turban, opened the door of their taxi with a flourish. A white-suited bellboy rushed to grab their luggage.

The newly renovated Raffles had been artfully rebuilt, capturing brilliantly the 1920's feel. The bed in their room was a massive four poster. Michiyo gasped when she entered the bathroom with its free-standing old-world bath, carved mahogany cabinets, stunning white marble walls, and delicately patterned black and white floor tiles.

'Oh Spencer, this is truly exquisite. Do you realise this'll be the first *proper* holiday we've had together?' She examined the luxury toiletries. 'This is just perfect. They think of everything.' Her eyes shone with pleasure.

Spencer swept her into his arms. 'I really need a shower,' he whispered, nuzzling her neck. 'And,' he added solemnly, 'did you realise Singapore has a water shortage?'

Michiyo was momentarily puzzled. 'A water shortage?' she laughed. 'So, in the interest of conservation we need to share a shower?'

'Absolutely.'

Emotion and desire threatened to destroy the delicately patterned shower screen. Their passion continued as Spencer swept Michiyo into his arms, carrying her into the bedroom. Their wet bodies tangled in the fine Egyptian cotton sheets. The past and his nightmares forgotten as they exhausted their passion. They lay in each other's arms, heedless of time.

'That was wonderful. You're wonderful.' Spencer laughed quietly

Eventually he glanced at his watch. 'I know it's a bit early, not quite lunch time, but hell, we're on holiday. It's time I introduced you to the famous Singapore Sling.'

They left their unpacked bags and headed downstairs to the hotel's, Long Bar. Spencer observed that it was certainly different from when he'd seen it last, when he'd met up with Harada and his officers and been confronted by the drunken Chilean arms dealer, Senor Cortez.

He shivered with the recollection that he'd been expected to converse in Spanish with Cortez. Luckily, Cortez had risen clumsily to his feet and immediately fallen back into his chair. He'd brought up his dinner, the vomit pooling around him. Cortez had instantly passed out, rescuing Spencer from exposure. Although at the time he'd been terrified, he now looked back at the incident and saw the humour.

Spencer motioned to the bartender. 'Two Singapore Slings, please.'

They sat perched on high stools at the bar. Michiyo took an exploratory sip of her cocktail, raising her glass in a toast.

'Here's to us—and to me not being at work.'

Michiyo's job was high pressure. Her Japanese employers were generous, but demanding. She had a high-powered job at the Perth branch of the Japanese corporation Matsu. Using her bi-lingual skills she was at the forefront of negotiations between hard-headed Japanese businessmen and equally ruthless Australian corporate high flyers.

Michiyo glanced at a couple of earnest looking Japanese

businessmen sitting at the bar who appeared to be going over some paperwork.

'Since I've moved to Australia, I've completely changed my outlook.'

'How so?'

'In Japan I was just a woman and … and I believed it.' Tears momentarily welled up in her eyes. 'When I think of my old boss Harada and what he did … just give me a few minutes. Please excuse me.' Michiyo put down her glass and headed to the ladies' room. Spencer watched her retreating figure with dismay.

Spencer had told Michiyo of his encounter with Colonel Harada in wartime Singapore. Michiyo had problems believing his tale, but when he told her the colonel was a doppelganger of her old boss, it just seemed this was simply a bridge too far. He remembered feeling foolish as he poured out his extraordinary tale.

After a few minutes a sombre Michiyo returned. She climbed back onto her stool.

'I'm okay. The thing is I'm never … comfortable talking about your … your … God, what do we call it? Your journey? I guess that's a good enough description. When you returned and you poured out that incredible story and how you met Harada's grandfather. Honestly, I just didn't know what to think. Anyway, it's all in the past.'

Michiyo laughed out loud. 'It's really in the past, isn't it? So, let … us … move on. No more about bloody Harada. Now I deal with guys like him on a daily basis. Initially I know they're thinking, "Ah a woman, I'll sort her out". Michiyo laughed holding her hand to her mouth in the Japanese manner. 'Now I know how to deal with them. They very quickly get the message this lady ain't no pushover.'

It was Spencer's turn to laugh. 'Ain't … ain't? You're really getting the hang of Australianisms, aren't you?'

'Well, I've had a good teacher, haven't I? Anyway, that's enough of bloody business.'

'Bloody?' Spencer echoed. 'There you go again.'

Michiyo put her hand firmly over his mouth. 'Spencer,' she said, 'we're going to have a glorious, carefree holiday and a beautiful, romantic wedding.'

As they sipped their Singapore slings, they helped themselves to the peanuts, throwing the shells on the floor in the time-honoured custom. Although the room was subtly different, the colonial era had been retained successfully, with its wood panelled ceiling, complete with ceiling fans, which Spencer considered were probably just for effect, as the unobtrusive air-conditioning guaranteed a perfect temperature. The rattan chairs were a nice touch, along with the oval, patterned floor tiles that could've been from any era.

Spencer's gaze fell on the full-length mirror with the clock centrepiece that'd been carefully relocated from the old building. He remembered when he'd gone back in time to 1942 and had raised a glass, toasting himself in that very same mirror. He shook his head, as other memories returned.

Spencer thought the male bar staff with their old-fashioned trousers, braces and aprons, didn't look at all like the original staff clad in black and white with bow ties. But overall, the past had been captured beautifully.

They spent some time exploring. The day seemed to be flying by. Since arriving on their early incoming flight, they'd already seen a lot of mainland Singapore. Lunching at Clarke Quay was a welcome and calming respite. The eclectic blend of Asian and other cuisines presented them with myriad choices.

Michiyo dabbed her lips with a serviette. 'That has to be the best chilli crab ever.'

Hunger satiated, they sat, relaxed and replete at a table

overlooking the Singapore River. Time lost any meaning as they watched the colourful bumboats wending their way up the waterway, looking like toy ships from an Enid Blyton children's novel.

As they discussed their plans for the afternoon, Michiyo took hold of Spencer's hand. 'Lunch was a delight, and now we are going shopping—together,' she added, a hint of steel in her voice.

Spencer gazed fondly at the beautiful Japanese lady before him. With her glamorous black suede baker boy hat set at a jaunty angle, cream silk shirt and black Capri pants, she looked the picture of casual elegance. The alluring subtlety of her French perfume gently teased his senses. With tenderness and a hint of a sly smile, Spencer took Michiyo's hands in his. 'Actually, I'd sooner endure a root canal without the benefit of anaesthetic.'

'What are you going to do?' Michiyo chuckled.

Spencer held up a slew of coloured pamphlets listing some Singaporean attractions. 'There's a photo exhibition at the Natural History Museum, and I'm keen to go.'

Glancing at the brochures he pointed out what had appealed to him. 'There's a photographic history of their late Prime Minister, Lee Kuan Yew.'

Spencer hesitated. 'All of that … stuff … I know is difficult for you but I feel really drawn to—well—everything to do with Singapore and Lee Kuan Yew. And I just feel that I need to see it.'

Spencer had told Michiyo of his meeting with Lee Kuan Yew in wartime Singapore.

Lee, known in those early days as Harry, had left an indelible impression on Spencer. His courage and his implacable vision for the future had been inspiring. Spencer's biggest regret was not being able to share this experience with anyone. Mention of his wartime adventure always resulted in an uncomfortable silence, because no matter how hard she tried, Michiyo simply couldn't reconcile the reminders of Spencer's adventure with the reality of twenty first century living.

Michiyo rubbed her brow. 'Spencer,' she said hesitantly, 'I know this is still tearing you apart. Why don't you just let it go? I know it's still affecting you, but it can't be helping … can it? Be honest! Is this why we met up in Singapore? What do you hope to find? What answers are you seeking?'

Spencer was momentarily lost for words. 'Michiyo, I don't know the answer. Can you please just accept that it's important to me. I'm sure this'll be … the finish. I'll check out the exhibition. We'll meet up later and as they say; Robert's your relative.'

Michiyo looked perplexed. 'What the hell has someone called Robert got to do with this?'

'Gotcha. It's an old saying—Bob's your uncle—meaning everything is ok,' Spencer chuckled.

'Just when I think I know all there is to know, you throw a winding ball,' Michiyo sighed.

Spencer couldn't help himself, he chuckled again. 'Actually dear, that's a curved ball.'

Michiyo playfully smacked his arm and with a smile. 'Ok you, bugger off to your silly exhibition then.'

They agreed to meet at the exhibition after Michiyo had exhausted all that Singapore had to offer in ladies' finery.

'I really don't know where to start. There are so many department stores, so many boutiques, really, it's … dazzling. I think that's the word. Perth is a lovely city but we've nothing like this. My problem is knowing where to begin. I know Tokyo like the back of my hand, but Singapore has a totally different feel, but I'll get the hang of it.'

'Take a taxi to Orchard Road. Start at one end and keep

going, that'll keep you occupied for the rest of the day,' Spencer said with a hint of a smile.

Michiyo squeezed his hand and spying a taxi slowly cruising past, she swept towards it.

'See you at the exhibition—after I've bought something exquisite to wear tonight.' Her mind seemed to be firmly focussed on her exploration of the wonders of Singapore.

Spencer remained for a few minutes soaking up the sounds, the sights and the piquant odours of the culinary delights forever tempting the tourist.

He had disembarked from the Chilean tramp steamer, the *Valdivia* on his way to see the sadistic Colonel Harada. His brief journey on the tramp steamer with its exuberant Captain Rodriguez was one of his fondest memories: the lively wardroom with the freely flowing Chilean wine, plates piled high with South American delicacies, and the pungent smell of Cuban cigars.

The Singapore of today, a city raised from the ashes of war, was truly a miracle, he reflected soberly.

It wasn't often Spencer allowed himself to dwell on his fantastic mission. Knowing he could never really confide in anyone made him force the memories to the back of his mind. Being in Singapore again, the memories were rising unbidden into his consciousness.

He thought of mission DNA. He thought of his comrades, Albert Lambert, Sam Willard and Irwin Lenane, Lee Kuan Yew, the driver Zhang Yong, Tommy Chan the waiter, the unfortunate Barney Yap, with his mouthful of glistening gold dental work, who'd been cut to pieces by machine-gun fire. Barney's canoe had been captured in the searchlight of the Patrol boat. Rather than fall into the hands of the Japanese he'd paddled away, an easy target for the deadly tracer rounds that'd ripped Barney and his frail canoe to shreds.

He remembered with absolute clarity the stealthy walk through the bomb-shattered streets of a defeated Singapore.

Trilby Lim had introduced him to the future prime minister, a youthful Lee Kuan Yew. Spencer winced at the memory of Trilby and Harry (Lee) discussing whether he was to be executed.

There remained a twinge of guilt when he remembered Trilby with her elfin beauty and her ability to overcome her fear, to play her part in the dangerous mission. Spencer had realised that being embroiled in war and danger had the effect of speeding up emotional responses. He recalled the moment their eyes had locked as they travelled in the lorry on their way to carry out the operation. They'd both implicitly known this could be the start of a love affair.

The feeling of terror returned as he dwelt on his near-death experience when the patrol boat had him in its powerful searchlights. He'd sat motionless in his canoe just waiting for the inevitable hail of machine gun bullets. Miraculously, the patrol boat had simply moved on. Spencer had sat his fear rendering him unable to move for what had seemed an eternity.

Spencer had read up on the career of Lee Kuan Yew, thinking sadly if things had been different, he could have visited him in the later years of his life. What would he have said?

Hey Harry, remember me, Spencer Marlowe? Yep, I don't look any older cos I'm a time traveller.

Spencer was proud of his contribution to Singapore's future, but in his mind, Lee Kuan Yew was the true hero, steering Singapore from British Colony to successful democracy, giving generations of people a peaceful and prosperous environment.

All of these thoughts cascaded unbidden through his mind. A kaleidoscope of faces, visions of destroyed ships, and the faithful Taipan that had transported his now long dead comrades.

Forcing a smile, he pushed them away. Life was for today and he was about to marry the love of his life.

One of the Comfort Delgro Hyundai Taxis was cruising slowly past the table. Spencer waved a hand, the obliging vehicle glided to a halt.

'Where to sir?'

CHAPTER FOUR

CONFRONTING THE PAST

Spencer faltered outside the museum, uncertain, knowing the past was in there waiting to be confronted. He paced up and down at the front of the building, his hands shaking, mentally chastising himself for allowing the past to fill him with this feeling of dread.

Spencer stepped nervously into the exhibition building and up to the counter, handing over ten Singapore dollars. 'One ticket, please.'

When he'd had a meal at the Raffles all those years ago, he'd paid with Japanese occupation currency. The past kept on resurrecting itself.

Spencer had a flash of déjà vu. He shuddered. *For God's sake move on, nothing can happen here.*

Spencer stood in awe at the impressive glass atrium housing the exhibition. Spacious, modern, and air-conditioned, the grand exhibition building helped to allay Spencer's unease.

School children, immaculately uniformed in blue shorts and blindingly white shirts, were being escorted by their teachers. Spencer smiled at the sight of the obedient children hanging on every word of their diligent instructors.

There were groups of service men and women who appeared keenly interested in the displays. Spencer recognised

British, Australian, and New Zealand uniforms. *I wonder Harry, if even you could have imagined just what Singapore would become?*

Spencer strolled from exhibit to exhibit: Lee Kuan Yew's barrister wig, the Rolex watch presented to him by grateful clients and so many other artifacts from this extraordinary man's long life. Spencer glanced at his own Rolex. The timepiece hadn't accompanied him on his journey to the past. He paused by a large black and white photo. It was stark and graphic, showing every detail of the stricken Japanese ships destroyed in operation DNA. The blown-up photo was mesmerising.

Spencer chuckled at the memory of how the operation came to be known as DNA. Spencer had carelessly mentioned the acronym forgetting DNA hadn't then been discovered. When he hastily said to their commanding officer Don Bidstrup that DNA was short for, *If captured Do Not Answer.* Bidstrup had seized on that, deciding to name the mission, Operation DNA.

The next exhibit, a life-size colour photo of Colonel Harada in dress uniform astride a white stallion, stopped him in his tracks. Standing close, Spencer examined every detail of the photo—the man who'd filled him with such gut-wrenching fear. His initial meeting with Harada had been the most dangerous part of his mission. If Harada hadn't believed his cover story, Spencer's end would have been bloody.

'This man was a butcher,' whispered an elderly Chinese woman standing next to him.

Spencer turned to the lady. She held a silver-handled cane firmly in her hand. He smiled politely. The woman gasped, dropping her cane. Holding her hands to her chest, the colour drained from her face. *'Spencer?* Is it really you? This isn't happening … it can't be happening.'

Alarmed, Spencer sprang to the lady's aid. Noticing a chair

standing against the wall, he guided her to it.

'Can I get you anything … some water? Do you need a doctor?'

The lady stared intently at Spencer. 'Who are you?'

'I'm sorry,' Spencer replied quietly, 'have we met?'

Her breathing was laboured. Her face was deathly pale, her eyes tightly shut as she muttered something in Mandarin, and then kissed a silver cross attached to a delicate chain around her painfully thin neck.

'Have we met? 'Spencer repeated, kneeling beside the woman's chair. He now suspected he knew who she was.

She was dressed expensively, in a tasteful fuchsia floral tie-back dress, court shoes, a Chopard watch, a diamond necklace and earrings that were subtle but clearly upmarket.

Retrieving an old-fashioned pair of pince-nez hanging around her neck and peering carefully at him, she hesitatingly, reached out, touching Spencer's face. 'It is you, it … really is you. Oh God! This can't be real, am I going mad?'

A multitude of emotions engulfed Spencer as he realised this was Trilby Lim, whom he'd known in 1942. Spencer took her other hand gently in his. 'I think you're confusing me with my grandfather. We never met, but I'm told we look alike.'

His mind flashed back to when they'd first met. Trilby had whacked him over the head and had seriously contemplated executing him as a spy. Although in the whole scheme of things their time together had been brief, there had been an unspoken understanding between them that, if circumstances had been different, they would have been romantically involved.

Spencer had seen similarities between Trilby and Michiyo. Spencer had a twinge of guilt remembering just how attracted he was to this intense beautiful and brave woman. Although her face was now aged, her fine features remained and her eyes displayed an intelligence undimmed by time.

'Of course, of course! It couldn't be the Spencer I knew. He would be well into his nineties. What's your name, Spencer's grandson?' she asked.

Spencer felt tears coming to his eyes. If circumstances had been different, Trilby could have been his wife. There was an immense sadness knowing that Trilby had lived her life without him, that she'd not known who he really was, and why exactly there never was the possibility of a relationship.

More than anything in the world he wanted to embrace Trilby and tell her everything. He reached out and was about to speak. His breath came in sharp bursts as he realised the futility of an explanation.

'My name is Spencer. I was named after my grandfather. What is your name?' he asked, knowing full well the answer.

'Trilby Lim,' she replied. 'I knew your grandfather during the war. Please tell me what became of him?'

Spencer hesitated. 'He disappeared after the war.' Spencer figured that was fairly close to the truth.

'I was more than a little in love with him,' she murmured wistfully. 'I thought perhaps he might have come back to Singapore after the war … but … Sadly, it was not to be.'

Trilby gazed at Spencer. 'What became of him?' she asked again.

'He disappeared without a trace after the war. It was quite a mystery,' Spencer replied, reflecting that at least that was true.

Trilby fished through her handbag. 'There is something I must show you.' She produced the silver cornicello, a good luck charm given to Spencer by the soldier he'd rescued from the clutches of Tiny Lewis the homophobic bully, at the Northam army camp. Spencer had given it to a petrified Trilby as she was about to embark on her mission to place limpet mines on the Japanese ships.

'This was given to me by your grandfather during the war,

as a good luck charm. It has been with me every day for the past seventy-seven years.'

It was Spencer's turn to be shocked.

He stood, feeling numb as the memory washed over him, seeing once again the brave Chinese girl he'd known and fought beside during the war, with her inner strength and determination to wreak as much havoc as possible on the hated enemy.

Trilby too, was silent—as if lost in her own thoughts—or perhaps the past.

'Excuse me, Madam.' A young Chinese man, dressed in a chauffer's uniform made his way around a group of people. He was tall and slim, wearing black trousers, a white shirt and black tie embroidered discreetly with the motif "Chong Limousines: Singapore's Finest".

Trilby focussed on the young man. 'Thank you, Chen. I will be a few minutes.'

She took Spencer's hand in hers. 'I can't begin to tell you how happy I am to have met Spencer's grandson.

'The doctors tell me I don't have long for this world,' she added with a wan smile. 'However, I would be delighted if you could come to my home for tea. I could show you some memorabilia that I'm sure would interest you.' Her eyes lit up. 'There are some wonderful photos. Photos of people who were on the mission with your grandfather. I also have photos of Harry … Lee Kuan Yew … taken before the war, when he was a student in England. So many photos … so many things …' Her voice trailed off.

She reached out and touched Spencer's arm. 'Do you know?' she said proudly, 'I have been here every day of the exhibition. A lot of these mementoes are from my personal collection. It makes me so happy to see the young people in particular, taking such an interest.'

Spencer felt the sadness of not having known this wonderful woman as she carved out a successful life after the horrors of the war. The urge to pour out his story was difficult to contain. This was the hard bit, he thought with a trace of bitterness, not being able to reveal his story.

'Unfortunately, my fiancé and I fly out of Singapore tomorrow.'

Trilby reached out and touched his face again. A tear slid down her cheek as she placed the cornicello into Spencer's hand.

'I won't have any further use for my good luck charm. It would mean so much to me to know that you have it.' She nodded to Chen, who sprang forward to help her to her feet.

Holding the cornicello in his hand was an extraordinarily moving experience. Examining the talisman, he realised that, inconsequential as it was, it was the only tangible link with his journey into the past.

Trilby and Chen slowly exited the room, Spencer reached out. 'Wait!' he said, but his voice lost in the general hubbub. Trilby and Chen disappeared into the crowded throng. Then the bitter reality hit home. 'What's the bloody point. She'll just think I'm a lunatic.'

The *tap tap tap* of her cane echoed through the modern as tomorrow glass and steel atrium. A forlorn finale. All that lingered was the subtle aroma of lilies hanging in the air. He hoped the cornicello would be an effective good luck charm for him. *God knows, I might need it.*

A wave of melancholy washed over Spencer, realising they would never meet again. For a brief moment he was consumed by a desire to run after her and tell her his fantastic story. As always, the harsh reality of his situation hit home with a jolt.

Once again Spencer turned to the full-size photo of Colonel Harada. He remembered Harada loudly bragging to his subordinate officers when they were having drinks in the Raffles how he personally executed some Australian servicemen. *I'm so glad I played a part in your demise, you bastard!*

The *clack clack* of high heels resonated off the parquetry floor. Michiyo appeared, weighed down with shopping bags.

'Spencer! There you are. So many people. The shopping in Singapore is just wonderful. I hope you've enjoyed yourself. I certainly have.' She glanced around the pavilion. 'My God it's popular, isn't it? People everywhere. I thought I'd never find you.' Placing her purchases on the floor she planted a kiss on his cheek.

Spencer smiled in delight. Michiyo's zest for life always made his spirits soar.

'You haven't noticed my new dress.'

'I don't wish to cast a pall over your day, but you really should look at this photo.'

Michiyo peered intently at the life-size image. 'Oh my God, it's him!' her hand went to her mouth, her face paled 'Let's just get out of here, I really don't need to be reminded of Harada or his bloody ancestors.'

Their pace quickened as they stepped out of the exhibition with barely a glance at the historical artifacts. An uncomfortable silence fell upon them. She shuddered.

'Change of pace, change of mood, c'mon, something different. Enough of this bloody rubbish. I don't ever want to mention Harada or his relatives ever again. For God's sake this is Singapore.' She forced a smile. 'And now for something completely different.' She intertwined her arm into Spencer's. 'I know … let's go to Chinatown.'

Spencer snapped out of his reverie. 'Cool! let's see the sights.'

CHAPTER FIVE

THE SOOTHSAYER

Let me tell ye your fortune, dear lady, today
and I'll tell ye a fortune ye wouldn't gainsay.
I'll read ye a page from the big book of fate,
and I'll tel o' yer love, and I'll tell o' yer hate.
but first cross my palm with ten strokes o' a shilling,
and I'll tell where he lives, and his name, if ye're willing.

C B Langston, *The Fortune Teller*

Michiyo and Spencer jumped out of the cab as it pulled to a stop outside the towering dragon gate that guarded China Town, excited to see the drama of colour and sound that welcomed them. Vivid flashes of light from exploding fireworks galloped across the night sky and the acrid tang of gunpowder hung heavily in the air. Camera-wielding tourists mingled with the bustling Singaporean families. Children perched on their fathers' shoulders, excited, eyes wide at the spectacle.

'My God Spencer, they're a noisy lot,' Michiyo yelled, her voice just managing to carry over the cacophony of sound. She grinned as a dragon paused in front of them, with a roar that sounded strangely human.

With cymbals crashing, drums thumping, and banners

waving, the procession wound its way noisily and colourfully through the streets as the enthralled spectators cheered them on.

Around them, street vendors hawked their wares, calling out to passing revellers and onlookers. The flavours and odours of the foods were exotic and tempting; the enticing smells of curries and spices, ginger, garlic, soy and onion, lured spectators to sample the vendors' cuisines.

Spencer paused at the front of one stall where a grizzled old Chinese man was skilfully whipping up crispy pork pancakes. 'Just have a whiff? Awesome.'

'Later big boy,' said Michiyo grabbing his arm and dragging him forward, keen to explore all the sights and sounds.

The spectacle helped Spencer, if not forget the experience of the museum, at least to put it onto the backburner. Michiyo's enthusiasm was contagious. Excited as a child on Christmas morning, she absorbed every nuance of the colourful display. She grabbed Spencer's arm again and pointed. 'Look! I haven't been to a fortune teller for years.'

"Madame Zu – Fortune Teller to the Stars" boasted the sign on the window. Spencer and Michiyo stood at the front of the shop of the self-proclaimed soothsayer.

'Let's get our fortunes read,' said Michiyo.

'One hundred dollars Singapore,' said Spencer, perusing the pricelist. 'You're kidding?'

'Go on, live dangerously. You don't have to be a believer but sometimes these people have an uncanny knack of coming up with some intriguing stuff. And … I've got a good feeling about this one. Your trouble is you're just a sceptic.'

Hand in hand they entered the den of the palmist. Spencer was in equal measure amused and suspicious. Michiyo, turned, giving Spencer a quick thumbs up as she strolled into the welcoming enclave of the mystic, while Spencer waited in an antechamber rehearsing a good-natured barb for Michiyo's return. He cast a jaundiced eye over the waiting room.

Absolute mumbo jumbo, he thought with a smile. Perhaps he should ask her for next week's lotto numbers. But then again perhaps his cynicism was misplaced. Maybe he, of all people, should have a healthy respect for the supernatural.

After some minutes, Michiyo swished back into the antechamber flushed with excitement, quelling immediately the quip that Spencer had formulated. 'Madame Zu said we were going to have a baby girl! Isn't that wonderful? Spencer, you must go and have your fortune read.'

'I'm going, I'm going. But you're a hard act to follow. My God, babies? What can possibly trump that?'

Spencer stepped into the inner sanctum. Immediately serenity enveloped him like a return to the womb. Wordlessly, Spencer handed over the fee.

Madame Zu gave a gentle smile and took his hand, gazing in quiet contemplation at the lines. 'In your pocket … there is something of importance to you?'

'Do you mean this?' Spencer took out the cornicello.

Madame Zu smiled, holding out her hand. Spencer felt a vague stirring of unease as he handed it to her. Madame Zu examined it, running her fingers over it. She then handed it back to Spencer, an odd look on her face.

'It belongs to you, and yet … it has been … missing for some time?' Madame Zu peered warily at Spencer. Clearly for some reason her suspicions had been aroused. Her eyes narrowed, she once again peered closely at the cornicello.

'I … I just don't understand. It's not right.'

Spencer momentarily had the all too familiar feeling of dread and he noticed his hands were cold and clammy.

'Yes, it was given to a friend, some years ago, and has been returned to me.'

'Something isn't right; it's been gone for too long. What is it that I don't know?'

Spencer almost poured out the whole story, but then thought better of it. Instead, he shrugged, smiled and said nothing.

'What you have is a precious and very special good luck charm.' Madame Zu's head tilted. 'This is ... puzzling? It is yours?' Spencer shrugged and nodded.

Madame Zu continued to examine the cornicello.

'Its potency has been increasing for ... oh, this is impossible ...' She appeared distressed. 'Its potency has been steadily increasing for at least the last eighty years. Madame Zu peered at him. 'I know it's yours ... but it was given to you.'

She pursed her lips, holding the charm close and squinting as she examined it.

'This makes no sense. It was given to you over ... over eighty years ago, yet you are a young man.'

Spencer believed he was a good judge of character, and as Madame Zu peered intently at him, he was certain that this mysterious woman was a power for good and no charlatan. The feeling of calm that had initially descended on him when he'd entered was like nothing he had ever experienced. He was impatient for Madame Zu to tell him all.

Madame Zu gasped. She held his hand tighter, peering intently at his palm before looking deep into his eyes. After a long pause she spoke. 'You must leave quickly,' she said in a quavering voice. 'Please, don't ask questions.'

She thrust the money back into Spencer's hand, then stood and pulled back the curtains behind her, revealing a teak door covered in strange carvings. With a swirl of her purple and chartreuse robe, she exited the room.

Spencer remained in his chair, momentarily stunned at Madame Zu's obvious distress at what his palm and the cornicello had revealed. He paced slowly back to the antechamber, his face revealing his confusion to a concerned Michiyo.

'What on earth did Madame Zu say?' Michiyo whispered, taking his hand in hers.

Spencer saw no point in further alarming her. 'Nothing of interest, you know, the usual stuff,' Spencer responded, managing a tight smile.

His initial sense of calm had been replaced by a numbing feeling of despair and foreboding. His instincts told him Madame Zu had the gift of foretelling the future and she'd seen something that was either outside of her understanding, or was simply too frightening to divulge. Spencer's fingers touched the hard outline of the cornicello in his pocket. On the one hand, it was strangely comforting to have it once more in his possession, but on the other, what should he tell Michiyo? There were no options available to him and no one to confide in.

'Let's get out of here,' he said. 'We'll go to the Stamford Swissotel for an early dinner. They have a spectacular restaurant with stunning views. You'll just love it.'

CHAPTER SIX

HAWAII

Aloha

Aloha means farewell to thee
Aloha means goodbye.
It means until we meet again
Beneath a tropic sky.
Aloha means good morning
And always to be true,
But the best thing that aloha means,
Is I love you

(Author unknown)

He spent an uncomfortable night. The mattress was like sleeping on air and the whisper quiet air-conditioning should have guaranteed a restful night, but he was plagued by vivid dreams of his wartime trip to Singapore and operation DNA. And now, new dreams held prominence in his subconscious. Scary dreams.

He saw Madame Zu with fear in her eyes and the terrifying image of a huge white pointer shark, its massive jaws about to devour him. He woke in a cold sweat, breathing hard, and feeling like he was in a bathtub full of ice. Silently, he pushed back the bed covers and felt his way to the unfamiliar bathroom. The wooden shutters kept the room in near total darkness. Shutting the door, he groped for the light switch. He peered at his distraught features in the mirror. Spencer was not in any way a religious man, but he found himself beseeching a greater power, than even Madame Zu. He wished, as he had done a thousand times before, for someone he could talk to. Someone to confide in. Finally, in the early hours of the morning, Spencer drifted off into an exhausted sleep.

***

Reclining in the cab as it set off to the airport early the next morning, Spencer glanced back at the Raffles Hotel. Staying at Harada's old watering hole hadn't been a good idea. The building stirred up too many memories. He decided to dismiss Madame Zu and the troubling encounter.

Spencer was relieved as their seven o'clock Singapore Airlines flight took to the air. A weight lifted off him. The past was the past. He had seventeen hours flying time, each kilometre whisking him further away from his frightening memories.

They dozed, periodically, watched movies and relaxed. Spencer was finally at peace. *It's done, finished with. The past really is the past.*

'Spencer, just look at that!' said Michiyo.

The jet had banked and now they could see the city of Honolulu sprawled across the horizon. Spencer could make out Waikiki Beach and the solemn, silent sentinel of Diamond Head. Spencer set his watch to 1 pm. Perfect.

For a brief moment, as Spencer savoured the scene below him, the vision of a monstrous shark with its open jaws flashed through his mind.

As they entered Honolulu airport's arrival hall, a portly man stood smiling and brandishing a board displaying their names and a welcome message. They approached him.

'*Aloha*, Spencer Marlowe and Michiyo Tanaka,' he said in a booming voice that echoed through the terminal. He draped a lei of fresh flowers around their necks, the fragrance of the tuberose bloom drifting gently upwards, sweet and soothing.

Effortlessly grasping the luggage in his ham-like hands he ushered them into the gleaming black Cadillac Escalade. As the Escalade cruised noiselessly along the freeway Michiyo peppered the obliging driver with questions about Hawaiian customs and language. Makani was an unlimited font of information about sport, politics and, of course where the best shops and restaurants were.

'Tell me Makani, is the Hawaiian language in common usage, is it taught in schools?'

Makani informed them that 'Ōlelo Hawai'i was a second language elective.

'And please tell me Makani, is there a Japanese cultural centre in Honolulu?' asked Michiyo.

'Of course! It's in Beretania Street,' the encyclopaedic Makani immediately responded.

Their car glided to a halt outside the Royal Hawaiian Hotel.

'It says here, the hotel was built in 1927. In the Spanish Moorish style,' said Michiyo, reading from one of the glossy brochures displayed in the limo.

'It's pink!' said Spencer, staring out the window at the hotel's façade.

'Supposedly it was influenced by the Hollywood heartthrob, Rudolf Valentino,' added Michiyo as she looked up at Spencer.

'Fond of pink, was he?'

'Who?'

'Valentino.'

'Oh him? Never heard of him.'

Spencer smiled. He'd never heard of Valentino either, not until he'd time-travelled back to 1942.

Two bellboys rushed to their vehicle. They were dressed in colourful costumes from a bygone era.

'Check out their outfits,' Spencer whispered to Michiyo as they climbed out of the taxi.

Spencer asked the bellboy holding the car door about their uniforms.

'Yes sir, we're having a back to the 1940s themed month here at the Hawaiian,' said one.

'We've done the best we can to recreate the ambience, the menus and the decor of that era,' parroted the other.

Michiyo clasped Spencer's hand. The scent of frangipani and hibiscus hung in the air. The pleasant Hawaiian temperature was a welcome change from the oppressive humidity of Singapore.

The porter escorted them to their room which had nothing 1927 about it. A flat screen television dominated one wall. The bathroom was a celebration of white and chrome with tropical blooms in a vase on the vanity. The bedroom was breathtaking, featuring an opulent king size bed with decorative pillows and a ruby flax doona.

'Spencer, it's magnificent and just look at this,' said Michiyo drawing back the curtains. The view of Waikiki Beach through the picture window was spectacular.

The porter hastened to demonstrate the various remote controls and features and then smiled as he held one hand out for the customary tip.

It was early afternoon. Both Michiyo and Spencer were jetlagged after their long flight. Spencer was also affected by his insomnia. The dreams once again had become an intrusive issue.

'I'm for a quick snooze,' he announced.

Spencer and Michiyo lazed on their balcony taking in the majesty of the Pacific Ocean. The surfers were out in droves, several outriggers could be seen just beyond the breakers, and the grandeur of Diamond Head added its majesty to the scene before them.

'*Awesome!* Look at those colours—the blue of the sky, the green of the ocean—even the beach umbrellas. Have you ever seen colours so vivid?' Spencer remarked, as he put his arm around Michiyo.

Michiyo held his hand tightly, a troubled expression in her dark eyes. 'Spencer, the colours are beautiful, of course they are, but no, I wouldn't describe them as unusually vivid.'

In the days preceding Spencer's journey back in time, the colours of the world around him had taken on unnaturally vibrant hues.

Again, Spencer felt as if a cold hand had grasped his heart.

'Are you ok?'

'Yes, of course I am.' Spencer thought Michiyo looked concerned. 'I'm just jet lagged … honestly.'

Spencer gazed fondly at his bride to be. 'I'm sure there's not a problem. I think I'm just tired. I'll just relax here for a bit, perhaps watch the TV.'

'I'm not sure I should be leaving you alone right now.' Michiyo put her arms around Spencer, looking a little subdued. 'Are you *sure* you're going to be, ok?' she asked again.

Spencer gave her a playful pat on the behind.

'Are you sure you don't want me to stay for a while—that bed looks inviting?'

'Oh, my God woman, don't do this to me … but you *are* beautiful and yes, I want you.'

Spencer wrapped his arms around her, kissing her neck and then slowly unzipping her dress.

'I thought you were tired?'

'Yeah, well I am, but this is going to be a new experience for both of us.'

'Really? Ooh now I'm getting excited. What exactly is new?'

Spencer smiled. 'Well, we've never done it in Hawaii before.'

***

Spencer relaxed back on the bed and closed his eyes, enjoying the afterglow of their intimacy. 'I'm exhausted.'

Michiyo said with a soft laugh. 'But when I return … I expect a re-run.'

Michiyo showered, then dressed slowly. Spencer gazed fondly at her with one eye shut.

'Okay, I'm out of here,' she said.

Spencer sprawled across the bed, immediately falling into a trance-like sleep.

CHAPTER SEVEN

NOT AGAIN

Spencer woke with a jolt. Looking over to the window he could see the last of the sunlight as it filtered through the curtains. Glancing at his watch, he noticed it was four minutes past seven. Momentarily confused, he called out for Michiyo, then remembered that she had gone shopping. How long had he slept? How long had she been gone?

He decided to explore the hotel. still vaguely disoriented, Spencer headed off down the darkened hallway.

He hadn't noticed the Art Deco wall lights when they had arrived earlier. Some weren't working.

The elevator clanked and rattled as it approached his floor. The door squeaked and clanged, protesting as it reluctantly slid on its noisy rails. Spencer gazed at the ancient contraption and shook his head. He didn't remember the elevator being this old. Perhaps he'd come down a different hallway?

The elevator door opened. The lively sound of a jazz band hit him immediately. *Wow that sounds ok. Wonder where that's coming from?*

He strolled out onto a landing with steps leading down into a vast and noisy room. The bar, made from cane, took up the whole of one wall. Old fashioned Japanese lanterns spilled their diffused light onto the wildly gyrating throng, dancing to an African American combo. The leader of the band was a short, slightly rotund man, playing a cornet. He paused to wipe the sweat from his brow with a snowy white handkerchief. After announcing the next number, he began singing into the microphone in a rough, raspy voice that Spencer had to admit was very melodic.

Spencer's earlier disorientation had evaporated. He started humming along to the words of "Mack the Knife". Truly a classic song. Then he remembered the nightmare in Singapore: the white pointer, the jaw, the teeth, and the cold lifeless eyes.

Spencer focussed on the charismatic musician playing his trumpet. He'd been addicted to American swing and jazz for a number of years and thought that he'd heard the best—but this guy—wow! He put them all to shame.

Spencer stood absolutely transfixed by the magical sounds, torn between wanting to sit and listen and wanting to find Michiyo so she could share this with him. If he could listen to this music every night they were in Honolulu, he'd be a happy man. He must find out if they had a CD for sale.

We're going to have an awesome time. The wedding ceremony will be amazing, and everything will be perfect.

In a darkened corner he could just make out a coterie of young women clamouring around a short young man, pestering him for autographs. Spencer thought he looked familiar with a wide easy grin, and a boy-next-door appearance. Got to be someone famous, Spencer speculated.

Spencer stood spellbound by the noise and the party atmosphere. He was staggered by the attention to detail. Everyone was in period clothes. Only in America, he mused. How much had it cost to put on this extravaganza? Spencer's gaze swept the room, looking for the cameras. Surely, they'd be filming this?

He descended the stairs and strolled over to the crowded

bar. The cigarette and cigar smoke hit him. He coughed. Authenticity was one thing, but seriously, was it necessary to have a room full of tobacco fumes?

He attracted the attention of one of the bar staff. Spencer smiled at her high waisted trousers, padded shoulders, bright slash of scarlet lipstick, and the name *Rosie* embroidered on her blouse.

'A beer please.'

With a quick smile, the young woman deftly poured Spencer a froth-topped tankard.

'Twenty-five cents,' she rasped, in a broad Brooklyn accent.

Spencer laughed. 'You're not serious? Twenty-five cents … really?'

The smile on Rosie's face disappeared. 'You got a nerve criticising our prices. If you don't like it, go to Lee's joint down the road,' she snarled.

The colour left Spencer's face. His eyes flashed around the room.

He stared again at the band. The motif on the drums read, "The Louis Armstrong All-Stars". The young, short guy in the corner with the ladies clamouring for his autograph, he now recognised as Mickey Rooney.

There was no camera crew. There was no retro dressing. This was the 1940s. He stood in shock, trying to grasp the enormity of the situation. Madame Zu's concerned features flashed through his mind. She *knew* this was going to happen, he thought bitterly.

The nasal Brooklyn accent of the barmaid cut through his thoughts like a knife.

'Listen Mac, it's still twenty-five cents. You don't want to mess with Mr Zelinski. Pay up or you'll find out how Mr Zelinski got his nick name, "Ivan the Terrible". He's the manager of this joint and he don't stand for no welchers.'

Ivan Zelinski appeared behind Rosie. 'Hey pal! You order: you pay,' he commanded in a hoarse voice.

Spencer was in no doubt there'd be consequences for noncompliance.

Ivan was a fearsome figure, standing well above average height, with the broadest shoulders imaginable and biceps so large few shirts could comfortably accommodate them. He had a sharp, watchful gaze with eyes that never seemed to blink; a robot programmed to nip trouble in the bud. Ivan had managed bars from the Bronx, the south side of Chicago, even the blood-soaked dens of iniquity of the notoriously violent Barbary Coast, and the San Francisco water front.

There wasn't going to be trouble in Ivan's bar.

'Sorry, no offence intended,' Spencer mumbled. Reaching for his wallet, he handed Rosie a dollar note. 'Keep the change.'

Her eyes lit up. 'Thanks mister.'

Spencer grabbed the tankard, his mind in turmoil and no idea of what to do next.

Then came the unmistakeable sound of trouble. Spencer's attention was drawn to an angry raised voice and a woman pleading, 'I didn't do nothing Butch, honest.'

'Listen sugar tits, I don't believe nothing you say.'

Spencer had no way of knowing the man uttering these words was Butch Larson, a longshoreman on the Honolulu waterfront.

The man's face was contorted with rage. Whatever the unfortunate young lady had or hadn't done, Mr Larson was not amused. And no one seemed prepared to help her.

Butch grabbed the woman by the throat. She screamed, throwing her hands about wildly. 'Please Butch,' she croaked, 'I done nothing. Honest.'

Spencer turned his gaze on the crowd. It was clear no one was going to come to the young woman's aid.

'Let her go!' Spencer stared squarely at Butch.

Butch wasn't used to other men telling him what to do. 'Listen circus boy, beat it if you know what's good for you.'

Circus boy? Curious choice of words. He glanced down at his clothes. His Hawaiian shirt didn't look out of place, but his chinos definitely didn't pass muster. But still, *circus boy* was a little unkind.

'I won't tell you again,' said Spencer.

Something in Spencer's voice made Butch pause. He appeared confused. Letting go of the woman and turning to eyeball Spencer, he prodded him in his chest with one tattooed forefinger. He scowled, then revealed a mouth full of teeth that resembled a row of condemned houses. 'You're messing with the bare-knuckle champion of the waterfront. Not so tough now, are you, Mac?' he snarled, prodding Spencer again and again. The anger and aggression built up in his features until his face distorted and the veins on his neck stood out.

Spencer grabbed the offending hand, gnarled and scarred from numerous brutal encounters. Using the Kokoro technique, he squeezed Butch's hand—and kept on squeezing.

Butch didn't speak, but stood with sweat pouring from his brow, baffled as to how the stranger had so quickly taken control.

Spencer knew he was capable of applying pressure until Butch's hand was crushed, but this was not the outcome he wanted. He applied downward pressure on Butch's hand. Butch, now groaning, sank to his knees.

A crowd had gathered watching the battle. Butch upped the ante. With his other hand, he grabbed a switchblade from his pocket. With an audible click, the razor-sharp blade sprang out.

Spencer brought his knee up hard, breaking Butch's jaw. Butch collapsed unconscious, blood seeping out of his shattered mouth and pooling on the carpet.

Ivan had watched with rapt attention. Ivan didn't tolerate trouble. From the East Coast of the USA to the West Coast and Hawaii, Ivan had never tolerated trouble.

As Spencer looked down at the unconscious Butch, he was unaware of Ivan standing behind him with his trusty cosh. Ivan's cosh was simply made but effective. A rod of lead encased in an eighteen-inch length of common garden hose. He brought the cosh down on Spencer's head with precision. The precision that was Ivan's trademark meant Spencer now joined the unconscious Butch on the floor.

'Call the cops, Rosie.'

CHAPTER EIGHT

A NEW DAY DAWNS

'Hey there, lazy bones wake up. You've been asleep for ages,' Michiyo implored. 'It's early in the evening. I'm hungry, let's go to Duke's.' Spencer peered in the half light at his watch, a twenty first birthday present from his late father. It was four minutes past seven in the evening.

He ran a hand over the back of his head. No blood, no bruising, no pain. He sat up, glanced around, the memory of the brutal encounter with Butch Larson imprinted on his mind in graphic detail. Every moment of his encounter in the bar felt completely real. Spencer wanted to pour out every detail of the drama to Michiyo. Spencer had conflicting thoughts, a combination of embarrassment and even perhaps shame, at the way the dreams with their frightening reality were once again creating havoc. He couldn't bring himself to once again burden Michiyo with his latest nightmare. Already he was trying hard to convince himself it was just a dream, just a dream.

'Ok, let's go. I'm hungry too. Duke's it is.'

They strolled down the brightly lit corridor and pressed the lift button. The high-speed elevator doors opened noiselessly. Soft muzak entertained them as they were transported to the spacious lobby. The reception bustled with new arrivals. Friendly staff waited to attend to their every need. Spencer strolled over to the concierge, 'tell me, do you have an entertainment room, with a bar? Perhaps a jazz band performing?'

Michiyo and the concierge stared at Spencer.

'No sir,' replied the concierge. 'We do have a piano bar on the fifth floor that is intimate and very romantic. Perfect for a couple,' he added with a broad smile.

Spencer's stomach churned. He was still trying to reconcile his encounter with Butch Larson. It was so real in his mind. He could still remember Butch's bad breath, relieved only by the pungent cigarette and cigar smoke in the air. He even recalled Louis Armstrong singing and wiping his brow with his handkerchief.

Spencer tried to pull himself together. He frowned and swallowed hard. He was just grateful to be back. With a tremendous force of will he focussed on the night ahead.

They ambled hand in hand along the colourful Kalakaua Avenue. It was like party night. The broad thoroughfare teemed with people, all in high spirits. A world of bright colours, men in Hawaiian shirts strolling along the sidewalk, convertible Mustangs cruising down the street in some sort of procession. They heard the occasional roar of customised Harley Davidson motorcycles, each one more outrageous than the last, with stunning artwork on their petrol tanks and mudguards as well as intricate and lavish chrome work, their riders trying very hard to look like hard-core outlaw bikers.

Spencer and Michiyo paused outside an ABC store. This chain of shops seemed to be unique to Hawaii, stocking a curious blend of tourist artefacts, fast food, and clothing. There was an endless array of Hawaiian souvenirs.

'Let's check this out. I'd like to pick up some tourist rubbish,' said Michiyo.

More than just cheap Chinese manufactured souvenirs, there was an amazing array of quality, take away food, and even

Australian wine, Spencer noticed.

In the middle of the store was an elaborate display of photos blown up in size depicting the attack on Pearl Harbor seventy-nine years earlier. Rather tasteless Spencer thought, as he examined mugs and other souvenirs commemorating the devastating airborne attack that had almost wiped out the American Pacific fleet. Michiyo was silent as she pored over the photos. A tear came to her eye. 'This is just awful, I'm so ashamed of what my country did.'

'It sure as hell wasn't your fault. Let's go to dinner,' Spencer said.

They strolled further along Kalakaua Avenue, then paused to admire an old building; the old Moana Surfrider resort. With its ancient banyan tree and its white-painted timber façade, it looked slightly incongruous amongst the modern concrete structures of Honolulu.

'What a magnificent building!' said Michiyo. 'Spencer this hotel is famous. I'm sure I've seen its photo often in magazines. And look, I can see their famous tree in the courtyard.'

'Just ahead, there's the Outrigger.' Spencer pointed at the equally famous hotel. 'I think Duke's is inside.'

The short stroll to Duke's, renowned for its steaks, seafood and exotic cocktails, had heightened their appetites.

Duke's was full of energy with happy people enjoying the ambience and the view over Waikiki Beach. The world-class chefs kept on creating culinary masterpieces.

Spencer gave their names to the concierge and then he and Michiyo managed to find a seat at the bar. 'I'm glad I booked. There isn't a spare table. 'Our usual?'

'Of course.'

Spencer had introduced Michiyo to the classic cocktail, the sidecar, on their first date at the lavish Ritz Carlton in Tokyo, and it had been their signature drink ever since.

The carnival atmosphere of Duke's lifted Spencer's spirits. The frenetic pace of the bar staff was practically entertainment in itself. Bartenders in brightly coloured Hawaiian shirts whipped up cocktails, throwing glasses and bottles into the air, before pouring the alcohol into the mixers, and theatrically placing the bottles back on the shelf. They looked like jugglers. And it was all accompanied by humorous banter between the bar attendants and patrons. No wonder the tips jar was overflowing.

A waiter appeared. 'Excuse me folks, your balcony table is ready.'

Michiyo glanced sideways at Spencer. 'And we've got the best view in the house.'

Drinks in hand, they followed the waiter to their balcony table with the view over Waikiki.

Spencer leaned back in his chair turning to Michiyo. 'I'm so glad we chose Hawaii for our wedding,' he said, 'it really is paradise. Everything about this place is perfect … the weather …' Spencer waved a hand expansively at the beach scene below. 'There's still people swimming and partying. What a great place.' Spencer was trying hard to be positive, but his fears remained.

Everything about the food was superb: the fresh local seafood, and the Californian chardonnay.

Michiyo placed her hand on Spencer's arm. 'This should be the happiest of times, but you look so preoccupied.'

Spencer gazed thoughtfully at Michiyo. He hadn't told her of his nightmare. Michiyo was right, he was preoccupied. Spencer feared his brief and brutal encounter with Butch Larson was the prelude to another extended trip back to the past. Spencer wanted to be married, he wanted the intimate ceremony on a Honolulu beach to go ahead as planned.

He couldn't confide in Michiyo about his trip back in time

and back again. There was no anger or even disappointment in Michiyo not being able to grasp the reality, his reality. Spencer reasoned that, if the boot was on the other foot, he would find it impossible to grapple with the concept.

'I'm fine, really,' he assured her.

In fact, he was not fine. He'd noticed a waitress in a brightly coloured sarong, colours that were vivid, too vivid. His sense of logic told him it was just a sarong, colourful yes, but just another sarong. Bile rose in his throat as his sense of impending disaster grew. He felt the fear rising again. Michiyo held Spencer's hand tightly. 'Maybe … maybe it's a jet lag thing? Let's go back to the hotel for an early night.'

CHAPTER NINE

A BRIEF RESPITE

Spencer heard a scream. A world of sound and light surrounded him. He was slipping, sliding like a child on an endless fairground slide, sucked into a vortex of sounds and faces. Before him loomed an impassive and resolute Ivan, Rosie with her nasal Brooklyn twang ordered him to pay for his beer, a sneering Butch Larson pointed a finger at him and jeered, Louis Armstrong belted out "Mack the Knife". Then there was nothing. Only the merciful oblivion of sleep descending on him, obliterating his thoughts, dreams, and memories.

CHAPTER TEN

A NEW WORLD

His head hurt. There were loud intrusive sounds of anger, whining, sobbing, complaining, and threatening. Spencer lay stretched out on a stained thin mattress that covered a hard, unyielding bunk. Nausea, made worse by the persistent noise, made him gag. Two men were arguing, their angry voices rising in a crescendo of fury. Another man was crying out, as if in pain. Yet another called loudly, 'Guard, how about some breakfast? I know my rights.'

Spencer turned his face to the wall trying to will himself back to his hotel, his bed, and Michiyo. The feeling was similar to coming out of a general anaesthetic, and not knowing where you were. Slowly consciousness returned. Spencer gazed around. He was in a large cell with at least a dozen men. The smell of sweat, urine, vomit, and faeces only exacerbated his nausea.

His cellmates looked like down-and-outs. Vacant stares, grubby clothes, an air of hopelessness, but most disturbing to Spencer was an attitude of … what? Spencer cast his gaze around. Acceptance. They were accepting of their lot, this was their life, their normality. He shuddered at his introduction to skid row—Hawaii style.

These were people accustomed to waking up dirty. Some

were still drunk. Many showing signs of violent encounters, probably from the night before. There were black eyes, bruises, cuts and abrasions, some with makeshift dirty bandages applied in haste and without care.

'Jeez, I couldn't hit a river if I fell out of a boat. What's your secret pal? You ain't lost a hand since you started dealing.'

'My poker face,' was the laconic reply.

'Yeah, well even your poker face is ugly. I'm watchin' ya, see?'

'Sonofabitch! You callin' me a cheat?'

The dealer was a mountainous Polynesian. The other card player gazed at him, then his face paled. 'No, no, just sayin, I guess ya just lucky.'

Spencer listened to the prisoners' hard-edged banter as they played stud poker.

He had a headache that stopped all other traffic in his brain. Spencer lay there waiting for the lights to turn green. He had no idea where he was or what he should do next. What was the time? A quick glance at his wrist, the Rolex was gone.

'Hey, you! Sleeping Beauty? Yeah, I mean you, Marlowe. Get up! Ya made bail.'

The guard stood there; a large man clothed in a shapeless uniform in need of a clean. A cigarette dangled from his mouth and he carried a truncheon in one hand. 'Hey, you, I ain't got all day.' The guard's demeanour was one of a man with power. The undisputed king of the lock-up. Obey me or else.

Spencer sensed the guard would expect immediate compliance or the truncheon would be wielded. The other men in the lockup were now quiet as if they knew instinctively that violence by the turnkeys was normal. And guards had long memories.

All eyes were on Spencer. It was obvious that the prisoners feared this particular officer. It was as if he would welcome an outburst. He smiled mirthlessly, his tongue licking his fleshy lips. It was easy to imagine that at the smallest indiscretion, violence would be enthusiastically metered out. The truncheon certainly appeared as if it was well used.

Although most of the men were hardened criminals with little empathy, they silently willed Spencer to get to his feet. They knew any sign of tardiness would almost certainly result in a barrage of blows.

'Are you gettin' up you sonofabitch, or perhaps you need a bit of hurry up?'

The jailer swung his well-worn nightstick, slapping it into his open palm.

Spencer cautiously staggered to his feet, surprised to find that he was able to remain upright. He shuddered at his own noxious odour, he screwed up his nose. *Christ you bloody well stink.*

'About time. Now move it.' The guard shoved Spencer in the back with the end of his nightstick, propelling him forward. He seemed disappointed he hadn't had the opportunity to administer some jailhouse discipline.

'I'm looking forward to next time, pretty boy,' he whispered into Spencer's ear.

There was still a sense of unreality, Spencer felt like he was moving like a sleepwalker. His sense of logic kept hammering. *Everything's ok, you're going to wake up. It's alright. Michyio's beside you. Breakfast, a stroll on the beach. You're going to wake up. You're going to wake up.*

Spencer followed the guard into the front office of the jail. An attractive woman stood at the counter, her face a picture of worry and concern.

Spencer silently took in his surroundings. Everything confirmed his fears. A section of one wall had a collection of wanted posters, all of whom looked like extras from an old movie. The officer's uniform looked like it had come from central casting.

The clothes, the hair, the office, everything was … different. No computers, no mobile phones. It was warm. Spencer felt ill. The feeling of dread intensified with every minute. He was back in the past—but when exactly? Everything was not alright.

The guard slid car keys, a wallet, and the silver cornicello across the counter. Spencer clutched at the cornicello, his one tangible link between the past and the future.

'Check the contents, and sign here.'

These things aren't mine surely? Car keys, an unfamiliar leather wallet? He scanned the room.

The guard tapped his fingers, glaring at Spencer, his impatience obvious. 'I haven't got all day.'

Spencer signed the release form and slid it across the wooden counter, noticing the worn and stained bench top, with brown rings from carelessly placed coffee mugs and grease from hastily consumed hamburgers. It was like the rest of the lockup—grubby and uncared for.

Spencer felt lost, alone, and vulnerable, but to have the cornicello once more in his possession was a comfort. He wanted the world to go away. For a brief moment he felt a surge of anger. The reality, the awful reality, was still filtering through. He didn't want to go through this again.

The woman still stood there. Was she somebody's wife or girlfriend? Stepping forward, the woman threw her arms around him, kissing him lightly on the cheek.

'Spencer! Thank God you're ok. Phew, you smell something awful. Let's get you out of here and cleaned up.'

He stared at the woman before him. He saw an exceedingly attractive brunette, wearing a plain pleated skirt, a businesslike shirt with padded shoulders. Particularly noticeable was her hair, which was long and lustrous, curled and pinned in a typical 1940s style.

'Oh, my God! This place is awful, and you spent the whole night here?' The lady shuddered and glanced sideways at him. 'And that dreadful guard, he looked like Boris Karloff. We've only heard a bit of the story. Vic said you got into a fight. Is that true?'

We? And who the hell is Vic?

Trying not to be obvious, Spencer did his best to sneak covert glances at the woman. He observed open honest features with a sprinkling of freckles, an aesthetically pleasing countenance, Spencer decided. A face that suggested hay rides barbeques and swimming in the local river or lake. The intelligence he saw in her deep blue eyes indicated a natural curiosity.

But who the hell was she? She obviously knew him—and *that* was a problem.

'Do you feel ok? Do you need some breakfast? You look terrible … and you smell worse.' The lady prattled on 'You wouldn't believe it, Vic actually lent me his car to pick you up and drive you home. Mind you, the tightwad will probably charge you … or me, for the gas.'

They made their way to a large, sleek, bottle-green car. 'I can't believe I've actually got Vic's auto,' she laughed. 'Hop in, I'll drive.'

'What model is it?' asked Spencer. He thought he should contribute something to the conversation.

'A '39 Packard. You wouldn't believe the extras.'

Spencer and the mystery woman slid into the front seats.

'Just look at this.' The lady pressed a chrome button on the dash and withdrew a glowing cigarette lighter which she used to light a Lucky Strike; she'd fished out of a soft pack.

'How about that?' she said as she flourished the now glowing cigarette.

Spencer was puzzled. 'How about what?'

The woman looked sideways at Spencer. 'Don't tell me you've

seen a car with a cigarette lighter before? I don't believe it!'

Spencer focussed on the car, the lady, the traffic, and the pedestrians. His nightmare was a reality. He recognised Hawaii. This was Hawaii in the 1940s.

'There's more. Just listen to this,' she gushed, as she switched the radio on. She grinned. 'Isn't that something?'

A commercial came on. Hawaiian music, and then the message, "Kemp and Tai, Kemp and Tai, straight from the ocean, canned fresh for you!", accompanied by a Hawaiian band.

'Kemp and Tai, the canned fish people! That's all you ever seem to hear,' she snorted.

The lady expertly propelled the vehicle through the light morning traffic. Spencer recognised some landmarks. They were on Kalakaua avenue. He recognised the Royal Hawaiian. Still pink and looking much the same as the previous night—or whenever the previous night was?

The previous night was *the 21st century.* He held his head in his hands.

Spencer gazed back at the *Royal Hawaiian* as it receded into the distance. The sight of this grand hotel just increased his melancholy.

He just wanted to be out of there, back in his hotel room having breakfast with Michiyo and preparing for their wedding ceremony. Despair washed over him in waves.

As they drove, the lady gave a running commentary on people it was assumed Spencer also knew. Spencer stared fixedly on the road ahead, not knowing what to say. His emotions were on a rollercoaster, a rollercoaster that twisted and turned. He closed his eyes and willed himself to focus on his surroundings.

Again, he cast a surreptitious glance at the lady, and forced himself to try and take a positive spin on his situation *You are in no immediate danger. Whoever this lady is she isn't a threat. You're not being led to a house of torture where some mythical beast is going to torture or devour you. Focus … focus … Try and glean as much information as you can. This lady is a potential ally.*

They'd left the city behind and were driving along a palm-dotted beach. The beach was the only thing so far that didn't look out of place, but the parked cars looked like an event featuring American vintage vehicles. Spencer was no expert, but he recognised Chevrolets with their running boards, Buicks, Studebakers and even an old, battered model A Ford.

'Nearly there.'

They turned into a limestone drive.

Nearly where?

Spencer observed a weather board cottage with a shingle roof, a broad verandah with a hammock tied to the wooden columns. As the car bounced up the rough drive, he could see a paperback on a stool next to the hammock waiting for the reader to come back, suggesting that the bookworm had been hurriedly called away. A lean-to carport stood at the side of the house with a maroon convertible Ford with its hood down and a long surfboard poking out from the back.

This quaint and charming dwelling that hadn't made up its mind whether it was a house or a shack, overlooked the rolling thunder of the Pacific Ocean. The expansive view was marred by a huge billboard that pictured a Caucasian man on the left-hand side wearing a chef's hat and holding a platter with a tuna on it, with the words, "I'm Stan Kemp". The centre of the billboard pictured a trawler on the ocean. On the right of the sign was a smiling obese Japanese man holding a similar platter with cans of tuna on it. The caption beneath him read, "I'm Lee Tai". The bold lettering underneath proudly proclaimed, "Kemp and Tai, straight from the ocean, canned fresh for you!".

'Well, we're here.'

Spencer was completely confused.

The lady jumped out of the car. Spencer followed, not knowing what was expected of him. She retrieved a key from under the mat.

'How about I make us a cup of coffee. You still look awful. I might add a shower wouldn't go astray.' She placed her fingers on her nose and grimaced, 'You do pong, you know.'

The cottage was pleasant, if a little basic. They walked straight into the living room, furnished with comfortable, well-worn pieces. To the right was the kitchen and dining area, which led on to a passage-way with a bathroom at one side and two bedrooms on the other side.

'This really is a terrific cottage. The view of the ocean is just fabulous. You never did tell me how you acquired it.'

Spencer's jaw dropped. He'd also like to know the answer to that. He gingerly lowered himself onto one of the chrome steel dining chairs.

'Where do you keep your coffee?'

I guess that's where the coffee would be. Spencer pointed to what looked like a pantry.

'Coffee, coffee … gee whiz, you don't exactly have a full larder, do you?' She rummaged through the cans and packets. 'You know what's missing, don't you?' She gave him a wink.

Spencer managed a slight grin.

'Ah no … not really. What's missing?'

'A woman's touch,' she announced triumphantly. 'And while we're on the subject, my God your clothes! I mean the shirt sort of looks ok … ugh … filthy, but sort of ok. But the trousers … they look like they belong in a circus or something.'

'Yeah, funny. You're the second person to say that,' said Spencer cast a disparaging glance over his apparel.

'Do you have any milk in the ice box?'

Spencer shrugged.

'Milk! For the coffee?'

Spencer managed a weak smile and shrugged again.

The lady went to the refrigerator. She shook her head. 'Men … honestly! Why *bother* to have a refrigerator? All I can see is a wedge of smelly cheese and something on a plate that's turned green. Oh, *yuk.*'

The lady prattled on about the office. Vic Smith was mentioned a number of times. Was Spencer going to the cookout out at someone named Fred's house on the weekend? What did he think of the chance of the Warriors winning the next game? Fortunately, the one-sided conversation didn't seem to require answers. Spencer was able to get by with a few nods, grunts and smiles.

'You were missed at tennis yesterday. That new receptionist, what's her name?'

Spencer's face was a blank mask.

'Rita. Yes, that's it, Rita … she was asking after you, the little …' The lady was clearly going to say something uncomplimentary about the mysterious Rita.

'Vic's hopeless. Once these Veronica Lake look-alikes give him the come on, they get the job.' Her face clearly registered disgust at the perfidy of men.

Spencer gazed at her blankly. Who the hell was Veronica Lake?

Spencer focussed on what was apparently his kitchen. There was a ghastly olive-green floral wallpaper, and a Pennsylvania Dutch Kitchen cabinet displaying plates, cups, and saucers. Bilious-looking olive green curtains caught his attention next, followed by a small cream refrigerator, and what appeared to be a gas stove in a hideous green enamel. The table and chairs he actually thought were quite attractive, made of chromed steel with an appealing dull red laminate finish on the tabletop. The lady clicked a switch on the wall and a ceiling fan lazily sprang to life.

They sat at the table drinking their coffee.

'Spencer, you've said virtually nothing since I collected you from the lock up,' said the lady, her face clouded with concern. 'Are you ok?'

Spencer gazed dispiritedly around at the cottage and rubbed his hand across his stubbled jaw. He felt dirty. His mouth was dirty, and his clothes were dirty. He turned to the woman and with a voice weighted with melancholy, he finally asked the question he'd been putting off since they'd met.

'Who are you?'

CHAPTER ELEVEN

A STEEP LEARNING CURVE

'I need a cigarette.' Out came the packet of Lucky Strikes. 'Spencer, do you have a light? Sorry, I forgot you don't smoke.' Rummaging through her handbag she found a book of matches. After lighting the cigarette, she threw the book of matches to Spencer.

'You can't get away from them, can you?'

Spencer picked up the matches advertising Kemp and Tai canned tuna.

After the lady inhaled deeply, she pointed her cigarette at Spencer.

'I know you copped a whack on the head last night at Ivan's place. I can only assume that it's affected your memory. So tell me, what do you remember?'

Spencer thought for a minute. 'I remember being at a bar. I remember a band playing.'

'That was the Louis Armstrong All-stars aren't they great?' the woman cut in.

Spencer nodded.

'I'd never seen them before, but yes they were the best,' he said truthfully.

'What else can you remember?'

'Mickey Rooney was there signing autographs.'

The woman tapped her cigarette onto an old bakelite ashtray sitting on the table. 'Really? It was Mickey Rooney? I heard he was in town. Is that why you were there? Trying to get a story? I've seen every one of his movies. I think he's cute—short—but cute. I do prefer tall men.' She looked Spencer up and down appraising his six-foot four-inch height. 'Did you get to talk to him? Did you get a story? I'd just love to know who his current girlfriend is, and the readers would just love to hear some real live Hollywood gossip. Wow! If you got a story on Mickey, Vic would probably give you a raise—well—probably not.' She laughed and almost choked on her coffee.

'Hang on a minute,' said Spencer, holding his hands up. 'Why would I be trying to get a story? I've no idea what's going on here.'

'Ok, tell me what's happening. I'm confused,' asked the woman, before drawing deeply on her cigarette and waving it around. 'Why did you ask me who I am? You've known me for months. Spencer, are you ok?'

Spencer was stunned. *Months, how could it be months?* He tried to get his thoughts in order.

'When I woke up in the cell, I had absolutely no memory of anything. I don't know who you are, I don't know who this guy Vic is you keep mentioning, and I don't know whose house this is. I also don't know …' He paused not knowing how best to phrase this delicately. 'I don't know what our relationship is.'

Roxanne sat forward on her chair; her arms folded on the table. 'I guess you're telling me you have some sort of amnesia?'

'It's not some sort of amnesia. It's full-on amnesia. I simply don't know anything.' Spencer grimaced.

'Oh, my God!' she said, her hand covering her mouth. 'You poor thing. This is terrible. I've read about amnesia, but I've never actually come across it. Oh *dear*. This is awful.' She looked like she was about to burst into tears. 'Well,' she said firmly, 'we'll just have to sort things out, won't we? I think perhaps … this better go no further. How about we don't tell anyone. Particularly that little twerp Victor. And I'm sure that over time your memory will come back. Ok let's get things sorted.' She sat back in the chair with her hands intertwined behind her head.

Spencer was impressed by her no-nonsense, let's-get-on-with-it attitude. She jumped up and started pacing the room. 'Ok, well, where to start? Stop me if I cover ground that you're aware of. My name is Roxanne, Roxanne Gething.'

'Pleased to meet you, Roxanne.' He leaned over and shook her hand.

'Your name is Spencer Marlowe. You're Australian. You've been in Hawaii for … Well, I'm not exactly sure how long. You've been at the newspaper for mm, I don't remember exactly. Six months I guess. You work at the *Hawaiian Chronicle*. You're a reporter. You apparently have a fiancé back in Australia. But because of the war Australia's involved in with Japan and Germany, it's been difficult for you to get back. Stop me if I'm going too fast.'

Spencer shook his head.

'As for us, well unfortunately there is no *us*.' Roxanne frowned. 'It's no secret that I would like there to be an *us*. But I respect that you have a fiancé and you're loyal to her.'

'You mentioned war?'

Roxanne shook her head. 'You really don't have much memory, do you? Australia along with Britain has been at war since, 1939 I believe. It's now 1941. The US isn't involved.'

'Can you fill me in on my job. I imagine they're going to want me back at work?' Spencer sat, his elbows resting on the table his hands steepled under his chin.

'Ok. You're a reporter for the *Chronicle*, Honolulu's biggest newspaper. The owner is one Victor Smith. Where do I start with Vic?'

She sat back down at the table and leant back in her chair. 'Our boss is a small fussy little man. A hypochondriac. An absolute tightwad. One of the most annoying individuals you'll ever meet. He repeats everything he says.' She rolled her eyes 'I'm the photographer. You and I … oh, and Horse are often on assignments together.'

Spencer's eyebrows rose. 'There's a horse?'

Roxanne laughed. 'Claude Demmer, affectionately known as, Horse.'

'Why Horse?'

Roxanne shook her head. 'I'm not entirely sure if it's because he eats like a horse, or looks like a horse, or perhaps has the brains of a horse. He's not the most literate person in the world. He's from Brooklyn and I suspect he probably worked for the mob. What I can tell you is, he has a heart of gold. He's a general dogsbody. He comes with us on assignments, particularly if we have to deal with nasty customers.'

'I gather he can handle himself?'

'When there's trouble, Horse sorts things out. Very quickly.'

Spencer and Roxanne spent the rest of the day going through every detail of Spencer's life.

'I think we've just about covered everything.' Roxanne leant back in her chair, hands behind her head.

'That's awesome, I'm sure you must have covered just about everything.' Spencer scratched his head, feeling overwhelmed.

'I think the word "awesome" might be a bit of an overkill, or is that an Australianism?' She laughed.

Yep, gotta be more alert.

'As I said earlier, reckon it'd be a good idea not to confide in Vic about your memory loss, I don't think he'd handle it too well. What do you think?'

'Yep, cool.'

'Cool? There you go again. You sound like a New York be-bop musician. That knock on the head has made you kinda weird.'

'What can I say, I really don't know where that came from.' *Pull yourself together. Think before you open your bloody mouth.*

'Umm, I'm sure I'll be ok in a day or two.'

Spencer was trying hard to focus on all the information that Roxanne was divulging. But at the same time his head was swimming with questions he knew he wasn't about to get an answer for. How long had he been here? How in hell did he deal with this? Would he wake up any time soon?

Roxanne tapped a pencil against her teeth and leaned back in her chair, 'I think that just about wraps things up. I'm sure I've covered every aspect of your job at the *Chronicle*.' She threw her hands in the air, 'I've never heard of anyone with this amnesia problem. It's a real doozy, isn't it?'

'You should see it from where I'm sitting,' Spencer grimaced. He didn't mention his fears that 1940s technology, or lack of it, would present some problems.

CHAPTER TWELVE

THE FOUR HORSEMEN

The muffled sound of Swing music filtered through to where four men occupied an office. The background noise was hardly noticed by the four men. One stood by the door, maybe preventing anyone from getting in or perhaps not letting anyone get out. Japanese by birth, everything about him was scary. He gave the impression he was someone ready to spring into action on command. And if that wasn't enough, the Colt 0.45 semi-automatic pistol in a shoulder holster concealed under his well-cut coat would certainly guarantee compliance. He contributed nothing to the conversation.

The other three sat at a table where an obese Japanese man held court. Sitting in an elaborate teak embossed chair drumming his fingers on the tabletop, he listened with thinly disguised impatience to one of the other men seated at the table.

'Honestly Mr Tai, I gotta stop. I think they may be on to me,' the man whined plaintively.

He was dressed in civilian attire, creased chinos, a military style casual shirt and canvas deck-shoes. Sweating profusely, he constantly dabbed his face with his damp handkerchief. He smelt of fear. His hands shook. He looked like he was ready to burst into tears. He was a little man. Not small in stature, but a little, snivelling man. A man of no consequence. A man who had been sucked into a world of greed and larceny. A man who had believed that the baubles and trinkets that Lee Tai had bestowed upon him would somehow transform him from nothing, into a man of respect, in short—a big man.

Lee Tai stared at him contemptuously. He giggled. A sound that was as incongruous as it was bizarre. To those who knew him, the sound didn't herald a moment of humour or warmth.

'Mr Farris you were more than happy to take my money. Whatever happens you will make sure no suspicion falls on me.' His voice, no more than a whisper, had the ability to drive fear into men's hearts.

Farris, the man in the chinos was petrified. Was it his imagination or had the Japanese man standing by the door move imperceptibly to the middle blocking any exit?

His mouth moved but no sound came forth. Eventually the words crawled out of his mouth, a jagged croak, 'No, no, no, Mr Tai. I guarantee you; I'd never squeal on you, honest.'

Also at the table was a tall pale man languidly smoking a cigarette, and giving the appearance of being slightly bored with the proceedings. This man was dressed in a flashy yellow pinstripe zoot suit. A garment favoured by the criminal fraternity of New York and Chicago. Not common attire in 1941 Hawaii, but this man was a pretentious wannabe.

Lee Tai continued to stare. The object of his scorn squirmed under the unflinching gaze. 'You may leave,' he said abruptly, and waved his hand dismissively. 'Let me know if there are any developments.'

Farris sprang to his feet, his gaze quickly flicking from one face to another. Was it a trap? Trying not to appear desperate, he exited the room with his head down, avoiding eye contact.

The man in the zoot suit stubbed out his chesterfield cigarette in a costly looking onyx and gold ashtray.

'G'night Mr Tai, I'll get going as well, ok?' This man had an Australian accent, unusual in Hawaii in 1941.

'Sit down.' Now it was the man in the zoot suit's turn to be nervous. The fat man's cruelty was legendary.

'Sure, Mr Tai, whatever you say.' Then a little surprised at his own assertiveness he spoke up. 'I don't suppose I could have a scotch and water, with ice?'

Lee Tai nodded to the man at the door who silently glided across the room to the well-equipped bar and poured a large scotch into a crystal tumbler and topped it with ice and water.

Lee Tai watched quietly as the man gratefully savoured the thirty-year-old single malt.

'Thanks, that's a nice drop.'

'Farris is a liability. He has to be gotten rid of,' said Lee Tai coming straight to the point.

The man gulped a mouthful of scotch, momentarily choking on it. 'Hey, wait a minute. You don't mean me?' He pointed a thumb at his chest.

'You've made a lot of money, Kitchener, but—as they say in America—it's time to pay the piper.'

Kitchener shook his head vigorously 'Sorry Mr Tai, but no way.' He shook his head again, jumping to his feet, and hastily drained his scotch. 'No! Absolutely *no* way.'

He turned towards the door; the Japanese man now stood blocking it with his arms folded.

'Sit down.' Lee Tai's voice was a whisper. 'I would like to show you some photos.'

He had a foolscap-size brown envelope in his hand. He slid out a photo, a glossy eight by twelve inch black and white picture and handed it to Kitchener.

'A swimming pool! That's nice,' said Kitchener clearly puzzled. He shrugged before handing the photo back.

Lee Tai gave a brief smile: no more than a curl of his lip. He drew out the next photo, slipping it to Kitchener. This was a picture of the same pool. A man's head could be seen floating like a discarded beachball, its mouth agape, its lifeless eyes fixed in an expression of sheer terror.

'Oh, my God.' Kitchener recoiled in horror, the bile rising in his throat.

'This is what happens to people who disobey me,' Lee Tai whispered.

CHAPTER THIRTEEN

A NEW LIFE BEGINS

Spencer gazed out of his living room window, captivated by the gentle surf washing over the sandy beach. The timeless palms added their own beauty. The tranquil scene was marred only by the billboard, Kemp and Tai, straight from the ocean canned fresh for you.

There was something about the sign he found disturbing. It wasn't just that he thought it was crass, and the sight, particularly of the jolly obese Japanese man was annoying. There was something else that niggled away in his memory.

I don't get it. Why does an obviously Japanese man have a Chinese name? It's not just a Chinese name it's … what … it's something else?

Spencer shrugged and for the moment, threw the oddity of the billboard into the too hard basket. *Move on. You have one hell of a day in front of you. A stupid billboard is the least of your worries. A nice hot shower is what the doctor ordered.*

The bathroom was certainly not what he was used to, having floor to three-quarter-height green tiles with a black border, small hexagonal floor tiles and an Art Deco-style pedestal hand basin: also, green.

The mirror was stylish, taking up half of one wall also in an attractive Art Deco design. The shower was placed over the old-fashioned claw-footed bath. Suspended above was a clumsy circular plastic shower screen. What was lacking was hot water. Spencer searched everywhere for a switch, a knob, anything that might direct a flow of hot water onto his person. Nothing, zilch, nada. *Oh well, at least I'm not in Alaska.*

Spencer showered and then padded back to his room and the wardrobe, leaving a trail of damp tell-tale footprints on the wooden boards. He grinned from ear to ear at the range of 1940s apparel.

He selected a pair of pleated trousers in a light fawn. They were certainly different from trousers in his century. The fabric was a mixture of wool and rayon. The shirt was a particularly attractive cream in a very heavy cotton. Spencer gently ran his fingers over the fabric. *This is nicer than the cloth I'm used to.* Next came the tie. There was a choice. Bold bright colours, and all of the ties were wide. He looked askance at the in-your-face colours and designs. He checked out the selection of hats on the top shelf. Spencer knew the well-dressed man in 1941 wore a hat. He chose a light brown fedora with a chocolate brown hat band. He smiled at his image.

Now how, I wonder, does the hard-bitten reporter wear a hat?

He tried pushing the hat back on his head, then pushing it to one side on a rakish angle.

Spencer saluted the mirror. 'Here's looking at you kid,' he mouthed.

What about shoes? Oh boy, just look at the shoes. Spencer decided that fashion in his century was bland compared to what was on offer in the 1940s. Sitting at the bottom of the wardrobe was a pair of two-tone chocolate and tan oxfords.

After donning his shoes, he stood in front of the mirror laughing at the image of a movie gangster. In the '40s the ties in particular made a statement. They were wide, bold, and worn short as the trousers were high waisted.

Clothes maketh the man.

Feeling buoyed by his first excursion into the world of another century's fashion, he decided it was time for breakfast.

He checked the pantry. 'Oh well, beans, toast and coffee perhaps.' Spencer had rifled through the sparse contents. A loaf of bread, at least a week old sat in a cream enamelled metal container with a rolling lid, conveniently marked "Bread" in embossed green lettering. A jar of hot sauce, labelled *Texas Pete*, added a bit of excitement. Some *Vermont Maple Syrup*, and a bottle of *Tabasco* sauce seemed to Spencer to be a little incongruous. A forlorn string bag full of mouldy onions, rested on one shelf. At last, something that looked like breakfast, a can of *Bush's Pork and Beans*.

'Now, what about coffee? Can't start the day without coffee.'

Spencer's search through the pantry revealed a round metal container advertising *C D Kenny Co Baltimore, Mammy's Favourite Coffee*. The colourful container sported a picture of a plump African American lady with a headscarf, holding a tray with a pot of coffee on it. 'Just add hot water' it boasted.

'I guess we're going to try Mr Bush's product.'

Rummaging through a drawer, Spencer found a can opener, but not the sort he was used to. The pointy end apparently you stabbed into the can and then sawed through the metal lid.

'You're kidding me. They call this a can opener? He speared the opener into the can, and sawed the lid open. 'Now we have to heat the damn thing.'

Spencer glanced around the room. Microwave? He laughed out loud. 'I don't think it's been invented.'

Can opened, contents tipped into a saucepan and heating up nicely on the gas stove. Mission accomplished.

'Well, what happens now?'

Sitting on one of his chrome kitchen chairs, he ate his meagre breakfast and paid attention to his surroundings. Yes, it was basic but not without charm. The kitchen floor was constructed of wide Robusta hardwood floorboards polished to a deep lustrous finish. Initially he had recoiled at the awful green wallpaper and curtains, but as he sat reflectively, he decided it was bit like clothes. You sort of got used to it.

Gathering together his few possessions, thinking, life in this century was certainly different. He grabbed his keys, his wallet … and of course … Spencer held the cornicello in his hand. He remembered again when Bert Weadley had given it to him, in the Northam lockup and what little importance he had attached to it.

Climbing into the car he glanced at the dashboard. It showed minimal instrumentation. He pressed the starter button. The flat head V8 responded with a satisfying growl. The Ford then appeared to have a change of heart as it lurched, coughed, and spluttered.

'Doesn't seem to like mornings,' Spencer muttered. He sat for a few minutes, gingerly revving the motor until the engine settled down to a rhythmic beat.

'Temperamental sod, aren't you?' He patted the dashboard. A gesture of affection for a machine that was as archaic to Spencer as a black and white television set.

'Dammit,' Spencer cursed successfully managing to crunch the gears as he forced it into reverse. There was a lot to be said for automatic transmissions he decided. The Ford bounced and rattled as Spencer gently accelerated down the rough limestone drive. He remembered a quote from Henry Ford, "A Ford generally has about fifty-two different rattles, when a Ford driver hears only fifty-one, he goes back to see what's fallen off."

Well, so far so good. Let's hit the road. *Hawaiian Chronicle* here we come. Can I pull this off? How in hell can I be a reporter, what in hell do I do?

Being an optimist, Spencer couldn't suppress a smile as

another random thought occurred to him. It'd be worse if he were expected to be a brain surgeon.

The directions to the office Roxanne had given him were easy to follow. He settled down to enjoy driving the convertible. He powered along the broad boulevard with the top down, his fedora resting on the passenger seat. The wind ruffled his hair. The subtle odours of frangipani and the colours of the hibiscus, combined with the tang of the Pacific as it gently rose and fell with rhythmic ease, helped to settle his nerves.

Slowly but surely, his natural optimism took hold. By hook or by crook, he was going to make a fist of it. He was ready to embrace his new life, a life that could be for days, weeks, months, years, or perhaps forever.

CHAPTER FOURTEEN

THE CHRONICLE

'I'm telling you Mabel, they're all the same. All men are creeps. He takes me to the movies. Buys me a hamburger and expects—well you know what he …'

The nameplate on the desk read, Rita.

'Good morning Rita,' Spencer nodded.

Rita was a bottle blonde. She was dressed in an A-line plaid skirt, and a white button-down blouse with padded shoulders.

'Good morning Spencer,' she purred, eyelids aflutter. 'We haven't seen you at tennis for a while. Are you coming this weekend?'

Before Spencer could answer, Roxanne appeared behind Rita's desk.

'Rita, if you have nothing to do, I've a whole lot of photos that need collating.'

Roxanne's tone and body language were as subtle as a hit on the head.

'Sorry Miss Gething,' Rita mumbled, blushing as she tried to look busy.

Roxanne smiled sweetly at Spencer and crooking her finger, she motioned him to follow her.

Spencer had watched the interchange between Roxanne and Rita with amusement. If nothing else, it indicated that

Roxanne was in a position of authority.

'That girl could easily find herself out of a job,' she muttered darkly.

'Hang on,' Spencer protested, 'Rita was only being polite.'

Roxanne shook her head and sighed. 'Honestly, men are such idiots.'

Spencer wasn't sure whether this comment was directed at him or perhaps men in general.

CHAPTER FIFTEEN

SPENCER THE JOURNALIST

The printing press clanged and hissed, the ancient metal runners sliding noisily into place. Hoarse cries from the typesetter rang through the print room, rising above the cacophony. Spencer just had to visit the basement and see for himself the spectacle that was a working newspaper, enthralled he made his way through the newspapers nerve centre. The noise, the clamour, it was like nothing he'd ever seen. Roxanne had explained the *Chronicle* not only distributed to Hawaii, but virtually the whole Pacific region with a strong following even in California.

There was a measure of relief as he entered the relative quiet of the office, it gave the impression of organised chaos, but with less noise.

But even here his workplace was a maelstrom of harassed staff running in all directions to meet deadlines. Reporters and journalists seemed to compete as to who could yell the loudest. Strident voices shouted, 'Copy boy, copy boy,' over the background clatter of countless typewriters.

Spencer's hands were clammy, his heart pounded, what exactly did a journalist do?

The sports journalist in another office was embroiled in a heated argument with someone on the phone. Dressed in a business shirt, loud trouser braces, an even louder tie, and using a huge cigar to punctuate his sentences, it was like watching a scene from an old movie.

'I tell ya, he's a bum! I saw your guy shadow-boxing and the shadow won.'

Spencer pretended to be busy, but the conversation of the journalist was gold.

'Yeah, yeah, I accept he's a great hitter, but there's more to boxing than hittin'—there's not getting hit.'

Cigar smoke eddied its way up to the ceiling as the journalist listened to the promoter's reply. 'Listen Joe,' the journalist said, 'I gotta tell ya, your boy has everything he needs, except speed, stamina, a punch, and … oh yeah, I forgot—the ability to take punishment. In other words, he owns a pair of shorts!'

He slammed the phone down, winking at Spencer.

'Don't ya just love the fight game?'

Spencer battled to keep a straight face.

A few typists gave Spencer a wave and a smile. The smell of newsprint and ink permeated the air. Spencer felt like a fraud, following Roxanne as she led him to his office. He wondered again, exactly how he was going to survive in this unfamiliar world when he didn't have a clue of what was expected of him.

At the back of the building were a number of smaller individual offices divided by wood and glass panelling.

'I'll show you your office. It's right next to mine,' Roxanne whispered.

Trying not to be obvious about it, Spencer took stock of Roxanne. He decided she worked hard at the image of being a hard-bitten newspaper woman, but she favoured dangly earrings that clinked as she turned her head. He suspected this was a lady with enormous capacity for fun. She was dressed for business and yet a soft femininity lurked not far below the surface.

'There it is.' Roxanne indicated his workplace. 'Now if there's anything you need … anything, and I do mean *anything* …' She gave him a wink.

Spencer studied his remarkably small and spare office containing a desk, three chairs, a filing cabinet, and a box with a collection of writing implements and bottles of ink. A round-shouldered wooden coat rack stood in one corner. A wire-framed in-tray sat with a stack of files and next to it a matching out-tray, waited to be emptied. An old typewriter had pride of place in the middle of the desk. Spencer gazed in horror at the antiquated piece of technology with its alphabet keys, matt black steel case, and innumerable awkward alloy levers looking like they'd been stuck on as an afterthought. He gingerly placed a hand on what he was to learn was a carriage return. *Jesus H, it has a ribbon, what on earth does that do? Well, just another part of the learning curve.*

Spencer decided to momentarily put the typewriter into the too hard basket. He patted the metal contraption emblazoned with the name, *Underwood.* 'You're not going to defeat me, sweetheart,' he muttered to himself. 'Now what else is there?' His eyes flashed around the office—his office.

'What the hell?' He grabbed a black and white photo of a smiling Spencer Marlowe, clad in well-worn khaki shorts and a t-shirt holding a forlorn-looking fish as a trophy. Spencer held the photo, examining it carefully. When was it taken? Who was the photographer?

Carefully placing the mysterious photo back on his desk, Spencer glanced around helplessly, scratching his head. Once again, he felt completely out of his depth. He'd been thrown in at the deep end and was flailing like a non-swimmer about to be caught in a rip tide with no life belt.

He gazed around the office at the busy people, toiling in the high-pressure newspaper business.

This can't be that hard. He took some deep breaths and found his natural optimism start to filter through. *Now what does a journalist actually do?* Spencer had no idea of what to do next, but he didn't have to wait long for an answer.

'Well Spencer, Spencer, yes, yes, Spencer good to, yes good, good to see you up, that is, up yes, up and about.' This had to be Victor Smith, the boss.

Spencer smiled, almost laughing at this fussy character bustling around. Clearly, Victor was impressed by his own self-importance. *This guy looks bloody ridiculous. Check out the comb-over, the built-up heels. Guess what? You're still short Sunshine. With that nervous tic you look like a demented rabbit, caught in a spotlight.*

'I don't, that is, I don't, yes, yes, I don't … I don't actually approve, that is … I mean … I don't approve of my staff getting, that is I mean … getting into fisticuffs. Now … now … I mean. I don't want this happening again.' The unprepossessing Victor blinked rapidly, then stared owlishly at Spencer.

Good lord, every conversation is going to take hours. This is worse than chronic stuttering.

'I'm afraid I'm going to, going to, yes I'm afraid I'm going to, going to have, yes …' His eyes darted around the tiny office as if searching for something sinister.

'You're going to have to …?' Spencer prompted.

This elicited another round of "yes" and "I'm afraids". Eventually Victor managed to get his message across that Spencer was to be docked a day's pay.

It was all Spencer could do to not laugh out loud at the bumptious newspaper man who gave the impression of being overawed by his own importance. He wondered if he could put up with this convoluted speech for much longer. Before Spencer could comment, an office girl knocked on the door. She grinned at Spencer, winking. Spencer immediately took heart at the friendly gesture, chuckling to himself. *A co-conspirator?*

'Excuse me Mr Smith, Mr Marlowe, there are two gentlemen

here to see Mr Marlowe. I think,' she grimaced, 'they may be, police.'

'Thank you, Deborah. Show the, yes show, well show …' before Victor could finish, Deborah disappeared, probably she was used to his painful longwinded verbosity. 'Well,' Victor snorted. 'You're probably, that is … I'm sure, yes, yes I'm sure that …'

Spencer was grateful the two men dressed almost identically in sombre suits, each carrying a fedora hat and a leather briefcase, had saved him from more of Victor's excruciatingly long-winded dialogue.

'Mr Marlowe?' The bigger of the two unsmiling men spoke authoritatively. 'We would like a word.'

Spencer had been anticipating a visit from the police, fully expecting to be charged with the assault on Butch Larson. He wasn't looking forward to being locked up again.

Victor Smith puffed out his chest, rocked on his heels and did his best to look tall.

'Now look, I say look, I mean, what I mean is …'

'We're here to talk to Marlowe. Would you give us some privacy?'

CHAPTER SIXTEEN

INTRIGUE

Something in the demeanour of the two suits convinced Victor discretion was the better part of valour. He scuttled off. Spencer laughed to himself. If ever the term "with his tail between his legs" applied, this would be it.

'Yes, well I mean, well I mean.' The endless stream of verbal diarrhoea could be heard disappearing into the distance.

Spencer smiled his most disarming smile. 'Gentlemen, if this is about the unfortunate incident with a certain Mr Larson?'

The larger of the two rolled his eyes and chuckled. 'Hell no. We were both tickled pink when we heard about the unfortunate Mr Larson.'

'Apparently, he'll be drinking through a straw for some time,' the other one chimed in, grinning from ear to ear.

The big man held out his hand. 'Matt Spinetti.'

Spencer shook the proffered hand.

'Walter Crabtree,' stated the other man.

Matt Spinetti's Mediterranean heritage was obvious, but his mannerisms and speech were pure American. A second generation American, he'd won a sports scholarship to Harvard, having the hard-muscled physique that went with years spent taking part in the brutal sport of college football. Matt excelled at all sport including boxing. His years in law enforcement had honed a keen athletic prowess into a very competent street fighter.

Walter Crabtree had the appearance of an academic. Like his partner, he epitomised the new breed of crime fighters. A college education mixed with street smarts. Fearless and a deadly shot with his cumbersome Colt 0.45 semi-automatic pistol.

Spencer wasn't familiar with what secret-agent-type people wore, but he couldn't help smiling at the apparel worn by Crabtree and Spinetti. Both wore suits. One a pale fawn, the other a pale green. Identical cut with wide cuffed pleated trousers, both with white shirts. One tie was a chartreuse green, the other a rather daring chestnut brown. Both wore identical tie pins with the obligatory white handkerchief in the left breast coat pocket, with three points protruding. The only thing missing was a sign emblazoned with the words "Government Agent—handle with care".

The two men informed Spencer they were with an agency working in counter espionage. They declined to give any more details.

Without asking, Spinetti and Crabtree both grabbed a chair, motioning Spencer to have a seat. Spinetti's gaze swivelled, making sure no one was in ear shot.

'What we're here to talk about is the murder, *or*,' he rolled his eyes, 'the suicide of Lieutenant Marty Farris, some months ago.'

Spinetti studied Spencer his eyes boring into him. It was if he thought, by staring long and hard enough Spencer would crumble.

Matt Spinetti, Spencer decided was one tough customer. *These guys are quietly running their bullshit meter over me.*

Spencer suspected, as a reporter, he would've been expected to be aware of the case. He nodded as if he already knew some of the details.

'As I'm sure you're aware,' Crabtree said, 'we're holding one of your country men on suspicion of the murder. But frankly we won't be able to make it stick, we'll probably have to let him—'

'What we want,' Spinetti cut in, 'is for you to visit him in the naval brig at Pearl and see if he'll open up to you. I might add this is top secret. There's a hell of a lot more to this story than it appears.'

Spencer held up his hands. 'Hang on just a minute. Look, I'm very pleased I'm not in any trouble over the unfortunate incident with the delightful Butch Larson. But gentlemen, why me exactly?'

Walter glanced at Matt Spinetti. 'Look Marlowe, I hate to admit this, but we are … there's no other way to put this, we are desperate.'

'Our sources told us there was an Australian journalist at the *Chronicle* and … well we figured …' Spinetti, rolled his eyes and looked a little sheepish.

Walter jumped to his feet, leaning his hands on Spencer's desk. 'Marlowe, we figured you being an Aussie, you just might be able to get the slimy rat to talk.'

CHAPTER SEVENTEEN

A SINISTER AND SHADOWY WORLD

'We'll fill you in with all we know,' said Spinetti, peeling off his jacket and hanging it on the coat rack. Spencer was bemused to see the shoulder holster now in plain view, with the shiny steel Colt 0.45 semi-automatic pistol slotted into it.

'And probably what's more important, what we suspect,' Crabtree chipped in.

Crabtree and Spinetti took turns to fill Spencer in with the details. Spencer listened to the story of intrigue, murder, and espionage.

'And the dead US serviceman was the quartermaster at the Marine Corp base at Kaneohe Bay. Spinetti glanced around making sure no one was in earshot. We'd just got wind of a massive amount of ordnance that was missing.'

Spencer was stunned at this story of grand theft and murder that had all the ingredients of a best-selling spy thriller. 'Just refresh my memory. How long ago was the quartermaster killed?'

Stretched out on his seat and trying to display a nonchalance he didn't really feel, Spencer's mind was in turmoil. Would he be expected to know about this?

Spinetti snorted. 'It was last year; your countryman has been in custody all of that time. We deliberately made sure it was kept quiet. In fact, you may possibly remember it was just a by-line in the *Chronicle.*' He waved his hands, 'That's when we found out about the missing ordnance.'

Spinetti cleared his throat. 'Look Marlowe, what I'm driving at is, why? A small quantity of handguns and long guns would easily be disposed of. Sold to the local lowlife. But what the hell could anybody want with the amount of weaponry that's been lifted?'

'So, what exactly are we looking at? I would've thought that missing ordnance would be a fairly regular occurrence? You're always going to get some smart guy who's going to buck the system. I'm surprised this isn't a local police matter, or a job for the MPs.'

Crabtree's lip curled. 'Whoa, hold it right there. We're talking crates. I mean several crates of grenades, handguns, Garand rifles, Thompson sub machine guns, ammunition—'

'Enough weaponry to outfit a small army,' interjected Spinetti. 'But here's the thing—what's the point?'

Spencer's eyebrows lifted. 'I'm sorry, I don't follow?'

'What Matt is saying is—why in the Sam Hill would anyone want this amount of ordnance? I mean, a few handguns, sure, maybe some Thompsons, but seriously, crates of grenades?' He stood up, running his fingers through his black locks in frustration.

'Maybe our Japanese friend with a Chinese name is involved, but once again why? Whatever Lee Tai is or isn't, he's certainly no fool. I mean, why steal enough weaponry to outfit an army?'

Spencer gave a tight smile. He was aghast. This seemed to be a story of murder and intrigue on a grand scale. 'How long has this been going on?'

Spinetti winced. 'It seems that it's actually been going on for some time.'

It was Crabtree's turn to look embarrassed. 'Just when we got a hint of the scale of the operation, and we were about to question—'

'Yeah,' Spinetti snarled, 'just as we were about to reel in the late suspect … *Kaboom!*'

'Here's where it gets interesting,' Crabtree continued. 'Before Farris's murder or suicide, we'd been following him, and who we suspected was his accomplice. And just guess who they were regularly seen with?' Without waiting for an answer, he growled, 'Yeah, you got it. *Lee Tai!*'

'That's surely not the Lee Tai that I've seen in all the ads?' Spencer cut in.

'The very same,' Spinetti said, a bleak expression on his face. 'We've long suspected Mr Tai is rather more than a fish canner. He operates Lee's joint on the outskirts of Honolulu. He also has accommodation at the back of the bar for when he comes to town. Lee's bar is a hangout for all the thugs and lowlife of Hawaii. Mostly his clientele is Japanese, or Japanese Americans. Most of the local Japs are ok, but you're always going to get some bad eggs.'

Spencer scratched his head. 'You say, *when* he comes to town. Wouldn't he live here most of the time?'

Crabtree emitted a mirthless laugh. 'Mainly he lives on Molokai. That's where his fish canning business is. He has a big, swell house and at least twenty trawlers based there, but Molokai, that's another story in itself.' Crabtree glanced at Spinetti who just shook his head, adding nothing.

'Isn't that where the leper colony is?' Spencer had read a brief history of Hawaii in a tourist brochure when he and Michiyo had been on the plane to Honolulu.

Spinetti looked pensive. 'Yes, and nobody goes there. Mr

Tai discourages visitors. We can't prove anything, but there are reports of people who got too close and they just seemed to disappear.'

'Disappeared?' Spencer echoed.

Spinetti tapped a pencil on his teeth. 'Yeah! Well, there just hasn't been enough to warrant an investigation. We know that people have been silly enough to go diving and spearfishing in the area, even though locals are well aware the area is infested with sharks. They're attracted to the offal from the fish factory. The local authorities even found a thirty-foot launch floating in the area with no crew members. It was assumed the guy, or whoever was on board, had gone for a swim and simply been taken by sharks. I mean there was nothing there for the local police to see the point of taking it further.'

Spencer glanced at the two men. 'What about Tai's partner, the other name on the billboard, Stan Kemp?'

Crabtree snorted. 'We've tried our darndest to locate him. No dice. It's as if he doesn't exist.'

'Is there anything else you can tell me about Tai?' asked Spencer.

Spinetti glanced at Walter. 'We've long suspected that he's involved in other illegal activities.'

Matt snapped open his briefcase and handed Spencer a folder. 'Just have a peep at this.'

Spencer skimmed over the page, emitting a low whistle. 'You seriously think he's involved in prostitution, loan sharking, extortion and drug running and yet you can't pin anything on him?'

'Our problem is that nobody will testify against him. We come across a wall of silence. It's obvious everyone's terrified of him.' Crabtree sounded a little embarrassed.

Crabtree leaned back in his chair. 'Although Matt and I are convinced Tai isn't what he makes himself out to be, it's always possible that he has deliberately crafted this … er … what would you call it? I suppose you'd call it an air of mystery. Of … well, call it a persona of violence. But it may be just that. It may be part of his business strategy, but our gut feeling is he's deeply involved in criminal activities.'

Spencer looked at the two men. 'What's the story on his alleged accomplice?'

Spinetti's eyes darted around, once again making sure nobody else could hear. 'Here's where the story gets bloody. Farris, while in the company of your fellow countryman, puts a gun to his head to see what it sounds like. Blew his brains out all over the furniture. The Australian says, "nothing to do with him."'

'You don't believe him?'

'We believe Farris and the Aussie were in cahoots. They knew Farris was about to be arrested. The Australian figured Farris would've done a deal and put him in the frame, so—bang!' Spinetti made a gun out of his hand, placing it at his forehead.

'Tell me about my fellow countryman?' Spencer asked.

Crabtree opened a file. 'He's a warrant officer in the Australian Army. Seconded here to demonstrate a sub machine gun to our military. It's called an Owen gun.'

Spencer knew little about sub machine guns, 'Is it any good?'

Crabtree continued. 'Apparently an excellent weapon. It can be dragged through the mud and still work. But it fires a 9mm round that doesn't have the stopping power of the 0.45 used by our Thompson.'

'So,' Spencer declared. 'You want me to see him in the clink. Try and get him on side, try to find out where the weaponry is, and what's his involvement?' Spencer smiled. 'That's a fairly big ask.'

'Look,' pleaded Crabtree. 'Sure, it's a long shot. But it's all we've got. We simply don't have enough evidence to charge him. The military have managed to get him on to a Catalina leaving next week, taking him to Sydney, Australia.' Crabtree ran his fingers through his hair. 'Frankly, we're desperate. We can't hold him and once he's back in the land of the kangaroo …'

'The most important thing is to find out where all this weaponry has gone,' Spinetti chipped in. 'In the wrong hands the potential for disaster is limitless. The other thing is, the general public don't know about the missing weaponry, and they're not going to know.' His eyes narrowed. 'Understand?'

'I think your message is pretty clear. You're telling me it's out of bounds. Classified.'

'Yeah,' Spinetti continued. 'Look, I'm sorry Marlowe, but this is about national security. At this point we're not asking you sign the Official Secrets Act. We've always had a good relationship with the press. For the moment this is all going to be hush-hush. Got it? We have to make sure some things stay secret. But,' he added brightly, 'at the end of it, there's going to be one hell of a story.'

'We think some of the answers might be found at Lee's bar,' Crabtree added. With all the lowlife there, someone must know something about those weapons. We can't impress on you enough just how important this is. This amount of weaponry is … well it's so God damned extensive that the possibilities are endless. Honestly, you could just about start a war with what's gone missing.'

Spencer glanced at the two men. 'Have you been there to talk to the customers?'

Spinetti gave a bitter laugh, 'Those bozos won't talk to us. But they might talk to you. Particularly if you mention the reward.'

'Reward?'

'Yes,' Spinetti replied. 'A reward of one thousand dollars.'

'Well, they say there's no honour amongst thieves,' Spencer chuckled. 'And that's one hell of a reward.'

Spencer knew in 1941 a thousand dollars was a small fortune.

Spinetti and Crabtree sat for a moment leaving Spencer to digest the information. Spinetti then threw in. 'If you're going to Lee's, take back up with you.'

'Any suggestions?' Spencer enquired.

Crabtree laughed. 'I'd reckon the Neanderthal would be a good choice.'

'Neanderthal?'

It was Spinetti's turn to laugh. 'I think Crabs is referring to one Claude Demmer, who goes by the handle, Horse.'

I think calling him a Neanderthal is perhaps a little unkind. Anyhow Marlowe, you of all people would know all about the man called Horse.'

Spencer smiled in acknowledgment. He remembered Roxanne telling him about Horse's encounters with some of Hawaii's criminal elements.

Crabtree sniggered. 'Let's face it Matt, he didn't quite make it to the end of the assembly line.'

Spinetti pointed an accusatory finger at Walter.

'And how would you like to go ten rounds against him?'

Crabtree shook his head and laughed. 'I think we're both agreed. If Horse were any more stupid, he would have to be watered once a week. But if it comes to a fire fight, a fist fight, in fact any sort of fight, reluctantly, I guess he's your boy.'

Spencer once again felt he was being sucked into a vortex of intrigue and danger. *How the hell did I get into this situation?*

'Ok, first things first. I'll go and pay a visit to my fellow Aussie. I'm sure he'll be pleased to see me. And then I'll take Horse and pay a visit to Lee's joint.'

Spencer glanced at the two secret service operatives.

'Can you give me everything you've got on the Australian suspect?'

Spinetti delved into his briefcase, pulled out another folder and handed it to Spencer.

Spencer stared at the black and white photo of an Australian serviceman dressed in a warrant officer's uniform. The bold, black print under the photo jumped out at him—*Warrant Officer, Wayne Kitchener*. His mouth went dry. He was speechless.

Spinetti's eyes narrowed. Spencer's look of amazement was clear to see. 'Are you ok, buddy? Do you know this guy?'

'Sorry,' Spencer mumbled. 'Bit of a shock really. I don't know him, but I've heard of him.' Then by way of some believable explanation he added, 'We're both from Perth, on the west coast of Australia.'

CHAPTER EIGHTEEN

A FELLOW COUNTRYMAN

The military police sergeant scrutinised Spencer's pass, at the same time staring at Spencer with eyes that were clear and hard. The checkpoint guard post was a smart business-like structure of white painted timber with a boom gate barring entry. Spencer glanced at the guard. *This is a different species from the turnkey at the police lockup. Get a load of the spit and polish. I'll bet he spends hours making sure the outfit is just right. That's one very smart khaki uniform, Yep, white belt, white steel hat, MP armband, and truncheon, and just check out the bloody Colt 0.45 on his hip. Step out of line and I'll shoot. And have a look at the private on the other side of the driveway. His rifle and bayonet are certainly not for show.*

He was escorted by a private through numerous checkpoints. They marched without speaking along a concrete pathway that ran through a well-tended, grassy area, then another checkpoint. This, Spencer assumed, was now the prison proper. High, cheerless concrete walls surrounded them. Above, officers with rifles could be seen patrolling. The guard's hobnailed boots clattered, the sound of metal on concrete announcing their arrival at the next checkpoint. A steel mesh door banged open and the private saluted. The first lieutenant, now standing in front of Spencer, took particular interest in him and his press credentials.

Another hard stare. 'Ok, private. Proceed.'

Spencer's papers were scrutinised at every post. The smell of overcooked cabbage, hash, and stewed coffee permeated the air, along with the overpowering smell of disinfectant.

With an eruption of noise, the prison telegraph sounded the alarm. Tin mugs clattered against the steel bars, competing with the strident voices of men with too much time on their hands.

Spencer followed the grim-looking guard down the long corridor which was lined with cells on either side. From the questions and comments shouted their way as they passed, it was obvious the prisoners welcomed this unexpected diversion.

Spencer smiled as he listened to the chatter.

'He's a Hollywood producer, gonna make a movie about our excitin' lives,' said one.

'No, he's Government. Look at the clothes. He's here to do a report on the garbage they call chow,' responded another.

Spencer gazed at the sleeping Wayne Kitchener, stretched out on the bunk of his cell, seemingly without a care in the world. With a clang that would awaken the dead, the MP whacked the bars of the cell with his baton.

'Hey, Kitchener. Wake up. You got a visitor.'

Kitchener opened his eyes, spotted Spencer, and smirked.

'Step into my office,' he commanded.

Kitchener was clothed in the US Navy hickory-striped prisoner's jacket and blue jeans. Spencer quickly appraised the supine Kitchener. In a word, shifty. He was tall, thin, pale as the skin on a glass of milk, his features gaunt and hardened. Small watery-blue beady eyes, darted from side to side as if looking for a weakness. Spencer immediately felt this was a man who was always on the take.

The guard jerked the cell door open. Spencer stepped in and perched on the edge of the opposite bunk, extending his hand. 'Spencer Marlowe.'

Kitchener fixed Spencer with a shrewd stare and warily proffered a limp, moist hand.

'An Aussie, eh?'

'Yep. An Aussie news journalist keen to make sure a fellow countryman is getting a fair deal. I'm not convinced you've been fairly treated. I may be able to help you. I can use the power of the pen to make sure the US Army doesn't try to railroad you. I've looked at the evidence, and it's clear they don't have much of a case.' Spencer forced what he hoped looked like an empathetic smile.

Kitchener's eyes narrowed as he weighed Spencer up.

'Well, what can I tell you?' he shrugged. 'I'm not sure I need to talk to you. They got nothing on me. Hells bells, I done nothing. Some stupid drongo shot himself and they wanna blame someone, so they set me up as the fall guy, see?' Kitchener lapsed into a sullen silence. He sat up on his bunk, leaning against the wall. He smiled. 'Tell you what cobber—give me some fags—and I'll tell you everything I can, ok?'

Spencer had anticipated that cigarettes might be useful. He pulled out three packets of Lucky Strikes and tossed them over to Kitchener. 'You have a deal.'

Kitchener ripped open one of the soft packs, put a cigarette between his lips and leant forward as Spencer lit a match. He drew the fragrant smoke deep into his lungs as he leant back against the cell wall, a smoke ring eddied gracefully towards the ceiling.

'Oh boy, I sure needed that. The mugs here haven't given me cigarettes or tobacco. Bastards.'

Spencer smiled sympathetically. 'Look Wayne … You don't mind first names?'

'Yeah, sure,' Kitchener nodded.

'The thing is, at the moment everyone's jumpy. Nobody knows what's going to happen. The Japanese are a bit of a worry here in the Pacific. And what concerns me, with your situation, is that due process may go out the window. I'm inclined to believe your story. As I said, there doesn't seem to be much evidence against you. Even if the Yanks send you back to Australia, there's no guarantee the Australians are going to believe your version of events. *As sure as God made little apples, Don Bidstrup won't believe a word you've said.* The Americans have told me what they have against you; how about you give me your version?'

Kitchener tapped another cigarette from the pack, lighting it from the previous one. He nodded. 'Sure, pal. I can only tell you what I told them. Me and Marty Farris were mates. I had no fucking idea that Farris was involved in the theft of weapons from the army.

'Look Marlowe, Marty and me went to bars together from time to time. Chasin' sheilas.' He laughed. 'They call them dames here. I'd no idea what else he got up to. I've been told some stories about him.' He shrugged. 'He always had plenty of money. He seemed to be a little out of sorts, then outa the blue he shot himself. And they wanna pin it on *me*,' Kitchener said, managing a suitably aggrieved tone.

Spencer decided this was Kitchener's rehearsed story and that his trip had probably been a waste of time. He tried a different tack. 'Do you think Marty Farris was seriously depressed? Maybe he had girl trouble?' Spencer grinned, as if he too knew that the fairer sex could be troublesome.

'I mean maybe some dame, *sheila* … gave him the heave-ho? It happens.'

Kitchener shook his head. 'Nah, we was both the same, me and Marty. You know … love 'em and leave 'em. There's always plenty more wahines where they come from.' He smirked slyly and scratched the side of his face. 'You know what I mean?'

'On the night he shot himself, he seemed a little down, you know, a little …'

'Depressed?' Spencer added.

'Yeah, yeah that's it. A bit depressed. Why? I got no fucking idea.'

Spencer suspected Kitchener was lying through his teeth.

'Anyhow, as I said before, they got nothing on me,' Kitchener bragged with a crafty grin. 'They're flying me back to Sydney in a few days. Can't happen soon enough as far as I'm concerned.'

'What happens back in Australia?'

'I imagine I'll be back at the Northam army camp as a weapons instructor.'

'You might find yourself fighting the Japanese.'

Kitchener laughed in derision. 'Mrs Kitchener didn't give birth to no fools. I won't be fighting anyone.' And he added with a broad wink. 'You can make a lot of money out of the army in war time. I guarantee when it's all over, Wayne Kitchener will be sitting pretty. *Yessir.*' Kitchener clasped his hands behind his head, smiling smugly.

Spencer winked, trying to give the impression he was struck by Kitchener's ingenuity. Rarely did Spencer take an instant dislike to someone. Kitchener was one of life's opportunists. The sort of man who would swindle little old ladies out of their pension money. A petty thief. Someone who'd always have his hand in someone else's pocket.

'You'd sure want to be careful.' Spencer tapped the side of his nose and smiled.

Kitchener nodded his head smirking, also tapping the side of his nose. For a brief moment, Spencer thought he was going to open up; spill the beans and dazzle him with some details of his nefarious activities.

'Well ... let's just say ... there's a lot of opportunities if you're smart about it. If you know what I mean?' Kitchener sniggered.

Spencer had been prepared to be sympathetic. The graphic,

stencilled inscription proclaiming Kitchener's death on the cell wall now seemed to make perfect sense and was probably justice well served. Spencer had always been philosophically opposed to the death penalty. But in speaking to the odious Wayne Kitchener, who was clearly prepared to put his own selfish interests over the lives of his fellow soldiers, he realised that he wouldn't shed a tear over his demise.

It seemed obvious to Spencer the scheming Wayne Kitchener had well and truly met his match in Don Bidstrup.

Momentarily, a picture of Don Bidstrup appeared in Spencer's mind. Bidstrup had been the mastermind behind operation DNA when Spencer had found himself transported back in time to Australia in 1941. Spencer believed the charming Bidstrup to be one of the most ruthless people he'd ever encountered.

Bidstrup would have signed the death warrant with relish, probably laughing while witnessing the execution. Spencer was a little disturbed at how quickly it seemed his own thin veneer of compassion had disappeared. His experiences on operation DNA had quickly led to adjustments in his thinking. *I think you might have got this one right, Don.*

Spencer rubbed his chin as he tried to get the measure of Kitchener. He was looking for some reason to like the man and found nothing. 'So, you fly to Sydney and then …?'

Kitchener grunted. 'I've had some telegrams from—let me see now.' He rummaged through the pockets of his prison jeans 'Yeah, some bloke called Bidstrup is meeting me in Sydney. Apparently, there's going to be a debrief. He's promised me a real nice spread. A "bang-up meal," he said. I imagine he's a nice chap who probably realises the Yanks have treated me badly.'

Nice chap? Oh, dear. Wayne, I'm sure the spread Don puts on for you will be first class. Sadly, I suspect it may be your last. Spencer decided to change tack. 'How well do you know Lee Tai?'

There was no mistaking the naked terror on Kitchener's face. The smug smile disappeared. His head turned swiftly from side to side as if someone might be in earshot.

Spencer was alarmed. What did this say about the shady Lee Tai?

'I-I … I hardly know him. He was a friend of Marty's.'

'Well,' Spencer persisted, 'I was told that you and Farris spent quite a bit of time in his company,' There was no doubt Kitchener had gone from confident conman to a man consumed by fear.

'I don't want to talk no more. Guard, guard! Get him out of here. I want to go back to sleep.'

Kitchener rolled over and faced the wall.

CHAPTER NINETEEN

A MAN CALLED HORSE

The interview with Kitchener was far from satisfactory. Spencer's impression of the man was exactly as Crabtree and Spinetti had portrayed him. A vicious, grasping opportunist. There was no doubt in Spencer's mind, even if he hadn't shot Farris, he certainly had the capacity to do so.

A light drizzling rain fell as Spencer floored the V8 to the *Chronicle*. The tyres made a monotonous hiss over the rain-washed roadway. The vacuum-operated windscreen wipers on the Ford seemed to have a lackadaisical approach to clearing the drops that spattered the screen. Screeching into a convenient space, he slammed the car door shut, sprinting into the foyer, grateful for his hat's protection against the elements.

Spencer had been unsure as to what exactly a journalist did in 1941. It now seemed he had plenty to work with.

Spencer glanced at the next office where Roxanne was talking to a tall, loud, brash character with a ridiculous black wig cut in a style, that by Spencer's reckoning, was at least twenty years out of date. Blonde eyebrows and stubble made the black wig look even more incongruous. His face was scarred. *A roadmap of gangster life, I'd say.*

The Brooklyn accent made him sound like a hoodlum. Was this Horse?

'Well photographer lady, how about you'en me go to de fights on Saturday? Lotsa girls will be there, so you'll have someone to talk to.'

Spencer didn't want to eavesdrop, but the glass partition wasn't sound-proofed, and he could clearly hear the conversation.

Roxanne was settled back in her chair, arms folded; her body language said it all.

'Horse, you know I hate boxing.' Roxanne shuddered. 'And in any case,' she, rolled her eyes as she turned her gaze briefly to Spencer. 'I think … I'm spoken for. And on top of that you're such a misogynist.'

Horse's face fell. 'What's a miso … misogist?'

Roxanne appeared to study the spectacle that was Horse. He appeared crestfallen. Then it seemed as if Roxanne took pity on him. She smiled. 'A misogynist is someone who's irresistible to women.'

Spencer decided to terminate the encounter.

'Horse,' he called out. 'Do you have a minute?'

'Hey boss, I heard that mug Ivan clobbered you? What a nerve. You want I should have a chat with him?'

Spencer pondered the man before him: tall, with muscles that suggested many hours spent in a gym, a red veined nose that looked like it had suffered many frontal attacks, and a pronounced cauliflower ear. All of this, Spencer concluded, meant Horse was no stranger to violence.

Spencer was grateful for the information Roxanne and the agents had already supplied about the nefarious Horse. He knew from Spinetti and Crabtree that Horse had spent his early years, when not in reform school or prison, as a successful heavyweight boxer. His home was originally the roughest part of Brooklyn. As a young man he'd drifted into involvement with the local mob.

If you're going to be a successful street fighter, there was perhaps no better learning academy than the New York mob. Spencer imagined to Horse, violence was as natural and normal as cleaning his teeth.

Escaping that life to be a seaman on a cargo vessel. Horse had jumped ship in Honolulu, deciding Hawaii was for him. For the first time in his life, he was going straight.

Horse came across as being semi-literate. Certainly not a man of letters. But apparently, he was a skilled tradesman. It was just, his skills didn't come with a recognised diploma.

Spencer shook his head at Horse's offer to chat with Ivan. 'No Horse,' he cautioned. 'It was just a misunderstanding. But I'd like you to come with me tonight to Lee's Bar. I want to chat with some of the people, just maybe they won't want to chat back.'

'Those mugs will talk to me; don't you worry 'bout that. Anyhow boss, I don't mind Lee's joint, they always got some sweet dames there. And I'm a misogyst.'

'Misogyst?' Spencer raised an eyebrow.

'Yeah, boss, you know—*misogyst*. That's someone who's resistible to dames,' he added proudly.

Spencer glanced across at Roxanne who had her hand to her mouth trying to stop her laughter.

CHAPTER TWENTY

LEE'S JOINT

Horse and Spencer headed out of town to Lee's joint. The V8 Ford burbled happily, disturbing the torpor of the beauty of the Hawaiian night. Spencer always thought of Hawaii as being synonymous with beautiful white beaches, luaus, and lovely ladies in grass skirts dancing to the rhythm of guitar, ukuleles, and drums. Tonight, there was little thought of such pleasures as they followed the long road out of town.

Spencer took advantage of their journey to surreptitiously ask questions about Horse and his life, both in Hawaii and on the mainland. Horse's easy, familiar manner suggested he and Spencer had spent some time together on assignments for the *Chronicle*.

Spencer nodded, smiling when Horse cackled, 'Hey boss, remember?'

Horse paused, wiping tears from his eyes. 'It was such a laugh I'm telling ya. The time when we was sent to talk to those bozos about their still up in the mountains, and that chump Mickey … can't remember his last name, pulled out a machete, and you …' Horse's abrasive laugh rang out again as he pointed a finger and guffawed. 'And you kicked him fair square in the balls. That's the first time I saw you fight.' He whistled a low, tuneless sound. 'I dunno what you call that fighting that you do, but that was ace, I'm telling ya.'

They were now passing plantations of pineapple crops, with the occasional farmhouse. As they rounded a bend, they disturbed a flock of Hawaiian geese fossicking by the side of the road, their low calls sounding like they were trying to start a conversation but had run out of something to say.

'Over there, boss.' Horse pointed at the beachfront roadhouse, its front open to the elements. People sat relaxing at tables on the lawn under coloured lights strung from palm to palm. On a raised bandstand, a five-piece Hawaiian band was playing. In front of the bandstand was a dance floor crammed with slow-moving couples. Waiters dressed in traditional garb were run off their feet, supplying thirsty patrons with jugs of beer. Spencer noticed some of the men were American service men, but most of the civilians appeared to be Japanese. There may have been war in other parts of the world, but here at Lee's joint they were partying like there was no tomorrow.

On the surface, the establishment appeared to be just your average happy juke joint, with ordinary people out to have a good time. But Spencer knew if Crabtree and Spinetti had concerns, they had good reason. Spencer was wary, glad he had the amiable Horse for back up.

A vocalist wooed the crowd with her angelic voice, singing a popular tune to the obvious appreciation of the mainly male clientele.

'I'll never smile, no I'll never smile again … Until I smile a smile at you again …'

The singer's hips moved provocatively, accentuated by her swishing grass skirt. Her long, lustrous black hair hung almost to her waist. She moved sensually to the sound of the music, her bare feet moving rhythmically.

Horse nodded approvingly. 'Say boss, ain't she a real glamour puss?'

'That she is Horse, but remember we have a job to do.'

Horse pointed to the front of the bandstand where an open, four-gallon oil drum stood.

'See that boss, that tin can is for the tips. Those mugs are falling over themselves to throw their money away. I seen her before. I reckon she'd wind up with a hundred clams easy.'

'Very interesting Horse, but the lady isn't the focus of our attention.'

'Sorry boss, just sayin' is all.'

Spencer had to admit the singer was a class act and he would have enjoyed joining the crowd, having a beer, but he had a feeling danger could be on the menu. The band finished their set.

'Thank you, thank you,' the singer breathed into the microphone, waving at the audience.

Horse nudged Spencer. 'This gal sure knows how to work a crowd.'

Spencer glanced briefly at the sultry songstress. *I think the Hawaiian girls are the sexiest on the planet, the way they move.*

Horse pointed at the rear of the building. Spencer glimpsed a large timber and thatch roof extension, partially illuminated by the feeble light of a solitary globe.

'That's where Mr Tai lives when he's in town. He's a real big shot,' Horse added unnecessarily. 'You ain't been here before boss?'

'First time. At least I think it is. Now, be prepared. There could be some trouble.'

Horse directed Spencer to a lane way at the side of the building. 'The car park's at the back.'

Spencer steered the Ford carefully down the narrow laneway. At the rear was parking for at least a hundred cars. It was packed with Jeeps, Buicks, Fords, even some upmarket Cadillacs and some very stylish Studebakers.

Horse gave a low whistle. 'Jeez boss there's some guys with a lot of lettuce here.'

Spencer glanced sideways at the big man. 'I don't think the guys with the "lettuce" are going to be a problem but be careful. I'm told that this is where some of the bad guys hang out.'

'Don't worry,' reassured Horse. 'There's nothing that the three of us can't handle.'

'Three?'

Horse chuckled. 'Yeah, boss you me and Smitty.'

Spencer shrugged. *Who in hell is Smitty?*

'Hey boss, you've seen Smitty before.'

Spencer stared at him with raised eyebrows.

Horse opened his jacket. On his belt was a pancake holster with a gleaming black, snub-nosed 0.38 Smith and Wesson.

Spencer frowned, realising he should have known all about "Smitty".

'Sorry Horse,' Spencer said, as he touched his forehead. 'This bloody amnesia … I don't remember …'

'That's ok boss, I forgot you'd lost ya marbles.'

Spencer grinned. His gaze settled on the gun. 'Ok, but only use the gun as a last resort, right? You know how I feel about firearms.'

'Sure, boss whatever ya say.'

Spencer and Horse strolled down the drive to the bar and restaurant. Spencer looked dapper in his high-waisted and pleated brown trousers and short-sleeved check shirt. He was particularly fond of his two-tone brown and cream saddle Oxfords. Horse was not quite so fashion conscious, sporting heavy-duty working man's trousers with braces, and a poorly cut jacket, to cover the holstered gun. His cream Panama with black band camouflaged his outrageous wig.

Spencer and Horse sidled up to the bar. Horse scanned

the crowd for local villains. There was a collection of mainly Japanese men at the bar. Night had descended and their working day was now over. Their stained dungarees and stout working boots gave the impression they were plantation workers finished for the day. Spencer nodded.

'Nice night for a beer.'

His friendly greeting was met with a stony silence, with some of the men at the end of the bar muttering amongst themselves. Spencer glanced sideways at Horse, who gave him the thumbs up, whispering, 'I told you we'd have fun.' Horse seemed to relish the threat of violence. Spencer didn't feel quite so comfortable.

'Two beers.' Spencer beamed at the Japanese barman.

The barkeeper poured their beers. No welcoming smile. Just a hostile stare.

Spencer paid for the drinks. Seeing a table with a couple of American servicemen and some Japanese civilians sitting with them, Spencer approached.

'Good evening gentlemen, my name is Spencer Marlowe. I'm with the *Chronicle*.'

'That's nice,' one of the Japanese sneered. 'Don't you think that's nice?' he repeated, smirking at the rest of the table. The other men glared at Spencer and Horse. The hard expressions on their faces made it abundantly clear that Spencer and Horse were not welcome.

Spencer began to think that maybe things weren't going to work out after all. He made a last-ditch effort. 'Did any of you know the late Marty Farris, or an Australian serviceman named, Wayne Kitchener? I'm prepared to pay for the right sort of information.'

The first man was villainous looking, with a vivid slash of a scar that ran from his cheek bone to under his jaw. He pointed a finger at Spencer.

'Beat it Mac, we don't like reporters,' he snarled.

Horse started to laugh, a loud braying laugh. The hard cases sitting around the table may have been prepared for many things, but not for Horse's laugh.

'You see something funny pal?' The man with the scar stared hard at Horse. In a voice little more than a whisper, he repeated, 'You see something funny, pal?' His buddies fell silent, fearful of the scar-faced man.

Scarface was tall for a Japanese, and had a muscular build. His rolled shirtsleeves revealed bulging biceps. His hands were rough and calloused and an assortment of gaudy rings adorned his fingers. Spencer shook his head at the sight of the knuckleduster jewellery.

'You think I'm funny Mac?' he sneered, rising slowly to his feet. 'Well, do you?'

Horse couldn't have looked happier. 'Yeah,' Horse retorted. 'I think you look pretty funny. In fact, I was laffin' at your scar. Ya look just like a Jap Al Capone, don't he boss?' He winked at Spencer.

'Wonderful,' Spencer groaned. Maybe bringing Horse hadn't been such a great idea.

For a moment the Japanese man seemed to have difficulty in grasping that Horse was poking fun at him. He then made the mistake of prodding Horse in the chest.

'Get goin' bud or I'm gonna hurt ya.'

Nobody had ever done that to Horse and not suffered the inevitable consequences.

'Whadya reckon boss?' Horse smiled, with enjoyment. He briefly contemplated the offending finger, turned again to Spencer.

Before Spencer could answer Horse unleashed an uppercut shipped direct from Brooklyn. The Japanese Al Capone lookalike collapsed in an unconscious heap. Horse stared at the prostrate form of the tough guy, with a smile not unlike that of an innocent child who'd just learned some new feat and was proudly waiting for its parents' words of praise.

The hard-faced barman whispered something to one of his staff.

Horse turned to the others at the table who gaped at Horse in a shocked silence. 'Any of youse guys wanna try your luck?'

Spencer tapped Horse on the shoulder. 'Time to go.'

Spencer and Horse strolled off as if nothing had happened. Turning into the shadowy driveway to the rear car park Horse nudged Spencer. 'We got company, boss.'

Four figures appeared from behind a large clump of bushes. One appeared to be carrying a meat cleaver, the other three armed with what looked like murderous blades. Spencer wasn't particularly alarmed. It was comforting having Horse as an ally. It was obvious Horse seemed to find the scenario amusing. He faced the men with relish.

Spencer shook his head. Seriously, these guys didn't look like professionals. Amateurs conscripted in a hurry. Meat Cleaver looked like a chef, big, clumsy, gangly legs and arms appearing to lack coordination, definitely not cut out for the job of assassin. As for the guys with the knives, one of them looked like he really didn't want to be there. The others looked like knife fights were not quite their thing. The question was, why?

The man with the meat cleaver yelled, careering straight at Horse, who grinned, as the man drew close, Horse bellowed, 'Hey, Mr Tai, Mr Tai,' as he pointed behind the thug. The thug hesitated, glancing over his shoulder. This was all Horse needed. Again, Horse's destructive right hook came into full force. There was an audible crack, the man staggered, collapsing, unconscious. The man with the meat cleaver was well and truly out for the count.

'Goddamn cream puff,' Horse snorted. 'What a schmuck.'

In the meantime, two of the other thugs cautiously advanced on Spencer. '*Atakku*,' yelled one of the knife wielders, waving the blade above his head as he suddenly bounded forward. He was big and awkward. His wild eyes gleamed as he raised his arm emitting another primal scream.

Spencer couldn't help laughing at this fearsome apparition hell-bent on turning him into hamburger. *I'll give you your due, your keen, but you sure as hell don't know how to use a knife.*

He was quickly and painfully immobilised with a knee strike. The other thug was despatched with a roundhouse kick. The last assailant looked wildly around for some backup, but seeing none, he fled into the night.

'Jeez boss, that's some pretty fancy footwork.'

Spencer smiled. 'And we didn't need Mr Smith.'

Horse guffawed again. 'That wouldn't been nearly as much fun.'

CHAPTER TWENTY-ONE

SEISMIC PHOTOGRAPHY

Eight of the clock in the morning, and the *Chronicle* team was going full pelt. Copy boys were collecting the morning contributions for the next edition. The clock was ticking, the deadline waited for no man. Victor Smith paced relentlessly, cigar in hand tut-tutting and muttering, 'Yes well, yes, I know.' Spencer was hunched over his typewriter finding the heavy weighted keys strange to his fingers, which were used to an electronic keyboard with backspace and delete keys. He came to the end of a paragraph and almost reached for the Enter key, *again*. Shit! He glanced around but no-one was looking at him. He hit the carriage-return lever and continued typing.

Journalism was a new career for Spencer; every minute piece of type that he painstakingly battered out on the ancient typewriter had to go to the research department for verification. He found the hustle and bustle of the newspaper invigorating. After the first couple of weeks, he discovered he was actually enjoying his new vocation; except for the bloody slow typewriters.

The shrill ringing of his phone broke his concentration. 'Spencer Marlowe. Can I help you?'

'Is that Marlowe?' A male voice, difficult to hear. It was muffled, nervous and insistent.

'Yes, this is Spencer Marlowe.'

'I know where the weapons are. Whadda I have to do to get the reward?'

It had been a month since the government reward posters went up and the phones had rung madly ever since. This was the fiftieth call this week. 'Who am I talking to?'

'Can't tell you that … too dangerous.'

The voice started to give instructions. 'Tomorrow at noon, go down Waimea Road, till you get to the Hamblyn pineapple plantation, make a right. You'll see a track about five hundred yards with a sign, Frogmore Mill. Drive to the mill. It's deserted. Wait for me there.'

'Hang on a minute.' Spencer wanted more information.

'Tomorrow. Noon. Bring the money.'

The line went dead.

Spencer sat motionless, collecting his thoughts. He picked up the phone and dialled.

'Is that you Matt?'

'You got it.'

'Spencer here. There's been an interesting development. We need to talk, ok?'

Spencer tore out of his office and ran to the coupe. Throwing it into first, he accelerated noisily down the busy thoroughfare, slamming to a stop at the front of the address he'd scribbled on a scrap of paper: 15 Acacia Place.

A number of offices stood along the street, timber and brick structures in need of paint and T.L.C. All with the same opaque white windows. Nothing looked like a government law-enforcement agency.

Spencer scanned the signs: *R J Montague, Attorney at Law*, *Vernon Huckerby: Tax Agent*, *Hawaiian Dentures*. He chuckled to himself at the sight of a painted wooden model of smiling teeth that perched on the roof of the dental prosthetist. Next to this a nondescript office with a sign announced in faded roman lettering, *Seismic Photography*. No further description or indication of opening hours, prices, or details of the services that Seismic Photography supplied. *This is the address all right, what's going on?*

Spencer shrugged, then pulled open the warped timber-framed glass-panelled door with a matching sign in plain lettering. What the hell was seismic photography anyway?

Inside, a business-like woman battered away on a typewriter while smoking a cigarette. An overflowing ashtray in front of her testifying to her love of the tobacco leaf. Placing the glowing cigarette into the ashtray, she looked him over.

'May I help you,' she asked, with a hard-edged stare suggesting, "don't mess with me buddy".

By now Spencer was confused. He observed a blown-up photo of a smiling woman in an aviator's outfit standing next to a bi-plane. Nothing about the premises suggested secret government agencies, spies in trench-coats with hats pulled down low over their eyes, just a sparse office, no advertising signs, nothing to indicate the nature of the business. Presumably the photo alluded to perhaps aerial photography that in some way was also seismic. Very puzzling.

'I've come to see Mr Spinetti or Mr Crabtree,' Spencer announced cautiously, not entirely sure he was in the right place.

The hard-eyed appraisal continued, as if she was figuring out whether he was friend or foe. Her cool stare reminded him of his third-grade teacher, it made him acutely uncomfortable. He had to stop himself from blushing.

Just then Matt Spinetti appeared from one of the offices. 'Marlowe, good morning. Welcome to Seismic Photography.'

Spencer opened the low panelled door, walking through to the office where Walter Crabtree waited. Spencer shook both proffered hands. The men took a seat in Walter's bland office, pulling up a chair each. Spencer noticed a walnut bookcase filled with official-looking, red leather-bound journals that took up an entire wall. A sturdy oak desk sat in one corner of the room and nearby, an ice box, and a steel safe. The sight of a grey steel gun rack holding two Winchester repeating rifles, two pump-action shotguns, and two Thompson sub-machine guns brought home to Spencer that these guys meant business.

From the plain grey-green linoleum to the heavy grey steel filing cabinets, the entire office said government. On the desk itself sat a number of utilitarian objects:an old-fashioned loudly ticking alarm clock, a photo of a smiling President Roosevelt, a desk calendar, in-tray, lamp, a pen rest, and large desk pad with green blotting paper; the top sheet, covered with blue ink marks and jottings. A framed copy of the constitution hung on the wall behind. This could've been one of thousands of offices across Hawaii and the United States except for the telephones which nestled side by side, close to Matt's right elbow. One was standard black, the other red. Spencer didn't have to be told this phone linked directly to the FBI's highest echelons of power in Washington DC.

'Seismic Photography, really?'

Spinetti and Crabtree laughed. Matt pointed at Walter. 'Seismic Photography was Crab's idea. By the way, seeing as you're on the team, first names, ok?'

Spencer gave a mock salute. 'Walter … Matt. So, what's the go? I'm now officially secret agent Spencer Marlowe?'

Matt laughed. 'I tell you what kangaroo man, Crabs and I are Number One and Number Two, you can call yourself Secret Agent Number Three, as soon as you shoot someone.'

'If you don't mind, I'll call myself 007. I think it has a nice ring to it. Now, moving right along, what exactly is Seismic Photography?'

'It came to me in one of my brilliant brainwaves,' Walter modestly proclaimed. 'I'd absolutely no idea what it meant, and I figured nobody else would. *So*, seeing as we don't want anyone knocking on the door, *voila.*'

'And what exactly is the significance of the Amelia Earhart lookalike?'

'Nothing really,' explained Walter. 'I just thought I'd throw the photo in for a little authenticity—nice touch, don't you think?'

'What about the delicate flower behind the typewriter? Is she in on the act?'

'Stella's far from a delicate flower,' chuckled Matt. 'She can shoot the pips out of a strawberry at fifty yards, and she has a loaded 0.38 with a silencer sitting in a drawer by her right hand.'

The secrecy surrounding the agents was understated but to Spencer, it reminded him of Don Bidstrup when he was involved in operation DNA. And like Bidstrup, Spencer was sure these two would cut corners, play any number of dirty tricks, and still remain unaccountable. The next hour was spent going over the plan for the next day.

'Now Spencer, you realise this could be a con: a trap?'

'Sure,' Spencer replied, with more confidence than he actually felt. 'But I reckon we've got all bases covered. And besides, remember I'm taking the "Brooklyn Brawler" with me. What could possibly go wrong?'

'Yeah, just don't get too cocky buddy, you just never know, ok?' Matt growled.

'Coke?' Walter opened the door of the ice box, extracting three bottles. Spencer gratefully accepted the drink, toasting the two agents. 'Cheers!'

Matt spilled a cigarette out of a soft pack, clicking his zippo and sending a plume of smoke towards the ceiling. 'It's a shame you drew a blank with Kitchener.'

Spencer glanced at the two men. He'd recounted his interview with the questionable Australian Warrant Officer the day after he'd visited Kitchener in jail. But like the agents, Spencer was certain Kitchener had been hiding something important from him. Probably lots of things, but still, he wondered if he should've gone to see Kitchener again.

Matt exhaled noisily. 'Without a doubt I believe your suspicions are correct. Slippery, slimy, in fact a real piece of work. We've been digging into his past. What the Aussies sent over only confirms our suspicions, as you know.'

Spencer shook his head. 'And nothing else has come up with his name on it?'

'Nope. But someone's paying for a lawyer. We've got nothing direct on him, so the lawyer has put a stop to our enquires. Kitchener's off limits—jurisdiction of your Aussie mates only.'

Walter looked glum. 'So, it looks like there's nothing we can do about him; he's as guilty as hell and he should hang, but ...' He shrugged, his face registering his disgust. 'He's on the next airplane we can organise back to Sydney. Out of touch and out of danger from US law I'm afraid.'

Matt held Kitchener's file in his hand. 'We haven't given up, though. We've been communicating with a captain in your security services.' He flicked through the pages. 'Yes, here it is—a Captain Bidstrup.' Matt emitted a low, rasping chuckle. 'I get the impression this guy Bidstrup has some pretty serious clout. I'm just hoping against hope he can succeed where we've failed.'

It was all Spencer could do to keep a straight face. He leaned back in his chair.

'Y'know guys, call me psychic or just an old-fashioned romantic, but I reckon Kitchener is going to get his just desserts.'

Matt just grunted. 'Yeah, well I sure hope you're right. Anyhow, let's hope for the best for tomorrow. If the mysterious caller is on the up and up and can give us the low down on the stolen weapons, it'll sure be a load off our minds.'

CHAPTER TWENTY-TWO

HORSE HAS A GOOD DAY

Spencer pressed a switch on his office intercom, smiling to himself as he thought what an asset the big man was if there was trouble. 'Horse? Mosey on down to my office, old sweetheart. We've work to do.'

'What's up boss?'

'I want you to come with me tomorrow morning. I'm not expecting trouble, but you never know. Oh, and … perhaps bring Mr Smith.'

Horse grinned from ear to ear. Spencer knew Horse would instantly connect the dots and without asking would figure there was a connection with their trip to Lee's Bar.

'Don't worry about a thing boss. Those guys are creampuffs.'

Spencer admired Horse's confidence.

Spencer and Horse set off, Spencer carrying an envelope containing one thousand dollars.

'Hey boss, you got the Jacksons and Grants right?'

'What the hell are Jacksons and Grants?'

'I figured the reward would be in twenties and fifties, you know? Andy Jackson's a sawbuck, and old Grant's a fifty.'

'Yeah, gotcha Horse. Remember I'm an Australian. I'm not up with American presidents.'

The Ford powered along the undulating blacktop of Waimea

Road, with plantations on one side and the shore on the other, reminding Spencer of his childhood in Australia. He spotted surfers on their long boards demonstrating their skills, while admiring girls waited under colourful umbrellas on the pristine white beach.

'This's the turn, boss.'

Spencer still had trouble understanding Horse's mangled Brooklyn speech.

'An' there's the sign—Frogmore Mill.'

The track they were now following was heavily wooded. 'Good spot for an ambush,' Spencer reflected grimly.

Horse was uncharacteristically quiet, the Smith and Wesson held loosely in his right hand as he scanned the surroundings, on high alert for any sign of trouble. The Ford crawled along the rough track at little more than a walking pace, bouncing and rattling over the bumpy surface. They'd now been travelling along the track for half an hour.

Spencer noticed the Hawaiian trees were covered in the creeping liana vines, very beautiful but also ideal for an ambush. As they plunged deeper into the rainforest, the sunlight struggled to penetrate the verdant foliage. The atmosphere was dank, dark and mysterious.

They pulled into a clearing, their eyes scanning the surrounds and the old mill. Rough and semi-derelict, it provided a number of hiding places for a potential ambush. Spencer brought the car to a halt and waited. Rivulets of sweat poured down his face. Roughhewn planks at haphazard angles gave the two-story structure the impression that a strong wind would blow it over. There was a large opening to the loft, where a rusty dilapidated windlass was bolted to a worn timber joist. Spencer could just read the faded sign on the ancient timbers: Hamblyn Pineapples. He figured the first storey would provide the perfect place for an ambush. It was in darkness. Spencer could imagine eyes watching their every move, guns in hand, waiting …

Horse's sweeping gaze scoured the first floor and the surrounding under-growth, his hand hovered over his revolver. 'This don't smell right boss,' he whispered.

A harsh rasping voice, rough with animal malice, a voice that suggested a large intake of cigarettes and whisky, bellowed out from inside the mill.

'Didja bring the cash?'

Spencer climbed out of the car, waving the envelope.

Four men snaked out of the mill. Bandanas covered their faces. Three of the men held carbines. The man with the revolver, barked again. 'Throw the money away from the car and reverse down the track.' This was a statement that didn't invite discussion or dissent.

'I can't do that, 'Spencer shouted.

Whisky Voice grinned, raising his revolver.

Horse was out of the Ford, crouching behind the door. In one swift movement he stood and fired. It was like seeing the violence unfold step by step in slow motion. Horse's 0.38. The cartridge exiting the snub-nosed barrel. Whisky Voice's scream. A hand clutching a stomach. Dark red blood seeping through fingers.

Completely unfazed, Horse yelled to Spencer. 'Jeez boss, what I tell ya? Creampuffs!' He shook his head in disgust.

Meanwhile the other creampuffs looked at each other uncertainly.

'Plug the bastards,' screamed the tallest of the trio.

A barrage of shots rang out from the undergrowth. The three riflemen fell to the ground, they hadn't fired a round. They lay there, an untidy sprawl of death.

'Not a bad shot, Horse.' Matt Spinetti's voice rang out from the scrub. Horse chuckled, giving them a salute.

Matt and Walter emerged from the tangled underwood,

their rifles still smoking. Walter cautioned. 'I'll check inside the mill, just in case.'

Another man sprinted out of the mill. A lean ferret-faced man. He dashed headlong into the rain forest. Horse raised his revolver, but the man had disappeared.

'Wotcha reckon, you want I should go after him?'

Spencer shook his head. 'Horse, you'd never find him, there's too many places to hide.'

Spencer had the merest glimpse of the man who'd run off into the scrub.

Spencer turned his thoughts to the graphic silent scream of violent death that lay before him.

The three riflemen were well and truly dead. The man with the revolver was breathing, in short, rasping, painful-sounding breaths, whimpering in agony, a small trickle of blood oozing from his mouth.

Horse contemplated his handiwork like a craftsman satisfied with the result of his labours. 'Not ya lucky day punk, is it?'

CHAPTER TWENTY-THREE

NO CLOSER TO THE TRUTH

Walter and Matt's obvious clout became evident, when the dead men were taken away in an unmarked police van. Whisky Voice was carried away in a city ambulance that cautiously headed down the rough track. The ambulance was accompanied by an unsmiling uniformed police officer, who gave the impression he would've relished an escape attempt by the now unconscious prisoner.

Later that day at Seismic Photography, Walter, Matt, and Spencer went over the morning's events. Walter, chalk in hand, was poised by a blackboard. He'd written names with links to the missing arms. He paused, lighting a cigarette.

'This is the info we have. At the top of the list, Marty Farris. Under that, Wayne Kitchener. Then these four other heavies.'

'They're the four dunces from the mill,' said Spencer pointing at the board.

Matt shrugged, seemingly indifferent to the demise of the bad guys.

'Do you know who they were?' Spencer queried.

Matt gave a half smile. 'They were all petty thugs with a rap sheet a mile long. We're inclined to think they weren't involved in the operation but got wind of the *Chronicle's* interest, deciding to exploit the situation for a few bucks.'

Walter glancing at Matt, chuckled. 'These guys really weren't too smart. Matt and I decided to get to the mill early. They didn't check around to see if anyone was there. I mean, how goddamn basic is that?'

Matt snorted. 'What Walter isn't saying, is that we'd been there since six this morning with creepy crawlies all over us. Ugh.'

Spencer grinned at the two agents. 'Well, on behalf of Mr Demmer and I, we both thank you from the bottom of … but meanwhile, what about the one that got away? Any clues?'

Walter groaned. 'That my Aussie friend, was I believe, the rather colourfully named, Joey Banana.'

'Spencer shook his head. 'Banana really? Where do these guys dig up these names?'

Matt pointed a finger at Spencer. 'Funny name alright, but a nasty piece of work, a standover man. He reputedly beats up and rapes the hookers, then steals their cash. He's a real sweetheart, that one.'

'Are you going to pick him up?'

'Well,' said Walter, scratching his head, 'we probably have bigger fish to fry. In any event no-one is prepared to make a statement. Anyway, he didn't pull a gun on us, his mouthpiece would argue he was an innocent bystander so …'

'Have you interrogated the man that Horse shot?'

Walter looked grim. 'I don't know if Horse carves notches on his Smith and Wesson, but you can tell him there's one more to go on.'

'Dead?' Spencer with raised eyebrows, knowing he was stating the obvious.

'Gone and unlamented. The now late, Jigsaw Kalua. Small-time hood and stick-up man. He was on parole. He just finished a five stretch for holding up a liquor store.'

'No problems, for Horse—legally?' asked Spencer as he glanced at the two men's faces.

Matt grunted. 'Officially, the coroner's report will read, the four men had a falling out and … Well as best we can tell, they got involved in a gunfight with each other.' Matt shrugged.

'No loose ends.'

CHAPTER TWENTY-FOUR

THE FACE OF EVIL

Strapped to a chair, Hiraku Sato was barely conscious. His only clothing; blood-soaked trousers. His body bore the marks of cruel and ghastly torture. His head was bent, chin resting on his chest, as if unwilling or unable to look at his tormentors. Two hard-looking men in Japanese military attire, stood wearily, on either side of Hiraku, their sleeves rolled up, and blood spatter staining their once pristine uniforms.

Hiraku's hands were swollen, his fingers broken, the tips where the fingernails had been ripped out were covered in congealed blood. Next to him a small stainless-steel table. It was the sort of table that you might find in a doctor's surgery, or in an operating theatre. On the table laid out neatly were the torture implements: a scalpel, pliers, an electric drill, and bottles of acid.

A fourth man sat on a comfortable padded chair, wearing a voluminous robe that did little to hide his vast bulk. The big man was smiling.

'Well, Hiraku, I do believe you've probably told us all you know.' The smile broadened. He turned to his subordinates with a giggle, as frightening as it was incongruous.

'Take him up to the big house. It's lunchtime.' He rubbed his hands together with obvious satisfaction.

Hiraku was dragged from the large packing shed to the impressive single-level home situated a hundred feet from the ocean. The manicured gardens had palms dotted throughout. A large pool dominated the front of the house. A scene of tropical beauty, marred only by the jarring sight of armed guards patrolling, watching the ocean for any sign of unwanted visitors.

Set out on the patio in front of this palatial home was a table laden with Japanese delicacies: tempura vegetables, whole baked fish, miso soup, and sushi. Hiraku was placed on a chair by the pool. The fragrant odours of the feast seemed to revive him. He hadn't eaten for two days. The supreme master, Lee Tai, surveyed the delicacies with satisfaction. A few feet away, a nervous servant waited for the signal to serve the boss.

At one end of the pool was a barrier leading to another smaller pool. What to the casual observer appeared to be only a swimming pool was in fact an elaborate structure, a pool leading to another pool. Hidden from sight was the pet—the white pointer.

With an imperious wave and like an emperor of old, the man watched, smiling as two men lifted up the barrier. The shark swam into the larger pool. This perfect killing machine was twenty feet long and weighed four thousand pounds. Hiraku was now conscious. He let out a long, pitiful wail.

Like a shogun of old, the big man again waved his hand. The men who'd carried the semi-conscious Hiraku from the packing shed dragged him to the pool's edge. Hiraku's face paled in horror. The pain from his damaged fingers forgotten, he struggled.

'No… please no, no, no,' he cried.

The men in an effortless motion, threw him into the water. It was a task they'd performed many times before. They were impervious to such unspeakable brutality. The shark circled.

Hiraku was ripped to pieces in moments. The first strike severed one leg. His arms flailing, Hiraku briefly rose to the surface, emitted a sickening scream, cut short as he was dragged below the water. All that was left was his life's blood discolouring the pool. The master licked his lips. His eyes gleaming with pleasure, he broke into laughter.

'Lunch please, Akihiro.'

CHAPTER TWENTY-FIVE

WE HAVE A PLAN

Matt and Walter rolled up Spencer's drive in their battleship-grey Plymouth. Spencer watched with mild amusement through his living room window. The conservative suits and hats and the ever-present briefcases were, he thought, as effective as a uniform broadcasting their occupations. The men's watchful eyes scanned constantly for potential trouble. Spencer found both men likeable, and he felt sure of their competence. He'd witnessed their decisive handling of the gunmen at Frogmore Mill.

'Come in! Coffee?'

'Thanks.' A grateful Walter shook Spencer's hand. Matt smiled, also shaking his hand.

They sank into the chrome framed, laminated kitchen chairs. Walter snapped open his briefcase. 'Ok, down to business. First of all, we need you to read and sign these.' Walter placed several sheets of official papers in front of Spencer.

Spencer picked them up and began reading. The documents were a copy of the Secrets Act. Nodding at the two agents and with a flourish, Spencer signed the papers with his latest acquisition, a Parker fountain pen.

Matt pulled a sheaf of photos out of his briefcase, laying them out across the table. 'Have a look at these.'

They were aerial photos of a house by the sea and others of a jetty, with a number of moored trawlers. A few hundred yards from the jetty, was a collection of sheds. Matt pointed to the photos. 'This is Tai's operation on Molokai.' He pointed at the house. 'This is where Tai and some of his servants live. Over here is what we believe is the canning factory.' He pointed to the other buildings, 'Here, we reckon are the workers' quarters, but these other buildings are a mystery. Altogether we know there are a disproportionate number of workers and buildings for the size of the operation.'

'What we're about to tell you mustn't go any further.' Matt glanced at Walter, who nodded his approval.

'Of course,' said Spencer and glanced at the two men.

'We have an operative working for Tai. We believe if his identity was known he would be … well' and he grimaced. 'We think he would be disposed of.'

'Why exactly are you showing me all of this?' Spencer waved a hand at the photographs. Walter and Matt gave a chuckle. 'Well, we have a sort of a plan,' said Walter as he leaned back in his chair. 'We believe Tai is going to be in his office on Tenth Avenue tomorrow. What we were going to suggest is you and your gorgeous photographer Roxanne, try to get an appointment to interview him. Take photos etcetera, say you want to do a story on him and his operation because … well… let's face it, it's an important local business. I mean, after all, he employs hundreds of people, and everybody here in Hawaii buys his produce.'

Spencer glanced at the two men. 'Well, as it happens, Lee Tai has been pestering Vic Smith to do an interview and write up on his fishing empire. The cheap bastard wants some free publicity.'

'That could work in nicely,' Matt asserted with a wink.

Spencer thought for a minute. 'You really think he'll go for it?'

'Gotta be worth a try,' Matt replied.

CHAPTER TWENTY-SIX

THE SMILING MR TAI

Spencer and Roxanne sped along Kalakaua Avenue on their way to Lee Tai's office on Tenth Avenue.

Roxanne was aghast at Spencer's account of the encounter at Frogmore Mill.

'My God it sounds like the *Gunfight at the O.K. Corral.* How about Horse?' Roxanne shook her head. 'There's absolutely no doubt he saved your life. What a lovely man. I feel bad about all the awful things I've said about him,' she said with a rueful grin.

She grasped Spencer's arm. 'Do you think you could stop behaving like a movie gangster? This isn't the silver screen. The bullets are real, and so are the bad guys.' Her voice was tinged with concern and emotion. She looked away, a little embarrassed at wearing her heart on her sleeve.

'Whoa, hang on Roxanne. I thought I was acting like a reporter who just happened to get caught in the crossfire? Let me tell you, I'm not overly fond of people taking pot-shots at me. You take photos, I write stories. It's always going to be the case. Some people aren't going to like what I write. Seriously, I'm not going to sit back and write about who was the winner at the latest flower show. I want to stir things up. Frankly I enjoy it. The pen is mightier than the sword and all that.'

The coupé powered along the roads the V8 emitting a dull

roar, an uncomfortable silence existing between them. After some minutes Roxanne the professional was back in control.

'Do you think Lee Tai is involved in any of this?' she finally asked. 'He is a respectable businessman, right?'

Spencer shrugged. 'Look, the fact is, there is rumour and innuendo but if Spinetti and Crabtree could have pinned anything on him, they sure as hell would have done so by now.'

'Ok then, what's the plan?' Roxanne had on a multi coloured scarf, tying down her locks, protecting her from the wind and sun. With difficulty she lit up a cigarette.

'Well,' Spencer yelled over the sound of the exhaust and the wind, 'I'm going to ask him about his rags to riches story. Ask him where his partner Mr Kemp is. You're going to take photos.' He shrugged. 'We'll see where it goes.'

Lee Tai's office was part of his old plantation house; a two-storey structure in white-painted timber and with a dark-grey shingled roof. A broad, timbered verandah wrapped around the house. Well-established stately palms were dotted throughout the grounds. White and yellow jasmine climbed up a wooden slatted gazebo, their sweet, rich fragrance scenting the air. The owner's love of horticulture was evident in the colourful blooms that surrounded the house, looking as though a thousand brides had strewn a thousand bouquets.

'Isn't this something?' Roxanne exclaimed. 'There must be money in fish ...' She paused, glancing sideways at Spencer.

'I don't want to sound paranoid, but seriously, I've heard so many rumours about this guy. Surely there has to be some foundation to all ...' she gazed searchingly at Spencer. 'God, I don't know! I really don't.'

'What can I say? I've also heard the rumours.' Spencer shrugged. 'But the fact is, this is our job. It's about questioning and interviewing dubious people. If this guy is a gangster, he's managed to stay on the right side of the law.' Spencer chuckled.

'Whatever Lee Tai is or isn't I don't think he's going pull out a gun and shoot us.'

Roxanne growled. 'I think maybe I'll shut up and take pictures.'

Roxanne paused, snapping shot after shot, pointing the camera in all directions. Spencer sauntered up to the front door. Before he could knock, a demure Japanese lady wearing a black silk kimono opened the door and bowed.

'You must be Mr Marlowe and Miss Gething. Please come in. Mr Tai's expecting you.' Her warm smile put both Spencer and Roxanne at ease.

Roxanne glanced sideways at Spencer, mouthing silently,

'I feel better already.'

Everything about the property exuded taste and wealth. The artworks adorning the walls and exquisite sculptures displayed on marble stands, were breathtaking.

'Can you believe all this stuff?' Roxanne exclaimed. 'It's got class written all over it.'

They were ushered into a spacious office, with a floor-to-ceiling window overlooking the manicured garden and the ocean beyond.

'Please, Miss Gething, Mr Marlowe, have a seat. Mr Tai will be with you in a minute.'

The lady bowed, smiling as she exited the room.

'I can't resist this. I'm sure Charlie Chan wouldn't object.' Roxanne snapped a shot of the garden framed by the office window, whispering to Spencer, 'Her English is perfect, I mean she couldn't have looked more Japanese if she tried, but she sure as hell doesn't come across like she's part of a criminal enterprise.' She shrugged. 'Well, what do you think, eh?'

Spencer drummed his fingers on the armrest of his chair, whispering, 'I suggest you change the subject. For all we know, someone could be listening. Why don't you talk about those?'

Behind the desk stood a bookcase carved from oak, with what Spencer thought was an extraordinarily diverse assortment of books. Spencer recognised such classics as Tolstoy's *War and Peace,* and *The Definitive History of the Roman Empire* by Gibbons.

Roxanne cast an eye over the overflowing bookcase. 'Now there's a surprise—he likes books.'

'I think there's more to this man than meets the eye,' said Spencer, pointing to one dusty tome just as Mr Tai swept into the room. 'Ah, Mr Marlowe, you're familiar with *The Tale of Genji?*'

Spencer was a little surprised at the vision of Lee Tai. Corpulent, certainly, and his robes seemed an odd choice for a business meeting. Spencer recognised the *yukata,* this one a subtle charcoal-grey silk with a wide black silk band. Lee Tai's demeanour exuded a persona of power and control.

'Mr Tai I'm impressed. I must admit I've never read it, but I understand it's regarded as the world's first novel.'

'Quite so Mr Marlowe. The Western world sadly doesn't appreciate or understand the depth of Japanese culture.'

'And I see you also have novels in Latin.' Spencer pointed to an ancient bound book, *The Selected Works of Cicero.* He knew the author wrote his novels at the time of Christ.

Lee Tai seemed pleased at Spencer's interest.

'Yes, Mr Marlowe we can learn much from the Romans. That is why I've learnt to speak Latin, along with a smattering of other languages.' He rubbed his hands together. 'Anyhow, that's enough about me. It's so nice to see you both,' he beamed. 'Can I get you anything, tea, or coffee perhaps?'

Spencer flipped out his notepad and unscrewed the cap of his fountain pen.

'Our readers get a kick out of rags to riches stories. If you could give us a little detail about ... you know, your early days. Was it a struggle? Was your family involved in fishing? All that sort of stuff,' Spencer said, and smiled reassuringly. 'If you can give us the broad outline. I can fill in the gaps. My job is to put in the colour, and the detail. All the stuff that people want to read.'

Lee Tai nodded. 'It's true I came from humble beginnings, but ...' he shrugged, 'it's just a case of a little luck, and a lot of hard work.' Lee smiled an oily smile, adding, 'I've found, Mr Marlowe, if you treat people well, and operate your business fairly and compassionately, others go out of their way to help you.'

Spencer proceeded to ask his host questions about his life and history. Spencer had the feeling he was listening to a rehearsed story, complete with the clichés about a poor boy succeeding against the odds. Something about the story didn't quite ring true, but Spencer had a hard time figuring out, just exactly why he felt that way. Lee Tai gave the impression of someone playing a game. Playing with them. But to what end? Spencer found the man an enigma. For a brief moment, his thoughts flitted back to the mysterious Madame Zu. What, he wondered, would the palm reader make of the inscrutable Lee Tai?

'Yes, indeed Mr Marlowe, the Gods have smiled upon me. I arrived in Hawaii some years ago. My family had a business in Okinawa. The climate there is not dissimilar to Hawaii. We'd been involved in fishing and canning, but in a small way. There were distant relatives in Hawaii, and they had told us there were many opportunities here and so ...'

Lee Tai droned on about the early days, the hardship, and his gradual climb to success. Spencer glanced at Roxanne, who looked like she was about to nod off. Lee Tai's story, as well as being boring, was so utterly predictable it sounded completely rehearsed.

Spencer then asked, 'What about Mr Kemp, where does he

live?' for just a moment Spencer thought he saw the mask slip and a flash of anger.

'Ah,' lamented Tai. 'Mr Kemp no longer involves himself in the day-to-day affairs of the business. He lives in California.'

Tai gave a little giggle. 'Would you and Miss Gething like to visit my operation on Molokai? I'm sure you'd both find it interesting.' He gave a sly smile. 'And of course, a write up in the *Chronicle* would be appreciated.'

Spencer quickly glanced at Roxanne, who gave him a nudge.

'We'd love to,' said Roxanne, 'wouldn't we, Mr Marlowe?'

'Yes, that's perfect Mr Tai. Miss Gething and I are at your disposal.'

'Splendid!' Lee Tai rubbed his hands together seemingly with unabashed delight. 'Please forgive me, I have some pressing business on a couple of the other islands. Time, tide,' he said, then chuckled, '... and fish, wait for no man.'

He picked up a small brass bell and rang it. Within seconds the door glided open, and the black kimono-clad woman appeared. 'Yes, Mr Tai?'

'Ah Ichika, would you please check my diary for three weekends hence?'

Ichika bowed, smiling as she exited the room. In a moment she was back with a large leather-bound diary. 'Yes, Mr Tai that weekend is free.'

'Splendid! Is that satisfactory, Mr Marlowe?'

Lee Tai promised to have them picked up at the jetty on the Saturday morning in three weeks' time. They would be transported in his luxury clinker-hulled motor-launch, with a photo shoot by Roxanne and Spencer writing a story on the fishing and canning operation being arranged. Lee Tai insisted they stay the night on Molokai, saying he was delighted with the *Chronicle* giving him free publicity, and his chefs would prepare a wonderful meal.

CHAPTER TWENTY-SEVEN

SPENCER LEARNS ABOUT AUTOMOBILES

'Just who does he think he is? The *creep*,' said Roxanne. Her voice changed to a poor impersonation of Lee Tai's voice. 'Oh yes, Mr Marlowe, does that suit you? How nice it is Mr Marlowe. Three bags full Mr Marlowe. Who does he think will be taking the goddamn photos? For Christ's sake! What a nerve. Wouldn't you think I had some goddamn say in it?'

Roxanne strode like a woman possessed to where the Ford was parked. Spencer quickened his pace to keep up, only just controlling his laughter.

'Where to, girl?'

'I don't really feel like going back to work,' Roxanne snarled. 'I'm so goddamn angry. But I guess we have to, otherwise Vic will be throwing tantrums. While we're at it, what's so *damn* funny?' she snapped, glaring at Spencer.

'Roxanne, Roxanne,' Spencer reassured, 'just remember that although Tai appears to have a veneer of culture, he's Japanese. In his world, women don't count for a lot. So, seriously, just get over it, ok?'

'Spencer, it's not just his attitude to women. Haven't you noticed; he makes no eye contact with me? It's as if I don't exist. It's … I don't know … I feel damn silly. Everything about him on the surface, looks above board. His secretary Ichika is charming and professional. I mean, everything seems to be exactly what you'd expect from a wealthy and honest businessman, but he still gives me the creeps. He's so … so … I don't know. So … *yuk*! I just don't *like* the guy.'

Spencer was silent for a minute. 'I don't disagree, but this is our job. It's what we do. What you have to keep in mind is, even if Tai is everything Matt and Walter suspect, what on earth do you think he's going to do? He's hardly likely to knock us off while we play Clark Kent and Lois Lane on Molokai. That just doesn't make sense. Sometimes I think Matt and Crabs are a bit paranoid. Trust me, it'll be an unforgettable weekend. Now let's get out of here.'

Spencer pressed the starter. The engine sputtered and then stopped. 'Damn thing, it often does that.'

'For God's sake Spencer, use the choke.'

Spencer experienced a moment of panic. *Choke, what on Earth is she talking about? Choke, choke what?*

Roxanne glared at him, pointing to a button on the dash marked with a large letter C.

'Ah yes … of course … yes. Choke.'

'Spencer, what's wrong with you?' Roxanne, grabbed the offending button, swiftly pulling it out. 'Now, pump the accelerator and start the damn car.'

The Ford obligingly sputtered into life.

'Thanks for that. I wondered why it was so hard to start in the mornings.'

Roxanne looked at him strangely. 'There wouldn't be anyone in the whole of the USA who didn't know what a choke was. Honestly, you really are a man of mystery, aren't you?'

Spencer shrugged, staring fixedly on the road ahead.

'Spencer,' Roxanne sighed. 'I don't care whether you know

what a choke or a carburettor is. Really, I don't, but it just adds another layer to this man of mystery bit … honestly it's …' She paused as if searching for the right words. 'It just doesn't make sense. It's just another thing that doesn't … God, I don't know. It's as if there are pieces missing. I wish you'd confide in me, because whatever your past is, I'd understand, honestly.'

Spencer gazed at this concerned and earnest woman. He was overcome with guilt and the unfairness of it all.

They were both lost in thought as Spencer drove back to the *Chronicle*. As always in Hawaii, the weather was perfect. A light breeze swayed the palms. They drove past workers toiling in the pineapple plantations. No-one seemed to work too hard. The fertile volcanic soil produced an abundance of staple crops, so nobody ever went hungry.

Roxanne broke the silence, 'That pig gives me the creeps. The very thought of him makes me shudder.'

Roxanne sighed as she placed her feet on the dash of the Ford. 'You're right of course, he can't help being what he is, and I guess there was no deliberate intent to insult me. It's just that I've been fighting this whole, she's-just-the-little-woman thing, all my life.'

And with a wink she added mischievously 'Well, I'm finally going away for the weekend with the mysterious Spencer Marlowe.'

Spencer glanced at Roxanne. 'It'll be a good story. The food will be spectacular.'

Roxanne rolled her eyes.

'Roxanne,' he said sharply. 'Ok, you don't like the guy— neither do I—but it is what it is. Look at the positives. A nice boat trip, we'll be staying in what I imagine is luxury accommodation, and we'll have a great time.'

Spencer didn't wish to alarm Roxanne, but he too didn't feel comfortable with the complex Mr Tai. He was no better informed than before their meeting with Lee Tai. The stunning residence and the obvious power and prestige that was on full view for the world to see certainly created an air of respectability. The charming Japanese lady who'd greeted them was the epitome of the well-groomed corporate meet and greet.

Logic seemed to dictate that the mystery swirling around Lee Tai was perhaps nothing more than rumour or superstition. Maybe Matt Spinetti and Walter Crabtree had an overdeveloped radar when it came to sussing out bad guys? After all, he reasoned, that was their job.

But he was confused. There was no mistaking the naked terror on Wayne Kitchener's face at the very mention of Lee Tai.

Still, until they found some evidence of wrongdoing, Lee Tai was in the clear.

The V8 emitted its distinctive growl. The gears crunched as Spencer changed into third. He was still far from expert with manual gearboxes.

Roxanne winced. 'These Fords have certainly got slow synchros.'

'Sure have,' replied Spencer, not entirely sure what a synchro was.

CHAPTER TWENTY-EIGHT

YET ANOTHER BAD GUY

The working day had finished, and the sun was heading west, throwing magnificent pink and orange hues across the clear sky. Spencer jumped into the Ford, pointing it towards town. No particular plan, maybe a cold beer, a nice meal, and perhaps listen to a band at one of the many bars. A light breeze carried the sounds of a Luau in progress. Spencer could hear the sounds of ukuleles, guitars and drums playing a lilting melody.

He was slowly adjusting to his life in the 1940s. He'd managed to push the memories of his past into the darkest recesses of his mind. There was an acceptance that there were things beyond his control. Mentally he ticked off the plusses of his current predicament: the climate, the country, even his job. Spencer could imagine forging long-term friendships with the cast of his current drama. But he was aware the same forces that placed him here could just as easily whisk him away again to the next century.

He thought of Michiyo and their last evening together in Hawaii. How long had it been now? Time seemed to play tricks with his mind. When he tried to envisage Michiyo, Roxanne's face would superimpose over hers, unbidden, like a mischievous imp wanting to be seen. Although only months had gone by since his awakening at the lockup, his past life was already hazy.

Spencer felt disturbed by just how much Roxanne occupied his thoughts. If he could be convinced, he was here to stay forever, he would unhesitatingly relish a relationship with this feisty, intelligent woman. He remembered vividly his previous journey into the past and how, when he'd least expected it, he'd found himself miraculously flung headlong back into the next century, back with Michiyo. The problem for Spencer was not knowing just where fate was taking him, meaning he couldn't contemplate being disloyal to Michiyo. This dilemma was tearing him apart. There'd been sleepless nights when he felt overwhelmed by his situation. He desperately missed Michiyo.

He headed into Waikiki. Motoring along Kalakaua Avenue, he spied the Moana Surf Rider Hotel, its classic white timbered structure seeming to beckon him. The Hawaiian, Union Jack flag, and Old Glory crackled in the breeze.

Although in this year 1941, Hawaii was yet to become the fiftieth state of the USA, in every way it was already America, happily embracing every aspect of the stars and stripes.

Strolling through the grounds of the Moana he admired the understated piece of colonial architecture. Wandering through the spacious garden to the beach bar with its magnificent banyan tree he could smell the simple smells of the sea. He noticed the odours: fishy, salty, sea weedy. Although the Surfrider in no way resembled the stately Raffles, it had that same air of tradition and permanence.

Feeling peckish, he ordered the Kalua pork, a wonderful dish, slow-cooked underground in banana leaves. Fragrant and enticing. Spencer's tastebuds were titillated as the waiter placed the heaped plate in front of him with a flourish. The pork was unbelievably tender and served with corn, carrots, and endives, washed down with ice-cold Hawaiian Primo pilsener beer. Perfect!

Spencer reclined in his chair overlooking the Pacific. The inviting beach still had swimmers and beach walkers in abundance. The golden disc of the sun was already touching the surface of the ocean. The white sand was illuminated by the soft glow of lanterns. Couples were stretched out on beach towels. Colourful umbrellas were dotted haphazardly as far as the eye could see. The swell of the waves revealed several surfers; he could just make out their long boards twisting and turning.

Spencer reflected on the turmoil he'd been engulfed in, thinking ruefully, there were certainly worse places he could be. Placing his hands behind his head, he felt a rare moment of contentment. Climbing to his feet and stretching, he searched his pocket for the cornicello. Pulling it out, he held it before him. *Just what part do you play in the life of Spencer Marlowe? Do you hold the answer to the mystery or are you nothing more than a trinket?*

Still lost in thought, Spencer ambled out to the Ford, not noticing a casually dressed Japanese man attired in worker's overalls who was watching him and following at a discreet distance.

With the top down and the warm breeze ruffling his hair Spencer headed into the twilight towards his cottage. A dark blue Buick followed stealthily. A pair of cold eyes focussed on the back of his head. Behind the wheel of the Buick was a man with a mission, a man indoctrinated from birth. A dangerous man.

Still pondering recent events, Spencer was almost home when the Ford sputtered, cut out, started again, then shuddered to a stop. Spencer had no idea what the problem was. He wasn't used to delinquent cars. In his world they rarely broke down.

Spencer jerked the bonnet catch, climbing out of the misbehaving vehicle he flung open the hood, peering at its innards, not having a clue what he was looking at.

The dark blue Buick glided to a halt behind his car.

A saviour? Spencer smiled at the man.

Spencer observed a compact, well-muscled man wearing new khaki work clothes, a wide-brimmed hat, and a welcoming smile. He rubbed his hands together as if itching to solve the issue of the misbehaving vehicle. 'What's the problem?'

The good Samaritan looked vaguely familiar. Spencer shrugged. 'She just stopped.'

'Let's have a look, I'm a mechanic.'

The man chattered on about the weather, football, and baseball. '…Yep, the Rainbow Warriors look like having a good year.'

Spencer knew the Warriors were a local team.

'I think I've found the answer. Have a look here.'

Spencer obligingly bent over the engine compartment.

'Yeah, Spencer, I think that's the problem.'

Spencer? How does he know my name? Spencer spun around.

A long-bladed knife gleamed in the half light.

With lightning speed, Spencer drove his rigid fingers into the man's Adam apple, using just enough force to immobilise the would-be-killer who collapsed, grasping his throat, trying desperately to breathe. Spencer's strike had been so swift the man hadn't seen it coming.

The double-edged stiletto clattered harmlessly onto the pavement. Unable to speak, the man's chest heaved, his eyes bulging and swivelling from side to side as he struggled for air. The sweat of terror glistened on his brow. Eventually breath began to fill his lungs. Desperation and resignation in equal measure were written across his face.

Spencer leaned back on the bonnet of the Ford, watching silently. Eventually the man's breathing began to even out.

Nondescript. That was Spencer's judgement. This thug didn't look like a decision maker. The more Spencer looked him up and down the more confused he became. The ordinary working man's clothes were all new. Spencer searched his pockets for identification, finding nothing. It was clear this was no random act of violence, robbery theft or murder. Very puzzling. 'I guess you must be what's known as a hit man. Not very good at it are you? Been doing it long?'

The man glared at Spencer, reaching into his pocket.

'No,' Spencer drawled. 'Don't do that.'

'I gotta heart condition, I gotta take a tablet.'

'Slowly does it. I don't think you want to see my next trick.'

Carefully drawing out a glass medicine bottle and slowly unscrewing it, the man paused, his hands shaking. Taking a deep breath, he tipped a tablet onto his palm. Hesitating for a moment he examined the pill, taking it between two fingers. He turned his gaze to Spencer. He smiled and swallowed.

In a split second and without a murmur, he fell backwards. His body thrashed uncontrollably as if struck by lightning. His face contorted, mouth open and eyes wide, saliva dribbling from his mouth. He clutched his throat as he struggled to breathe.

Spencer grabbed him and felt for a pulse. Nothing. There was a subtle odour of bitter almonds. Well, pondered Spencer, this gets curiouser and curiouser.

Heading off along the unlit road, the gentle sound of the surf a background murmur. Spencer jogged the remaining distance to his cottage. Hastily grabbing the phone, he dialled. 'Operator, would you connect me to Seismic Photography?'

'Walter Crabtree.'

'Walter, this is your favourite reporter. It seems we have another problem.'

'That being?'

'Well, it just so happens we have another corpse.'

Walter and Matt arrived with a screech of brakes. Their Plymouth had been pushed to excesses not recommended by the manufacturer. The car doors slammed shut with resounding thumps. Matt and Walter leapt out, guns in hand, scanning the landscape.

'You guys are always in a hurry.'

'Yes,' said Walter looking grim. 'Dead bodies do seem to give us a bit of hurry-up. I'm sure you've a good reason for icing this guy.'

Neither Matt nor Walter seemed concerned with the legal implications of what appeared initially to be a murder scene.

Spencer held up his hands. 'Whoa, hang on a minute I didn't kill him. He tried to kill me.'

'And now… he's dead,' chortled Matt, nudging Walter in the ribs. 'So, let me guess, our late Jap friend was so upset he decided to have a heart attack cos he was … let me see now, overcome with guilt?'

Spencer retrieved the medicine bottle. 'Guys, guys … he swallowed a tablet from this bottle. He said he had a heart condition.'

'Told you,' Matt smirked, 'there's your *heart attack.*'

Spencer recounted the episode in full. 'I've got no idea who he was or why he would want to kill me, but—'

'Spencer,' Walter said as he clapped Spencer on the shoulder. 'We didn't really think that you just decided to murder some innocent on the side of the road just for the hell of it.'

'For a moment you guys had me worried.'

Matt gave the body another cursory glance. 'So, you don't know this bozo? Never seen him before?'

Spencer had a closer look at the corpse. 'Look, I'm not sure. He may have been one of the guys at Lee's joint.'

Walter laughed. 'Yeah, I get it, all Japs look the same right?'

'It's not that. It's just this guy looks so … bland, so ordinary … so, nothing. He sure as hell doesn't look like your classic hitman does, he?'

Matt rolled his eyes 'Well, Spencer, Crabs and I have been in this racket for some time, and we haven't figured out what a hitman looks like. Have we Walter?'

Matt squatted, taking a closer look at the body. 'Spencer, I guess there could be endless possibilities. Journalists and newspapers are always upsetting someone. But why is it that behind everything we see or—'

'What's obvious,' said Walter, pointing at the hit-man's body, 'is that it wasn't random. Everything about this, stinks. You were targeted—the question is why?'

Spencer shrugged. 'The only person I've upset as far as I can see is the hard case that Horse slugged at Lee's joint. But seriously, that's drawing a long bow. I'd expect retribution from that quarter would be a little more basic. I mean, come on… No ID? Tampering with my jalopy? I don't think those clowns from Lee's joint would be that organised.'

Walter nodded. 'We seem to always come back to the jolly fat Japanese gentleman.'

Spencer rubbed his chin. 'I'm with you guys. Tai is certainly an odd bod, for sure. But,' he waved a finger at the two agents, 'tell me why he'd try to kill me so soon after inviting Roxanne and I to spend a weekend at his island estate?' Spencer shook his head. It doesn't stack up guys, does it?'

Before the conversation could go any further, the intrusive roar of police Harley Davidsons interrupted the discussion. Two motorbike patrolmen arrived, dismounting from their motorcycles and standing guard over the crime scene. Then came an ambulance, its revolving red light flashing eerie shadows onto the sparsely wooded surrounds. Two ambulance officers dressed in crisp white uniforms climbed out and walked quickly over to them.

Matt had a few words with the driver, while the other checked the prostrate body for a pulse. It seemed to Spencer everyone knew everyone in Hawaii. There was no checking for ID. Matt punched the driver good-naturedly on the shoulder.

A short time later a Ford Mercury skidded to a stop, siren wailing. A beefy middle-aged sergeant clambered out of the police car, gazing dispassionately at the proceedings. Spencer decided this was an old-fashioned copper; no nonsense, and accustomed to sudden death, who would show no sympathy for the bad guys. The sergeant pulled a huge stogie from his shirt pocket and bit the end off, spitting it onto the ground. A flame leapt from his worn Zippo emblazoned with a faded picture of the Alabama Crimson Tide Baseball Team. He turned to Walter, at the same time casting a curious eye over Spencer.

'Any idea who the stiff is?'

'No Eddy. I thought I knew most of the bad guys in Hawaii, but this one?' Walter shook his head. 'No idea. He's gotta be an outta-towner.'

Spencer thought the cop was probably a southerner. There was a trace of Mississippi or Alabama in his voice. Spencer watched the interaction, fascinated. The whole scene looked like something from old police TV shows he'd seen as re-runs: Dragnet or Highway Patrol. He could imagine Sergeant Joe Friday barrelling up in his V8 Ford, jumping out, insisting, "Just the facts ma'am, just the facts".

The sergeant well and truly displayed his southern background when he remarked to Walter. 'I think these nips could be a bit of a problem, a bit like the spics and niggers back home.'

Spencer gazed at the faces around him to see whether the sergeant's blatantly racist comments had ruffled any feathers. It was clear nobody saw anything amiss.

The sergeant yelled to his offsider, 'Danny, check the Buick, see if you can find anything, then drive it back to the station.'

'Roger boss.'

Spencer was intrigued to see the uniformed officers were deferential when speaking to Matt and Walter.

'Ok, anything else you guys need?' asked the sergeant.

'No Eddy, I don't think this little event's likely to go any further, if you know what I mean.'

Eddy grimaced. 'Yeah, well a dead Jap isn't that important one way or another.' He gave them a wink as he heaved himself into his police cruiser.

Definitely wouldn't want to get on the wrong side of these guys.

The ambulance officers unceremoniously loaded the body then, with red light flashing, headed off at a sedate speed.

CHAPTER TWENTY-NINE

SURF'S UP

The longboard powered down the A frame, it's rider tall and suntanned, grinning as he rode the monstrous swell. Spencer shouted in pure exhilaration at the excitement of the moment. As the wave flattened out, he edged to the end of his board until his bare feet reached the end. Then just as casually stepping back again, he demonstrated perfect mastery and control. His two companions either side of him, both young Hawaiian men, yelled encouragement.

'Go man, go! You're gonna wipe out.'

'You ever seen me wipe-out JoJo?' Spencer laughed, waving acknowledgement.

Eventually after the long run up to the beach, the three riders jumped off their boards. One of the men clapped Spencer on the shoulder. 'I can't believe it,' he groaned, 'a *Haole* better than a Hawaiian on a board, it's … it's not fair.'

Spencer laughed good naturedly. 'Well Kai I'm not going to apologise. I spent years doing this stuff.'

'Whereabouts?' the other man queried.

'Australia, JoJo.'

'No kidding?' Kai interjected. 'I thought Hawaii was the only place in the world people surfed. You coming down again? You and that sweet girlfriend of yours?'

'Not my girlfriend, Kai. A work colleague.'

'If you say so,' Kai sniggered.

Spencer decided not to pursue the subject. 'You bet, so long as I've time off. Friday's the Fourth of July, and I'm not working.'

He collected his long board dragging it up the beach to where the woman in the bright one-piece, flower-patterned bathers sat.

'Get your ice-cold Coca Cola here,' she called, waving.

Throwing the board on the sand and collapsing on the multi-striped beach towel, he lay on his side took the bottle of Coke from Roxanne and clinked it against hers. Then he stretched out onto his back, spreading his arms and legs like a starfish. His smile grew slowly into a broad grin. The only marker of time on this lazy day was the sun above them.

'Boy oh boy, that was great. There's nothing like surfing to blast the cobwebs away and clear the mind. These guys have so much enthusiasm. I tell you, it's a tonic watching them.' He hitched himself up on one elbow and pointed at JoJo successfully executing a walk-the-plank manoeuvre Spencer had shown him some weeks earlier. 'Just have a look at JoJo. He's going to be a great surfer.'

'He's had a good teacher. I've never known anyone to surf better than a Hawaiian. You're really a man of unusual talents, aren't you my Australian man of mystery?'

Spencer ignored the comment and deftly changed the subject.

'What gets me with Hawaii is there just doesn't seem to be any seasons. You lose track of time. I've been teaching these guys for months. It's been great fun.'

Roxanne mumbled as she set up her camera 'Yeah sure … seasons. Yep, doesn't change a whole lot.'

'What exactly are you doing?' Spencer pointed at her camera.

'Well, you're going to pose for some candid shots. You know, stand there, flex your muscles, show off that Aussie physique to all the wahines.'

'What on earth are you playing at?'

'See that guy over there, the tough guy with the straw hat?' Roxanne hissed.

Spencer glanced across the sand at a hard-muscled, lean whippet of a man, smoking a cigar and taking swigs from a hip flask. He appeared to be basking in the sun, staring fixedly at all the girls in their beach costumes. The stares were so intense several of the women spoke amongst themselves as they cast surreptitious glances in his direction.

Up until know Spencer hadn't paid him any attention. 'I see what you mean. The bloody creep. Talk about undressing with your eyes. How about if I have a chat, as Horse would say?'

Roxanne laughed. 'I would enjoy that, but no … I don't want to shatter your male ego. However, I won't be taking your photo. It's his I'm taking.' Roxanne nodded in the direction of the man on the beach.

Spencer was puzzled. 'Explain?'

Roxanne leaned closer. 'He fits the description of a guy who has been beating up the local … you know … the local … um …'

'Actually, I don't know. Give me a clue.'

Roxanne rolled her eyes. 'You know, street walkers, working girls.'

You mean hookers?'

'That's exactly what I mean.'

'Any idea what his name is?'

Roxanne shook her head. 'Not sure. I've heard the name Joey, a couple of times.'

Spencer took another swig of his coke, peering intently at the man. 'My God, I reckon that just might be Joey Banana.'

Roxanne stared hard at Spencer. 'The guy from the mill who ran off?'

'Yep. I reckon that's him. I'm not a hundred percent sure, but ...'

Roxanne, trying not to look too obvious, stared again. 'Are Matt and Walter going to arrest him?'

'They thought they probably didn't have enough to charge him. But whatever he is or might be, what's your interest?'

Spencer was now concerned for Roxanne. 'I mean what for? I mean, where is it leading? This isn't exactly part of your job as photographer on the *Chronicle*?'

'I'm going to show his photo to some of his victims and see if I can get them to talk to the police. Mind you, the police don't exactly have a lot of respect for the ladies of the night.'

'You're quite the crusader, aren't you?' said Spencer who was still puzzled.

Roxanne hesitated 'Believe me, I have my reasons.'

'Why don't you tell me all about it.'

To his shock, the hard-bitten camerawoman suddenly broke into a torrent of tears. 'I've never told anyone about it. Let me just do this and I'll tell you the story—my story.'

Roxanne wiped away her tears and attached a telephoto lens to the camera.

'Firstly, stand up, pose like Tarzan, while I take photos of this creep.'

Roxanne shot off a whole roll of film, muttering to herself as she did so. 'Just you wait you bastard, I'm going to fix your little red wagon good and proper.'

Finally satisfied with the number of photos she'd taken, she placed her camera in her bag. Spencer sat beside her and waited.

CHAPTER THIRTY

ROXANNE'S STORY

'I come from a small mid-western town in Wisconsin, a place of farms and forests and about as far from the glitz of Hollywood as you can get. As a teenager, I developed a passion for photography. I dreamt of becoming a fashion or movie photographer.'

Roxanne smiled as she remembered her teenage years and her childhood home. 'Honestly Spencer, life in Fond du Lac was just about perfect. It was … I tell you what it was … it was uncomplicated.'

Full of optimism, she'd left the safe, comfortable Mid-West and like so many before her, headed to the magical dream-world of Hollywood. Roxanne groaned, recalling how she'd worn her best skirt and blouse to the job interview at the movie studio.

Roxanne thought back to her big interview with the studio's publicity man, Mortimer Lester …

***

'Call me Mo,' he said, leaning across his desk and shaking her hand.

Opposite her sat a sloppy man in his fifties, sweat glistening on his brow and smoking the clichéd fat cigar. Everything about him was in bad taste; ill-fitting double-breasted suit, a grubby off-white shirt and a garish red satin bow tie. His face seemed to be set in a permanent leer.

'Yeah, yeah, these are pretty good shots,' Mo said with a smarmy smile, revealing tobacco-stained teeth and breathing a strong halitosis in Roxanne's direction.

'I'm glad you like them, Mr Lester.'

Roxanne surreptitiously scanned the small untidy office, heartened by photos of Mo with Sam Goldwyn, and another of him standing behind Gary Cooper. Day-bills from blockbuster movies adorned the walls.

He's a slob, but I guess he's one of the movers and shakers. I guess?

'Call me Mo, sweetie.'

Lester smiled, scribbling on a scrap of paper. 'Go to this address tonight at seven. There'll be a few people there, important people,' he added with a wink that made Roxanne uneasy. 'Bring your camera. You can take some shots.'

She'd alighted from the yellow cab just before seven. The California bungalow before her was not what she expected, a little down at heel, the lawn needed cutting, paint was peeling from the window frames, and the surrounding houses were down market.

'Come in Raelene, come in.'

'It's Roxanne.'

'Sure babe, sure … Roxanne.'

Lester was dressed in a smoking jacket, in faded red velvet with frayed cuffs.

Roxanne's stomach heaved as she gazed around the untidy room with its worn furniture and threadbare carpet. On the walls hung black and white photographs of voluptuous Hollywood hopefuls posing enticingly in lacy lingerie. Placed provocatively on a coffee table next to the divan sat a champagne bottle in a wine cooler, and two glasses by its side.

'Where are the other people?'

'They'll be along any minute now.'

Champagne. Only two glasses. No other guests. Roxanne remembered her parents' warnings about putting herself in danger by being alone with strangers. The penny dropped.

'I'm sorry, I've got to go.'

'Listen girlie, you wanna get on in this town, you gotta play the game.'

With that Mo grabbed her, trying to kiss her and at the same time forcing her onto the stained divan. She struggled, but he was bigger than her and practiced at what he did.

He laid across her, pulling up her dress. He undid his trousers. The man's foetid breath made her want to vomit. She screamed at him to stop. In desperation she raked her fingernails across his cheek. Droplets of blood spilled onto her face.

'You bitch,' he screamed, grabbing her by the throat.

For a brief moment memory her life in Fond Du Lac flashed through her mind; swimming in the lake, the old wooden jetty, screams of laughter as she and her friends splashed in the cold water, her father in his old jeans, smoking his corn-cob pipe.

Roxanne's hands, groped for the champagne bottle. With an almighty effort, she grasped the cold glass and slammed the bottle hard down on his head. *Crack.* Mo slumped forward on top of her.

Sobbing and gasping for breath, she heaved his bulk off her. He collapsed on the floor, a vicious gash on the side of his head, blood already seeping out onto the floral carpet.

'It's surprising, the thoughts that go through your mind. At that moment it looked to me like a crime scene from a B-grade movie. I had a vision of a judge intoning "guilty" before I was led to the electric chair, my pleas of innocence falling on deaf ears. I had no idea how much damage I'd caused by belting that bastard over the head. My sense of revulsion was so strong I hadn't been able to bring myself to touch him … you know, to feel for a pulse. I had no feeling of guilt. All I wanted was to get away as far as I could from the scene.'

Roxanne gathered her bag and camera and lurched out of the front door, her breath coming in short, sharp bursts. She stumbled down the steps and along the pebbled pathway.

In a blind panic she ran down the street, keeping to the shadows, trying to collect her thoughts. Roxanne suspected in Tinseltown her word against that of someone working for a major studio would be worthless; just another small-town girl. Only this one hadn't played by Hollywood's rules. And she suspected she wouldn't have many friends in her corner.

A feeling of terror and abject hopelessness threatened to overwhelm her as she made her getaway, sobbing and with her dress torn, Lester's blood splattered over her. She knew she had to pull herself together.

Don't draw attention. Walk normally, you're not out of the woods.

Gradually her common sense prevailed. Adjusting her clothes, she glanced around.

This was a quiet suburb, in a city that she was unfamiliar with. And Los Angeles was a big city. She wanted to put as much ground between her and her attacker as possible.

There was a good chance nobody knew her name or identity or where she lived. A plan started to formulate in her mind. For what seemed like an eternity she walked. When she spotted a Chevrolet sedan with Yellow Cab insignia coming towards her. She hailed the cab and breathed a sigh of relief when it pulled over.

'Good evening young lady. Where to?'

She sat in the cab, her eyes focussed on the back of the cab driver's head, a man in his late fifties she guessed, grey hair, a Yellow Cab peaked cap on his head.

'Sunset Boulevard please.'

'Are you OK, Miss?'

'I'm fine.' Her voice was barely a whisper.

'Well, take it from me, you shouldn't be out on your own like this. I'm from Kansas and let me tell you, LA ain't Kansas. I've gotta daughter about your age, and I wouldn't let her out on her own like this, no sirree.'

Relief surged through Roxanne like a powerful drug. The cab driver was one of her own, a caring small-town guy. Kansas and Wisconsin were peas in a similar pod. She latched on to his mid-western drawl like a drowning person thrown a life preserver. By the time the cab reached her destination, it felt like they were old friends.

She woke in the morning, the warm California sun streaming through the window of her cheap hotel on Sunset Boulevard.

Checking out of the hotel she ventured onto Hollywood Boulevard. For the first time she noticed the real Hollywood. She strolled past Grauman's Chinese Theatre, the Hollywood Walk of Fame with the stars' names embedded in the concrete paving: Shirley Temple, Clarke Gable, Mary Pickford, Lionel Barrymore, Charlie Chaplin.

Roxanne entered the Musso and Frank Grill at 6667 Hollywood Boulevard with its homely faded pink façade. Its high ceilings and dark wood panelling created a comforting ambience. The red leather booths afforded her some privacy while she carefully checked her dwindling cash.

The world-weary waitress reluctantly put down her fan magazine, stubbing out a cigarette. 'What can I get ya? Today's special is eggs and bottomless coffee for thirty-five cents.'

Roxanne wondered, had the waitress once been a fresh-faced hopeful just like her? *She sure would have been a beauty in her day… just look at those cheekbones, and still a good figure.*

'Eggs over easy on wheat toast and black coffee please. And … if you don't mind me asking, are you an actress?'

'Honey. I came from Texas over ten years ago. I was Miss Lubbock 1925. You'll knock 'em dead they all said. Yeah, well my Hollywood dream died long ago.'

The waitress' faded good looks; dyed blond hair with black roots showing and cheap floral perfume, reinforced Roxanne's new understanding of the brutal reality of Hollywood.

Roxanne perused the *Weekly Mirror* someone had left at her booth, her eyes alighting on a steamship company's ad, *Travel to Sunny Hawaii*. Accompanying the story was a picture of a sun-splashed beach and a smiling young man holding a surfboard.

***

'Spencer, he just didn't look like a Hollywood wheel, but what the hell did I know? He was absolutely revolting but I thought, well, I guess this is Hollywood.'

Spencer nodded, shocked by what Roxanne had told him.

'And that's why I hate the Joey Bananas of this world. I've been in Hawaii a couple of years now, and of course I find even paradise has its fair share of creeps.'

'What about Mo Lester? Did you find out what happened to him?'

'There was a by-line in the Los Angeles times a few days later. He told police he was attacked by a burglar. Apparently, he had a fractured skull.' Roxanne sighed. 'Honestly Spencer I felt so stupid. I've used the *Chronicle's* resources to check the creep out. The bastard didn't work for a studio, he was simply a publicity man. You should've seen him, he had photos of himself posing with major stars. I mean he had an office. Christ almighty, it turns out, he was a nobody.'

CHAPTER THIRTY-ONE

THERE SEEMS TO BE A LOT OF BAD GUYS

'Cyanide,' Matt announced, throwing the green glass prescription bottle to Spencer.

Spencer examined the bottle searching for a vital clue.

Matt, Walter, and Spencer were at Seismic Photography mulling over the unsuccessful attempt on Spencer's life.

'What do we know?' Matt asked, looking thoughtfully at Walter then Spencer.

Walter scratched his head, staring moodily out of the window. 'It looks like a professional hit,' he said. He picked up the assassin's stiletto. 'You sure as hell don't carry this for peeling apples.'

His assessment was greeted by wry grimaces from Spencer and Matt.

'For a journalist you seem to be able to handle yourself?' Matt stared; his steel grey eyes unblinking.

'Yeah, what can I say? I don't know … I can tell you, I surprised myself. I guess it was just some sort of survival instinct.' Spencer stared back just as hard, at the G man. *This is starting to feel like a contest.*

'Are you sure you haven't had some sort of combat training?

Naturally, we did some checks on you. We couldn't find a damn thing about you.'

'Well, there's not much to tell really. I'm from Perth, Western Australia. Pretty humdrum background in fact.' Spencer laughed. 'Guys, I'm just a journo who wants to see the world. No special skills. No special talent.' Spencer felt distinctly uncomfortable.

'Sorry Spencer, it's our job to be suspicious. Neither of us think you're a thug, do we, Matt?'

His partner nodded and reached for a cigarette, blowing a smoke ring at the ceiling. 'You're the least of our worries and at the moment we need all the help we can get. Personally, I'm sure glad you're on our team.'

CHAPTER THIRTY-TWO

THE ENIGMA OF LEE TAI

Thankfully for Spencer, it seemed as if the mystery about his past wasn't going to be a problem. He didn't fancy a spell in jail while inquisitive law enforcement tried to unearth a history that didn't exist. He breathed a sigh of relief, absentmindedly examining the cyanide bottle again.

'May I?' Matt removed the bottle from Spencer's hand, turning it over and examining it closely as if there was a hidden clue about to reveal itself. 'An unknown Jap with no identification and … God dammit, equipped with a cyanide pill. I mean who'd believe it?' Matt flopped heavily onto his swivel chair, a file in hand. He shrugged, lighting up another Chesterfield and inhaling deeply, sending a choking plume of smoke in Spencer's direction, drumming his fingers on the tabletop.

'I agree, Spencer, what do you think?' Walter paced the room mulling over the issues.

'I'm far from being an expert, but although it may be silly to talk about things like intuition or sixth sense, I have to tell you both, Roxanne and I keep coming back to Lee Tai.'

'Unfortunately,' Walter cautioned, 'while I absolutely accept what you say, it ain't evidence.'

'I have an idea,' Spencer laughed quietly.

'And that is?' Walter raised an eyebrow.

'How about we send Horse to see Tai and he could have a chat?'

'Nice idea,' Matt cackled, 'but probably not.'

Walter sat on the edge of the desk, clearing his throat. Matt and Spencer glanced at him.

'Go on, out with it,' Matt chided.

'What I'm going to say sounds like heresy but … sometimes I wonder if we—and by we, I mean you and I Matt—perhaps we have an over-developed sense of … what's the word? Spencer you're a journalist help me out here.'

'Paranoia?' suggested Spencer.

'Yes, that's it, that's the word. Paranoia.' Walter laughed. 'C'mon Matt, let's face it! How many times have we been convinced some jerk's a crime king only to find his biggest felony is knocking hub caps off automobiles?'

'What are you talking about?' Matt snapped.

'Look Matt … it's our job to be suspicious, that's our stock in trade. I admit that Tai's a suspicious character—'

'Listen Crabs—'

'But the reality is,' Walter countered, 'we've devoted a lot of time digging the dirt on this guy. And what have we come up with? A big fat zero?'

I know we don't have any hard evidence,' said Matt, casting a jaundiced eye over his colleague.

'Yeah, well forget *hard*. We don't have *any* evidence full stop.'

Matt glared at his colleague. 'If it walks like a duck and quacks like a duck? Walter, the fact is, evidence or no evidence, he's all we have to work with.'

Matt had a number of files on his desk relating to the late Marty Farris and Wayne Kitchener. He picked them up, rifled through them, then threw them back on the table in disgust. 'I don't mind telling you Spencer, we're copping a lot of flak from Washington. They want answers, and they want 'em fast.'

'The thing is Spencer, Washington at the highest level, and I mean the highest level possible, is in daily meetings with the Japanese Government representatives.' Walter stood up, glaring at his partner for agreement.

'I'll just bet you're all hungry?' Stella appeared.

'Stella you're a darling.' Matt smiled as Stella wheeled in a trolley.

'We must make sure our guest is being looked after.'

Stella stared directly at Spencer, smiling, holding eye contact a little longer than necessary.

Walter noticed the look and gave Spencer a knowing wink.

The tray was laden with bowls of Hawaiian poke, a raw skipjack tuna salad with vinegar, sesame oil and various subtle spices which Spencer thought was sensational. They followed with the sweet treat of malasada, the exquisite Hawaiian doughnuts.

They sat back after their meal. Matt and Walter were drinking coffee and smoking, the air was blue with the smoke. Spencer knew in this day and age; cigarette smoke was something you had to accept. You simply had to tolerate it.

'Tell us about Australia, Spencer.' Matt drew on the last of his Chesterfield, stubbing it out on his ash tray.

A subject Spencer tried to avoid. He knew that in-depth questions were difficult for him to answer. 'Well, really it's a lot like the US. Nice beaches, nice girls, everyone speaks English.'

'But things aren't exactly the same, are they?' Spencer found Matt's unsmiling visage to be unsettling.

'What do you mean?' For a brief moment Spencer felt panic rising.

'You're not telling us the whole ... *story* ... are you?' Matt stared hard at Spencer.

Spencer felt the colour rise in his cheeks and the sweat beginning to bead on his brow. Both agents fixed him with a stern, unblinking gaze. 'I … I … don't know what you mean,' Spencer stammered.

'Yeah, well you forgot Australia's got kangaroos and koala bears.' Matt guffawed and slapped his leg.

'And … and don't forget Matt. Nice girls, lots of nice girls,' Walter chipped in.

Relief surged over Spencer. 'Did you guys learn "scary" in secret agent school? And by the way, koalas aren't bears, they're marsupials.'

'Mar … what?'

'Marsupials, they have a pouch.'

'Well, I'll be.'

Matt and Walter overall seemed satisfied with Spencer's superficial description of Australia. Walter wagged a finger at Spencer. 'Speaking of girls, I noticed Stella giving you the eye.'

'She's a delight, but I do have a girl back home,' Spencer laughed.

Matt swallowed the last of his coffee. 'Back to business, I guess. Now, about the other week …' He turned, nodding at Walter, who took his cue to continue.

'This unknown assassin probably put a small hole in the gas tank of your car, followed, waiting for you to run out of fuel—then—*voila.*'

'What I just don't get is, why suicide? If he'd been arrested, charged, and convicted, he might have done a few years, but *suicide*?' Matt shook his head. 'I just don't get it.'

'Well, someone doesn't like me. Any clues who?' Spencer glanced at the two grim-faced secret service operatives.

'The latest stiff is a cleanskin. New clothes. Nothing to identify him. Zip, zero, nothing.' Matt looked thoughtful.

'What about the Buick?'

'Doesn't help us. It was stolen. We don't have a clue who he was.'

'Well, I'm not a hundred percent sure, but I think he may have been at Lee's bar the other night,' Spencer suggested.

Matt sat forward at the desk, flicking through wanted posters. 'There's at least fifty suspects here, some from California, and one who's done some time in Sing-Sing. He's an evil looking bastard, but he has tattoos, and our little cadaver doesn't. A couple look a bit like our dead chum. I'll bet, even if we take a photo of the dead gook and show it to the chuckleheads from Lee's, we wouldn't get a bite.'

Matt stared at Spencer and Walter, his fingers steepled under his chin. He pointed a finger at Spencer. 'The bozo from last night—you may've seen him at Lee's joint? You and Horse go to Tai's, then some thugs try and take you out. A bit more than coincidence!' He rose from his desk, waving a hand. 'And then for Chrissake, we have the God damned late and unlamented Marty Farris, who we *know absolutely* was responsible for pilfering enough ordnance to start a revolution! And *who* has he been seen with on frequent occasions?'

'Lee Tai,' replied Walter and Spencer in unison.

'Goddamn slippery bastard!' said Matt, slamming the desk blotter with one hand.

CHAPTER THIRTY-THREE

HORSE HAS A BOAT

Spencer sat slumped at his desk frowning as he twiddled a pencil between thumb and forefinger, while all of the past events played through his mind, a half cup of cold coffee, sat untouched on his desk.

'Penny for them.' Roxanne stepped into his inner sanctum.

'I'm trying to put together the pieces of the puzzle.' Spencer scowled.

Spencer told Roxanne about the latest developments including the attempt on his life.

'Oh my God.' Roxanne held a hand to her mouth. 'You could have been killed.'

With a look of horror on her face, she started forward then stopped, as if she was going to throw her arms around him and then thought better of it.

'Call me paranoid but all of this seems to point in one direction,' she said. She tapped her fingers on his desk, a grimace on her face. 'It always seems to come back to Lee Tai. I do hope we're going to be ok visiting the lion in his den?'

Displaying a confidence he didn't feel, Spencer assured Roxanne that Lee Tai would be unlikely to try anything on his own turf, even if involved in something nefarious.

'What I would like, would be to take a boat to Molokai and

scout out the island with the aid of binoculars, just to get a feel of the place.'

'Horse has a boat. And the name of his boat is—wait for it—*Jailbird.*' Roxanne had a smile on her face.

'I guess that figures,' Spencer laughed.

CHAPTER THIRTY-FOUR

FISHING FOR MORE THAN FISH

A typically spectacular Hawaiian dawn with a fiery orange sun and stunning cloud formations was laid out before them as they boarded the *Jailbird*.

Spencer couldn't imagine they would be in any particular danger playing the part of tourists fishing for marlin, but if any craft headed their way from Molokai, he was prepared to beat a hasty retreat.

Horse proudly showed off his clinker-hulled motor launch with its white paint and polished cedar superstructure. Spencer admired its sweeping lines. The main salon was at deck level just behind the bridge. A line of portholes suggested cabins and a dining room below. It was a fifty-foot Famille B motor launch propelled by two 61XB diesel motors and would do a comfortable twenty-five knots. Polished brass lamps gleamed under a canvas canopy. It really was a thing of beauty with its natural timber trimmings and brass accessories. A classic Edwardian motor-boat. Spencer gave Horse a thumbs up. 'Nice boat.'

Spencer had filled the icebox with beer and Coke and had brought along the thermos flask, full of steamy coffee.

'Ok buccaneers hoist the Jolly Roger and we'll go and strike fear into the hearts of the great unwashed. Yo ho and a bottle of rum,' Spencer quipped.

Horse looked puzzled. 'Jeez boss we ain't got no bottle of rum.'

'Just a joke,' Spencer soothed.

Roxanne looked like a model in a fashion shoot with a blue and white striped top, deck shoes and a captain's hat set at a jaunty angle. Spencer still got a kick out of the fashion of the day. He wore a Hawaiian shirt with high waisted white trousers and rope-soled shoes. Horse went for the practical with rough working clothes: well-worn stained blue coveralls, a faded fawn gabardine work shirt and battered deck shoes completing his ensemble.

'Here's the plan.' Spencer glanced towards Horse. 'Let's get the Marlin poles out. I want this to look like a fishing trip. When we get close to Molokai, I want for us to look for the entire world like tourists.'

Horse frowned. 'Boss, ya don't want I should moor the boat on Molokai?'

'No Horse, we just want to get close enough to see what's there.'

'Yeah, boss cos they got leopards.' A clearly relieved Horse exhaled. Horse was facing the stern fixing the marlin poles in place.

'Leopards?' repeated an incredulous Spencer.

Roxanne giggled, whispering in Spencer's ear. 'Lepers.'

Spencer grinned back at Roxanne.

Molokai had been the home of a leper colony since the 1800s. Over eight thousand unfortunate souls had been banished there over the years. Taken forcefully from their families and loved ones.

One side of Molokai housed the infamous leper colony, the other side, the fishing and canning business of the mysterious Lee Tai.

This was turning out to be a great day. As always in Hawaii, the weather was perfect. Spencer and Roxanne were at the stern, drinking Coca Cola, the wake of the *Jailbird* the only disturbance in the otherwise placid sea.

'Tell me a little about your elusive girlfriend, fiancée, wife, or whatever she is? 'I'm not sure I *believe* there is a fiancé.'

'Well, you can *believe* it,' Spencer returned with a laugh and clinked their Coca Cola bottles together.

Spencer was silent for a few moments. Any discussion about Michiyo was venturing into deep dark waters where no reasonable explanation could be given. Honesty was important to him and he was deeply troubled about living a lie. He so much wanted to be honest and open about his predicament, but he knew it was impossible.

'There's not that much to tell,' Spencer confided. 'We had been under pressure as Michiyo had to finish a university degree. She had enormous family problems. And we thought it best for both of us to have some breathing space, and then with the war that Australia is embroiled in. It's been very difficult for me to get back there.' Spencer shrugged.

Even to Spencer this fabrication sounded a bit lame. Roxanne gazed searchingly into his eyes, as if weighing up whether to press the issue. 'Well, if that's your story and you want to stick to it?' Roxanne's voice was stone.

An awkward silence descended as they both wrestled with their inner thoughts.

'Shouldn't be long now boss. How's about a beer? The salt air makes a man thirsty.'

The ever-cheerful Horse took Roxanne's mind off their discussion. 'Coming right up Cap'n,' she said, and grinned.

Spencer was now relaxed. A beautiful boat, a beautiful day, what more could he want. He glanced at the lady beside him. He had no idea whether he was destined to live permanently in the past, or like his last time-travel experience, he would wake up one morning with Michiyo beside him. His personal regret was his attraction for Roxanne which was growing daily. Her quick wit and easy charm combined with grace, style and beauty, meant he spent more time thinking about her than was good for him.

'Roxanne, my compliments on the lobster salad,' said Spencer. Horse and Roxanne were sitting back relaxing on the deck. Horse's razor-sharp machete deftly hung drew and quartered a magnificent Hawaiian pineapple for dessert. As Spencer admired Horse's impressive skill with the blade, he idly wondered whether it had only been pineapples that had felt the keenness of its edge.

The twin engines roared to life.

'Ok Horse, Molokai.'

Horse grinned, gunning the motor, the powerful diesels propelling the craft to a very respectable rate of knots.

'So, I can get my bearings, would you circumnavigate the island?'

'Sure, ting boss, circa ah, circum … circagate,' he added brightly.

'Go round the island.'

Keeping a respectable distance, Spencer could make out through his powerful binoculars what he imagined was the leper colony. The scenery was spectacular with towering cliffs and verdant foliage. Spencer shuddered. Leprosy was a disease of the Middle Ages, not something which still existed in the twentieth century. No matter what problems you face there is always someone worse off, he thought.

The island was far bigger than Spencer had imagined. He could see the palatial home of Lee Tai coming into view. It was set back from the beach. The home was situated in a bay, a perfect semi-circle protected from the worst of any storms.

Spencer could clearly see a swimming pool, a long wooden jetty, a number of moored trawlers, and a motor launch similar to the one they were on.

Standing on the jetty also peering through binoculars was a man watching them, a rifle over his shoulder.

The *Jailbird* held its course, meandering lazily across the placid waters, with Roxanne holding one of the fishing poles, giving the illusion that they were on a fishing trip.

Past the wide spit of land was another sheltered bay, with another jetty and more trawlers. Set further back, Spencer could make out the canning operation and beyond that, a large, corrugated iron warehouse.

'I wonder what secrets that holds?' he murmured to himself.

'Look,' Roxanne pointed.

Heading their way was a single-engine monoplane. It flew low over the *Jailbird* and close enough for them to make out the features of the pilot. The plane circled back, flying over the canning factory, disappearing behind a small hill.

'Lee Tai has an airstrip ... the question is why?' Spencer turned to Roxanne.

'I don't like this place, and I don't like Mr Tai,' Roxanne grunted.

On the jetty by the canning factory there were a number of men loading or unloading the trawlers. Spencer observed them talking amongst themselves, pointing in their direction. Four of them hurried to a small launch, which powered off from the jetty, and headed their way, with its bow in the air.

Am I being paranoid? Spencer wondered. Ok they appear to be taking an unhealthy interest in our presence. But maybe they just want to go fishing. There's no law against carrying rifles. Tai could well be a respectable magnate with an overdeveloped sense of security.

'Time to go Horse,' Spencer said cheerfully. 'I think we

might get a visit from the ungodly. So how about showing us what the *Jailbird* can do?'

'Sure, thing boss.'

The reassuring bellow of the twin diesels accompanied the more raucous screams of the seabirds and the crash of waves hitting the hull.

CHAPTER THIRTY-FIVE

JOEY BANANA

'Dammit all!' Spencer leaned against his front door frame, coffee in hand, moodily surveying the breakers in front of him, and the ever-present Kemp and Tai billboard. He'd tossed and turned through another sleepless night, wrestling with his predicament and the uncertainty of it all. He'd adjusted to life in the 1940s. He liked everything about it. The relaxed lifestyle. The fact it was so uncomplicated. He was finding the slower pace, and the lack of technology a blessing, not a curse. He found more and more he was being seduced by Hawaii.

His recurring dilemma were the two people who meant the most to him: Roxanne and Michiyo. The two names kept bobbing up in his mind, over and over. There was no doubt in his mind he loved Michiyo absolutely, but he now tended to view her as somebody in the past. As the months flew by, he found it more and more difficult to even imagine going back to his old life.

He remembered to pull out the choke. The obliging side valve V8 roared into life. The Ford rattled down the limestone drive, he reversed onto the boulevard, and smoothly selected first gear. The coupe eagerly leapt forward. Perversely, Spencer had fallen in love with his maroon jalopy. There was nothing about it that compared with the vehicles from his century, but he enjoyed wrestling with the heavy steering. The slow synchro's had made him an expert at double de-clutching. He revelled in the crack of the twin exhausts when he put his foot down. '*Chronicle*, here we come.' He headed off to the job he was enjoying more than he ever thought possible.

Spencer cruised up to the *Chronicle*, adroitly reversing into a parking place. This time with no crunching of gears. He patted the dash of the Ford affectionately. 'Now I'm used to your funny ways, I think we've become good friends.'

He bounded out of the car, striding into the office full of *joie de vivre*.

'Good morning Rita. Is Miss Gething around this morning?'

'Morning Spencer,' she replied, patting her hair. Once again, her eyes were a-flutter. 'Did you have a nice weekend?'

Spencer had to smile at the flirtatious Rita, who only addressed him as Spencer when Roxanne wasn't in earshot.

'Miss Gething left a message for you.'

Spencer took the hastily scrawled message, reading it with dismay.

I have the name and address of that low life on the beach. I've taken Horse with me in case of trouble. The creep's name is Joey Banana. He lives above Smith's Union Bar in Fort Street.

Fort Street was in the very heart of Honolulu's vice and corruption square mile. This was where the opium dens were, the desperate, the down and out, the absolute underbelly of Hawaii's criminal element. Spencer took some comfort from the fact that Horse was her protector, but he wasn't happy. He sprinted out the door of the *Chronicle*. Punching the starter button and jamming it into first, he floored the Ford, and raced towards Smith's Union Bar.

Spencer pushed the coupe to its limits, thundering towards downtown Honolulu. The traffic was heavy by Hawaiian standards. Spencer found himself stuck behind one of the clanking, slow-moving orange trams, edging its way down the thoroughfare. Coloured lights and bunting had been strung between shopfronts and light poles, and fluttered in the breeze. Stilt walkers wearing colourful masks pranced along the street, waving and yelling at the delighted crowd. Children squealed as strings of firecrackers exploded in a flash of light and sound. Costumes as colourful as a summer garden clad the array of marching band members and people riding the floats.

Ordinarily, Spencer would have been entranced by the spectacle, but now he beat his fists on the dashboard in frustration at the slow pace of the traffic. This was the Aloha festival celebrated every August, the whole street seemed to be out celebrating. 'Some sort of wing-ding, just what I bloody well need,' He muttered.

A jeep stalled in front of him. 'For Christ sake move it, will you pal?' The driver managed to get it rolling again.

Spencer tried to pass a slow-moving tram, only to be stopped by a contingent of traditional Hawaiian warriors chanting blood-thirsty war cries and brandishing spears, their brightly coloured cloaks trailing behind them. His mind quickly cast back to when he and Michiyo were in Singapore's China Town, watching the dragon festival with excitement and awe. Another life: another century.

The streets were thronged with US serviceman and their families. They appeared to be revelling in the opportunity to let their hair down. Finally, he could see the bar. He managed to swerve into a vacant space and lurch to a stop at the front of the disreputable Black Cat Café a couple of doors down from Smith's Union Bar.

Spencer blinked as he entered the darkened bar. It was long and narrow with illuminated signs advertising Budweiser Beer. Black and white photos of heavy-weight boxing champions and a large US flag dominated one wall. The bar was packed.

A Hawaiian band with its pedal steel guitar poured out "Somewhere Over the Rainbow" bringing the house down.

Adrenalin pumping, Spencer breasted the bar. An unsmiling barman clad in a dirty Hawaiian shirt and a blue American navy cap gazed impassively at him.

'What'll it be?'

'I'm looking for Joey Banana.'

'Don't know him. You wanna beer or what, pal?'

Spencer was in no mood. He grabbed the barman by the front of his shirt, 'Listen *pal*—don't mess with me.'

Something in Spencer's hard-eyed stare made the barman a little more agreeable. He glanced around at the clientele, hoping someone would come to his aid. Nobody seemed particularly interested.

He shrugged, 'Out the front. The stairs on the left lead up to Joey's joint, ok?'

Spencer tore out of the entrance and headed for the stairway. He had a bad feeling. At that moment he realised just how important Roxanne was to him. She was … what? He realised that here in the 1940s, she was his everything.

He flew up the dirty stairwell with wings on his feet. The stairs were slapped against the chipboard wall as if they were an afterthought. The rail was simply a plank of wood wired in place. The whole structure bent and creaked. He bounded on to a small landing. On the left was a rattan door. He pounded on it. The old timbers threatening to snap as his fist hit it with a resounding clatter.

'Yeah, hold on! Where's the fire?' A gravelly voice rumbled from within.

The door jerked open. Spencer immediately recognised the man at the beach.

'Spencer he's got a gun,' Roxanne's voice rang out.

'Yeah, Spencer. He's got a gun,' Joey sneered. He held a

bright steel semi-automatic Colt 0.45 in his hand.

'Do come in, Spencer.'

CHAPTER THIRTY-SIX

JOEY AND SPENCER BECOME ACQUAINTED

Joey smiled, revealing surprisingly white teeth, with a big chunk of gold in one incisor. He held the Colt rock steady, pointing at Spencer's midriff. 'Aha, the boyfriend no doubt.' He paused. 'Hey, I know you. You're from the Chronicle. Sonofabitch! You're that goddamn Aussie reporter. You were at the mill along with Dumbo over there. Well, well, well, because of you, my buddies are dead. We gotta score to settle, don't we, Hank?'

As Spencer stepped into the squalid room, he observed Horse and Roxanne seated on a filthy divan, standing menacingly in front of them was presumably Hank.

'Hey boss, how ya doin'?' Horse smiled, he didn't look particularly concerned, which was surprising as Hank had them covered with a very businesslike German Luger. Hank was Polynesian and a good three inches taller than Horse. There didn't appear to be an ounce of fat, just solid muscle. He had a big head on top of a thick neck, traditional Hawaiian tattoos crept like snakes from the top of coveralls, which were bursting at the seams. Hank was obviously a man who pumped iron.

'I'm sorry Spencer, it's all my fault.' Roxanne appeared calm.

'I'm sorry Spencer, it's all my fault,' mimicked Joey in a high voice.

'Joey, what the fuck we gonna do with them?' Hank had decided to enter the conversation.

'Well Hank, I think they might be going for a ride, Chicago style, what do you reckon?' Joey scratched his head and thought for a second.

Right at that moment a barrage of fireworks exploded from the street below, followed by a roar from the crowd. Joey's gaze was diverted for a split second. 'What the fuck?'

In that split second, four fingers as hard as armour plate drove into Joey's Adam's apple with a sound like a sledgehammer hitting an over ripe watermelon.

The damage was catastrophic. Spencer's fingers were a crude and vicious battering ram. The Colt flew from Joey's fingers, clattering across the worn parquetry floor, and coming to rest under a scratched, walnut veneer sideboard.

Joey sank to his knees, his hands clutching his throat, trying desperately to suck in lifesaving air, but his damaged throat was never going to function again. Hank turned his gaze on Joey. 'For fuck sake Joey?'

It seemed sympathy wasn't Hank's overriding emotion.

Not being one to miss an opportunity, Horse sprang to his feet. 'Sit yourself down,' snarled Hank.

Horse smiled at Spencer, shrugged his shoulders and sat down. Hank surveyed the scene. Roxanne sat wide eyed; her hands held to her face. Joey now lay face down—lifeless.

'Well folks, plans have changed.' Raising his pistol, pointing it at Horse's centre mass. Hank grinned.

Spencer stood transfixed, his blood freezing in his veins as he waited for the inevitable, knowing even his remarkable reflexes were hopeless against the Luger.

Click. The Luger misfired.

Horse jumped up, swatted the Luger out of Hank's hand, then punched him hard in the solar plexus. Hank just shrugged as he absorbed the blow. The two men faced off. Horse grinned. 'Don't worry photographer lady. He's a cream puff.'

Spencer almost smiled. Is he kidding?

Spencer was about to enter the fray, but there was something about Horse's confident manner that held him back.

Hank feinted with a left, then swung a vicious right hook. Horse moved to one side, and Hank's fist glanced harmlessly off his shoulder. Horse jabbed Hank in the middle of his large face. Blood dribbled from his nose.

'How's that for starters, cream puff? And there's plenty more where that came from.' Horse turned and winked at Roxanne.

'Sonofabitch,' Hank bellowed as he swung a haymaker that went nowhere.

'Ok cream puff, pay attention.' Horse drew in close, feinted, following through with a jab to Hank's jaw. Hank shook his head, once again, seemingly unaffected. He threw himself at Horse, trying to wrap him in a bear hug. Horse laughed in his face, landing two solid punches again into his solar plexus.

Spencer was perplexed. These weren't the sort of killer punches Horse was renowned for. Hank threw a flurry of punches at the delighted Horse. Nothing connected.

'What I tell ya boss—a cream puff,' Horse yelled.

Horse again threw a rock-hard fist into Hank's solar plexus followed by a serious whack against his jaw. Still, Hank was upright, screaming insults.

Spencer glanced at Roxanne who watched the fight, not knowing what to make of it.

The penny dropped. Horse was playing with him. Hank was in fact a mouse. Albeit a very large mouse and Horse, the cat, cruelly playing with its prey.

'C'mon punk, ya gotta do better than that,' Horse taunted the desperate and tiring Hank, who by now couldn't land a blow.

Horse grinned at Spencer. Giving him a thumbs up, Spencer leant against the wall to watch the spectacle. This is what he lives for.

It seemed Horse was finally getting bored with the game. 'Hey… what's your name? I know, how about Dumbo? Well Dumbo, it's about time for you to say nighty night.'

The blood run freely from Hank's nose as Horse gave it a few more friendly taps. Hank breathed heavily, swinging desultory punches which, he must have realised were never going to connect.

'Rock-a-bye baby … ' Horse sang the old lullaby tunelessly, but with gusto.

He unleashed the uppercut that Spencer had witnessed at Lee's joint. Playtime was over. This was Joe Louis. It was Jack Dempsey. It was Gene Tunney. It was the punch no man could withstand. Hank sank without a murmur. His face was bruised and battered, and one eye was open, staring blankly at the ceiling.

Spencer felt for a pulse. He was alive.

INVASION PLANS

The room was large and impressive in the Japanese manner. The cyprus and pine timber floor and walls were unpainted, displaying their natural grain. The shoji screens had been opened to reveal the Imperial Palace gardens ablaze with late autumn colour.

At a rectangular conference table sat four solemn men clad in military army attire, generals, their uniforms festooned with medals. There was electricity in the air—the course of history was being decided. Four Admirals, clad in their finery sat at the table, contributing little. Two soldiers stood to attention behind the tables.

At the head of the first table sat an uninspiring looking man on a raised chair, like a throne. This surprisingly nondescript man, a modest five foot four inches with a Charlie Chaplin moustache, was the Japanese Emperor, Hiro Hito.

The Emperor, His Imperial Majesty, contributed little to the plans being discussed. War plans. The four men at one table were the heads of the army. At the other table were the heads of the navy. The commander in chief was Hideki Tojo, the other main contributors were Isoruku Yamamoto and Commander Mitsuo Fuchida. They were discussing the bombing of the American Pacific Fleet in Pearl Harbor Hawaii. If this bold plan were successful, it was agreed a full-scale invasion of the Hawaiian Islands would follow.

'Send in Saito,' Tojo whispered to one of the soldiers.

Lieutenant Colonel Saito, the head of the feared Kempe Tai, the Japanese secret police, entered the room. The men waited expectantly for Saito to speak.

'Tell us about Hawaii,' Hideki Tojo prompted.

'I am pleased to announce everything is proceeding as planned in Honolulu. Major Nakamura has everything in place. The Americans are more interested in their movies than the defence of the islands. We have every confidence that after the glorious Japanese Navy Air Service have done their job and the invasion commences, it will be over in days, perhaps hours,' he boasted.

CHAPTER THIRTY-EIGHT

WASHINGTON

The atmosphere was electric, the destiny of the free world hanging in the balance as two men, powerful men, pondered the fate of the nation. One sat upright in his wheelchair, the other paced the office, the most iconic office in the world; the Oval Office. The man in the wheelchair smoked a cigarette through a cigarette holder; the other was a tall, distinguished, grey-haired man who knew his president was frail and must receive the best possible advice.

The smoker was the president Franklin Delano Roosevelt, the other the secretary of state, Cordell Hull. It was late November 1941, but the Thanksgiving holiday celebrations were the last things on their minds. The President looked old beyond his years; polio had left him reliant on a wheelchair for mobility.

'For the sake of the American people I need to know that we have explored every possible diplomatic option. The signs I know are not good. Surely they wouldn't be rash enough to stage a strike against the US?' He fixed the Secretary of State with a baleful stare.

Hull was silent as he gathered his thoughts, knowing he must choose his words carefully. Before he could speak, the President turned his attention to the garden below, and after a few moments silence, turned his head to face him. 'What are they going to do?'

'Mr President, sadly I think war is inevitable.'

CHAPTER THIRTY-NINE

A PUZZLE INDEED

Spencer leaned against the door jamb of his cottage. His cottage had become his place of solace, but today he was oblivious to the calming influence of the ocean. As always, the first coffee of the day was in his hand. Weeks had passed since Spencer had killed Joey. As expected, Matt and Walter hadn't been at all concerned at the violent death of the small-time hoodlum.

Recent events swirled through Spencer's mind. The dead villains. What about Wayne Kitchener? What about Marty Farris? The men at the mill? The incompetent hitman? And Joey Banana—what was the story there? And what did Lee Tai have to do with all of it?

Spencer considered the Kemp and Tai advertising sign. Something about the sign still niggled away in his subconscious but it was time to go to work. Spencer put down his coffee cup/mug and grabbed his well-worn leather wallet.

For the whole morning, Spencer immersed himself in records and old newspaper stories, using the resources of the *Chronicle*, to unearth information on Kemp and Tai. From what he could find out, the company had been operating for ten years in Hawaii. The reclusive Mr Tai it seemed was a generous giver to charity.

His smirking face appeared in a number of archival records. He'd donated money to various good causes. There was no evidence of his partner, the elusive Stan Kemp. Spencer discovered Mr Tai had no criminal convictions, and in spite of no immigration records he was a Hawaiian citizen. He's a real sweetheart, thought Spencer. He doesn't put a bloody foot wrong. Yeah, right!

He scratched his jaw reflectively. Roxanne was typing in her office. Spencer marvelled at her resilience, the encounter with Joey and Hank didn't seem to have affected her.

'Busy?' Spencer enquired as he leaned against her doorway.

'Nothing important. Just doing a story on another blood-soaked encounter involving your old friend Ivan the Terrible. I tell you … ' Roxanne shook her head. 'That man's just a thug.' She reached for the cigarette burning in the ashtray beside her.

'Well, Ivan does at least maintain law and order on his own patch.' Spencer laughed, rubbing the back of his head. 'But right now, I'm trying to dig the dirt on Mr Tai. Also, his seemingly non-existent partner. So far, I hate to admit it, but he does come up smelling of roses. Not a hint of any trouble.'

Roxanne took a long drag on her cigarette. 'What about the stories of people who got close to Molokai only to disappear?'

'That's the problem,' said Spencer glancing at the sheaf of clippings in his hand. 'There's nothing confirmed. There's nothing more than unsubstantiated rumours. Maybe we got it wrong, I admit he's creepy. but there's no law against that.'

'Have you checked birth records? Immigration records? I accept he's a legit Hawaiian citizen. Obviously, he's of Japanese parentage, but so are a lot of Hawaiians. Was he born here or was he an import?' Roxanne was leaning back in her chair, hands entwined behind her head.

'Well,' Spencer paused, settling on one of Roxanne's office chairs. 'Figure this out? I can find absolutely no record of his birth in Hawaii, and no record of him entering the country. It's as if he doesn't exist.' At the same time the irony wasn't lost on Spencer that his own circumstances were not a lot different from Lee Tai's.

'I don't know that you can attach much importance to the no-record thing? The islands are full of people who've come from somewhere else, often with a hidden criminal history I might add.' Roxanne smiled, pointing at Horse who they could see through a window unloading a truck load of printer's ink.

'I take your point,' Spencer laughed.

CHAPTER FORTY

IVAN THE NOT SO TERRIBLE

Spencer's quiet night at home was interrupted by the insistent ringing of the telephone.

'Dammit, leave me alone.'

'Thank God, I've got you. We have a problem.'

Roxanne's voice jolted him out of his train of thought.

'Ok Roxanne, take a deep breath. Tell me all about it.' Her tremulous voice was raising alarm bells.

'Horse is in trouble.' Roxanne laughed nervously—a brittle sound.

'Bloody hell! How bad is it? I damn well hope he hasn't shot someone?' Now Spencer was alarmed. Any trouble Horse was in, could be big trouble indeed.

'I've had a call from Rosie at Ivan's joint. She's a spotter of mine. Horse is drunk, very drunk, and he's been causing trouble.' Roxanne sounded a little more composed.

'Oh really? Ivan's likely to belt him over the head like he did to me.'

This time Roxanne's laugh was pure humour. 'I guess you didn't know, but Ivan and Horse are actually buddies. But according to Rosie, Ivan's patience is wearing a little thin.'

'I'm on my way.'

Spencer tore into the Ford Coupe, noisily slamming its

door. He smiled as he remembered to pull out the choke. The flat head V8 responding gratefully, rumbling into life.

The Ford roared along the now familiar road into Honolulu and along Kalakaua. Avenue. Night-time in Honolulu and nothing was happening. He screamed to a halt outside the pink facade of the Royal Hawaiian.

Roxanne was pacing up and down her brows drawn together. She saw Spencer's Ford jerking to a halt and ran to it. 'Thank God you're here! Horse is absolutely spifflicated. I mean he's *gassed*.'

'Don't worry Roxanne, we'll sort it,' Spencer comforted. He wasn't in fact feeling very comfortable at all, but experiencing a severe case of déjà vu. He hadn't been here since Ivan had so unceremoniously laid him out with his faithful cosh.

Spencer paused for a brief minute gazing at the pink facade and the memories of Michiyo washed over him. How many months had it been?' *Move on, you're here now, nothing else matters. That life has gone, probably for ever.*

'Are you ok? You're as white as a ghost! Roxanne grabbed him by the arm and gazed searchingly into his face.

'I'm fine,' he said.

They flew up the steps, through the archway to the back of the hotel and Ivan's Bar.

Spencer scanned the room. Everything as he remembered, the Japanese lanterns, the cane furniture. Rosie was refusing an inebriated marine another beer. Spencer could hear her strident Brooklyn accent. 'I'm not your sugar babe, and no, we're not going to the movies, not tonight, not never. Ok?' She gave Roxanne a friendly wave.

It seemed a lifetime ago. Mickey Rooney signing autographs. Louis Armstrong singing "Mack the Knife".

It was almost closing time, the last of the merrymakers and drunks were being ushered out.

Roxanne tapped Spencer on the shoulder. 'There he is.'

Horse was propping up the bar, singing lustily.

'Every young girl likes a young man with an upstanding… Hey Bosh ssgood to see you… an'… you too Rox Roxah Rox, dammit, I'm smashed.' The sea shanty ended there, and Horse grinned a big toothy grin.

A now smiling Ivan sauntered over to them. 'Well, if it isn't circus boy and camera girl.' Ivan held out a gnarled hand which Spencer grabbed.

'I'm not sure it's safe shaking your hand after what you did to Butch. How the hell did you do that?' Ivan quickly withdrew his hand, pretending to examine it. 'Thank God! I still got all my fingers. Seriously, how in hell didja do that? It took Butch a month before he could hit somebody again.'

Spencer grinned. 'Just an old party trick.'

'Yeah?' Ivan grimaced. 'Some party trick. Anyway Superman, you betta get the boy outta here. Horse's problem is one drink gets him drunk.' Ivan laughed, pointing at Horse.

'One drink? That comes as a bit of a surprise,' Roxanne queried.

'Yeah, the problem is we've never been able to figure out which one!' Ivan roared with laughter. 'Good to see you again Horse, but you gotta go. Closing time.' Ivan clapped Horse on his shoulder.

'G'night Ivan ole mate, ole buddy. Man, I sure got ballast on board, I tell ya.'

Spencer tapped Horse on the shoulder. 'Time to go slugger.'

Horse put one beefy arm around Roxanne and the other around Spencer, and they staggered out of the hotel towards Spencer's car.

It was dark. Shadowy figures could be seen moving along the unlit Kalakaua Avenue. This was far different from Honolulu in the next century. This was the time of opium dens, small time hoods and stick-up men. It wasn't wise to be out at night in a town that law and order seemed to have forgotten.

Roxanne shuddered as she glanced at a streetwalker chatting up a drunken sailor. 'C'mon Horse,' she commanded, 'not far to go.'

Spencer noticed three Japanese men, two of whom were leaning against his Ford, the third, his voice loud and aggressive, appeared to be arguing with them.

'Sorry to interrupt guys, but you're leaning against my car and we have to go.'

The man who'd been arguing turned to face Spencer. His eyes lit up. Spencer could now see in the half-light the vicious scar Horse had laughed at when they were at Lee's joint.

'Well, well, well if it isn't the reporter and the guy who hit me when I wasn't looking. Now isn't this a nice surprise?' His cronies snickered.

One of them leered at Roxanne saying, 'I think the wahine would like a *real* man.' He winked at his buddies.

One of the men was tall for a Japanese, muscular and confident, with a nose that looked like it had been hit on multiple occasions. He had watchful close together eyes and a military bearing. All together a potential threat Spencer decided. The other man was shorter and running to fat, but with a hard, brutal face, suggesting violence was a part of his life.

'I don't see anyone here who fits the bill,' Roxanne sneered.

'Guys, we've had a big day. Our friend here isn't well. So, let's just move on and let bygones be bygones … ok?

'Just try and set the big guy down gently,' Spencer whispered to Roxanne.

Horse was still happily attempting to sing some bawdy tunes.

Spencer was now alone but unencumbered.

Scarface grinned, sliding out the deadly *Sai* knife, with its razor-sharp blade and two vicious side prongs. He turned to the taller man and in Japanese.

'Just watch this Tora, this gaijin's going to look like sushi.'

Tora laughed. An evil sound, flat, staccato and confident. 'Make it artistic, Seiji,' he crowed.

If anything, the Japanese men were relaxed. The odds so firmly in their favour. There could only be one outcome. And then, of course, fun with the attractive wahine. What could go wrong?

Spencer unleashed the jumping kick. The speed and power behind it was lethal. Seiji's neck appeared to elasticise as his head was propelled backwards, and then the sickening crunch as he fell, his head smashing into the concrete. The smile on his face became contorted into a sinister, twisted grimace, he was stretched out on the sidewalk, his sightless eyes gazing upwards at the pink facade of the Royal Hawaiian.

The taller Japanese man, Tora, sprung from his position leaning against the car only to be met by a knee strike.

Crack, the knee bone shattered, resonating in the tropical air. Tora screamed a blood curdling howl, he collapsed clutching his leg. Turning his head to the remaining thug, screaming, 'Shoot them you fool.'

The third man gazed around wild eyed at the carnage before him. He hesitated, then reached into his jacket. Roxanne dumped Horse unceremoniously onto the pavement.

'Oh no you don't.' She cannoned into the man, ramming him bodily against the car. He cursed, pushing her away. The moonlight glinting on the nickel-plated automatic which appeared in his hand.

Spencer grabbed the man's hand, then employing the Kokoro technique he squeezed. This was different from when he dealt with the unfortunate Butch Larson. This was life and death.

As in the mountains of Japan with his sensei Katashi

tutoring, Spencer felt as if his soul had left his body and he had become an observer. As Spencer squeezed, the unfortunate thug's hand was compressed against the hard metal of the automatic. He sank to his knees, sobbing. There was a horrible sound of bone, gristle, muscle and flesh being compressed. Blood oozed from the broken hand, which looked like it had been run over by a steamroller. Spencer was shaken from his reverie when Roxanne grabbed his arm.

'Enough Spencer, enough.'

Spencer let go of the hand. Even he was disturbed at the sight of the grisly, distorted appendage. Next to him, Tora lay on the ground, his arms clutching his shattered knee to his chest.

'Shay boss, how about we go somewhere for a liddle drink,' Horse, slurred, beaming owlishly at him.

CHAPTER FORTY-ONE

MOLOKAI

'Tell me again why we're going to Molokai?' asked Roxanne. It was Friday afternoon. 'The girls are having a tennis afternoon with some of the ANC nurses. What about my Christmas shopping? I haven't even made a start with that. Seriously, I've got so much to do. And I have a Goddamn mountain of photos to collate for the editorial we're doing on the seventh fleet. Why am I going off to a fish canning island to play footsies under the table with a creepy Jap with a Chinese name?'

'Because you're a professional, that's why. What's the bet that after this weekend, you'll be singing the praises of Lee Tai? What a lovely weekend. Fabulous food and your girlfriends will all be envious. Get a good night's sleep, it's going to be a big day tomorrow.'

'Yeah sure, big day, love it. Can't wait.'

Spencer spent a restless night, tossing and turning. He slept fitfully, haunted by myriad images, his previous adventures all morphed into one. A succession of villains taunted him.

Then it was Saturday morning when he could've been surfing. Sipping his coffee, Spencer glanced out of his window at the Kemp and Tai sign.

He and Roxanne were travelling to Molokai to interview

Lee Tai. He hoped they'd be shown the fishing fleet, and the inner workings of the canning operation.

Roxanne was already waiting at the wharf when Spencer arrived. She gave him a tentative wave. She clutched her canvas overnight bag, decorated with a picture of Madison the state capital of Wisconsin. Sitting next to her was the precious camera bag, containing her pride and joy, a Zeiss-Ikon Simplex camera.

She looked like a young college student in her white skirt, multi coloured top and her braided espadrille beach sandals. Spencer wore a pair of high waisted pleated fawn trousers, a sailor-type red and white striped t-shirt and deck shoes. He carried his small leather portmanteau.

Roxanne boldly looked him up and down, 'You look like a playboy sailor,' she said, laughing. 'I'm not sure why I'm laughing? I can think of better things to do with my time. You never know, he mightn't turn up,' she added hopefully, as she put a hand up to her eyes, scanning the ocean.

'He'll turn up,' Spencer assured her.

'I can seriously think of other places I'd rather be, in fact any other place would do.' Roxanne declared, as she shook out a cigarette from a soft pack.

'I admit the guy has all the charm of a fat toad, but I'm sure he's going to be hospitable. After all we're giving him free publicity for his operation.'

'Look Spencer, here she comes.'

Pulling into the wharf was the *Rising Sun* a twenty-eight-foot Chris-Craft with its gleaming white hull, mahogany deck and varnished cedar superstructure.

'Hello, I'm Riko. And you are Mr Marlowe and Miss Gething?' A broad welcoming smile lit up his features.

Riko was a young Japanese man with a Californian accent, his manner efficient but charming.

He bounded off the boat, grabbing their bags. 'Mr Tai sends his compliments. If you want anything to eat or drink, just let me know.'

Riko was immaculately turned out in white cotton trousers and shirt. His affable manner did a lot to make Roxanne feel more comfortable. She turned and grinned at Spencer.

'I feel better already,' she whispered.

This guy's too smooth to be a glorified chauffeur. He nodded at the suave Riko.

The trip to Molokai was pleasant, with the *Rising Sun* skimming across the waves. The soft breeze caressing their faces. His fears had largely been allayed. The spotless vessel, the articulate, well-presented Riko. Everything gave the impression of a slick well-run successful company courting the press for publicity. But still he had doubts. The slimy Wayne Kitchener, his obvious fear when Spencer had mentioned Lee Tai. Matt and Walter's absolute conviction that Tai was not at all what he seemed.

He turned his gaze on Roxanne. Observing her chatting and taking photos he thought, she still managed to carry around an aura of innocence.

She was photographing a smiling Riko at the helm, asking him innocuous questions about the boat. 'How much horsepower Riko? Tell me what's a beautiful craft like this cost? I'll bet the fuel bill's a killer?' Riko in turn laughed and chatted, perhaps even mildly flirted, Spencer suspected.

He felt uneasy, scanning the big house and the jetty as they drew closer. There were no armed guards; everything appeared normal, businesslike. In fact, exactly as it should be.

What is it, what's wrong, nothing looks out of place but … what is it … what am I not seeing?

Waiting on the jetty was a smiling man, bowing and repeating. 'Welcome, welcome, welcome to Kemp and Tai Fisheries. My name is Haru. I'm Mr Tai's personal assistant.'

Haru spoke English with a marked Japanese accent. He had the build of someone who worked out. And to Spencer's practised eye, something in his movement suggested martial arts skills. *This guy would be a worry if push came to shove.*

The jetty was broad and long, with enough moorings for a dozen trawlers. Spencer glanced around. *Everything ship-shape and Bristol fashion.*

'A bit of a stroll to the house I'm afraid Mr Marlowe.' Haru had a smile which appeared to be glued to his face.

As they drew closer to the house Roxanne nudged Spencer's arm. 'This is some shack.'

Spencer and Roxanne were escorted up the long pathway to Lee Tai's mansion.

A uniformed servant smiled, ushering them into the hall.

'This hallway is about the size of my apartment,' Roxanne whispered to Spencer.

'Let me take you to your rooms. Please follow me.' Haru bowed, leading the way.

Carrying their overnight bags, they were escorted to their guest rooms which were spacious beyond belief. Roxanne nudged Spencer, winking as she pointed a finger at the stunning Japanese watercolours adorning the walls.

'Well Roxanne you couldn't complain about the accommodation.'

'It really is lovely. Actually, do you know what?'

Spencer shrugged.

'This'd make a wonderful honeymoon suite.' She giggled. 'Just joking. I'm going to go and freshen up, must look my best before we go and see Toad Face.'

'Roxanne.' Spencer growled, and then grinned. 'Behave.'

'Oh, and I see we have connecting doors,' she murmured to Spencer, with another wink.

They were escorted to the living room. Both Spencer and Roxanne were staggered by the scale of it. Opulent, even showy, with floor to ceiling windows. A ninety-foot balcony with privileged direct access to the swimming pool and another sunny flag-stoned patio.

'I should have bought my swimsuit,' said Roxanne, gazing wistfully at the huge pool which sparkled and shimmered invitingly.

Lee Tai swept into the room, striding towards them, beaming, then shaking both their hands.

'Welcome, welcome. First, we will have drinks and a snack, then you'll be escorted around the factory, and you can see all there is to complete your article. You've brought your camera I see Miss Gething. Now please be seated.' Lee Tai pointed to cushions next to a short-legged *chabudai* table. Lee Tai was the perfect host as they were plied with various Japanese delicacies.

'Mr Marlowe, I've read some of your articles in the *Chronicle*.' Lee Tai clapped his hands together. 'And you have had a number of headlines. May I say, excellent work?' He then hastily added, 'Of course Miss Gething, also complimented by your very professional photos.'

Spencer noticed Roxanne now appeared to be relaxing. *Thank God for that, keep it up Mr Tai.*

Lee Tai seemed as if he relished their company as he mentioned different stories that had been in the news.

'Miss Gething do try the *wagashi*.' Lee Tai pointed to a collection of small cakes which had been placed before them. 'They are not as sweet as European desserts, but I think you'll find them very tasty.' He once again emitted his annoying giggle. He rubbed his stomach. 'As you see, they are my downfall.'

The chit-chat went on for a half an hour. Lee Tai glanced at his watch, then as if programmed, the smiling Haru entered the room.

'Ah Haru, there you are. I think Mr Marlowe and Miss Gething are ready for the grand tour. Haru will show you all there is to see. I must warn you, the grounds are extensive, so it's going to be a bit of a trek. I can guarantee you'll have quite an appetite for dinner.' Lee Tai beamed.

'Miss Gething, Mr Marlowe, please follow me?' Haru bowed. 'First, I must show you, our gardens. I'm sure you're going to agree they are stunning.' Haru waved an arm expansively, pointing to the magnificent tropical grounds which stretched between the house and the canning works.

'Mr Tai keeps everyone busy managing all of this. As you may imagine it's very labour intensive. What you can see is a botanical paradise.'

'The way it's been terraced, and the sheer variety of plants and trees—it's beautiful,' Spencer observed. He glanced at Roxanne who was clearly entranced by the artfully arranged display of plants, shrubs and trees. *She certainly seems to be relaxed. The gardens just go on and on.*

'Spencer this is absolutely lovely,' said Roxanne, as she focused on photographing the exotic plants. 'We've been walking for an hour, it's like being in another world. You get the impression these gardens go on forever.'

Haru appeared to have some knowledge of botany and was quick to answer Roxanne's questions.

'Tell me Haru, what do you call that?' asked Roxanne pointing to a delicate flower.

'The Illima flower.' He then added, 'The flower used for making leis.'

'Please have a look at this.' Haru pointed at an unusual species.

'I've never seen this one before.' Spencer examined this unusual plant, spiky with a tall stalk of maroon flowers resembling a sea urchin, or even a distant relative of the Australian Blackboy.

Roxanne moved closer. 'Wow, I've never seen that before either. I've got to get a picture of it.' She quickly snapped some closeups.

'Yes,' exclaimed Haru with enthusiasm. 'That's the Haleakala Silvers wood plant. It was almost extinct, and only grows in a few locations in Hawaii. If we walk up these steps, I'll show you the collection of rare ferns, and from there you'll see a beautiful view of the ocean.'

Roxanne grinned at Spencer. 'I didn't realise we'd have such a long walk.'

'Getting tired are we old girl?' Spencer mocked, with a laugh.

They were shown the Uluhe and Moa ferns, and the Naupaka flower. The scent from the exotic plants, the flowers, and the orchids was overwhelming. An array of palms provided welcoming shade. As they meandered along the terraces, the foliage so dense in places, they lost sight of the ocean.

Spencer found his relaxing stroll through this timeless array of Mother Nature's beauty both calming and relaxing. *Maybe we got it all wrong? Lee Tai is an oddball eccentric. Admittedly a little scary, but just an oddball.*

'We could of course spend unlimited time in these gardens, but we do have constraints, so I'll take you to the business side of things. After all that's what you're here to see.' Haru bowed as he spoke.

The next hour was spent inspecting the trawlers and talking to some of the fishermen. Then Haru took them across to the canning works. The thick, heavy odour of fish was everywhere.

In the distance Spencer could see the large shed.

'Can we see inside that building over there, Haru?' he said, pointing at the corrugated iron structure.

'There's really nothing of interest there Mr Marlowe, just

odds and ends. You know, fertiliser, a tractor and so forth.'

'Really Haru, that's one hell of a shed to just house a few bits and pieces. Surely it must have been erected with some other purpose in mind?'

'Perhaps later Mr Marlowe, but I assure you there's nothing to see.'

Haru led them through the factory where fish were being canned and then across to the smoking house. Everything was pretty much what you would expect from a business that was all about processing fish. Spencer noticed there were men everywhere, some in groups idly chatting, others simply wandering around. *Curious.*

'I think we're going to stink of this for weeks,' said Roxanne, holding her nose. 'What a disgusting smell.'

Roxanne opened her camera bag. 'Hold on a minute I have to put a new film in.'

'The factory's not operating at anything like full strength at the moment,' Haru, charming as always, was quick to explain. 'When the trawlers come back, the activity is intense. The fish have to be sorted and processed as quickly as possible.'

Relieved to get away from the stench, they made their way to the top of the hill behind the factory. High up, they had a clear view of the ocean and jetty. Haru waved his hand at the trawlers lying stationary at their moorings. He laughed. 'It's either feast or famine.' Spencer nodded, jotting down the information in his notebook.

Haru stood for a moment silently surveying the scene. Spencer glanced sideways at their affable guide.

What is it about you I can't quite grasp? A combination of smug, of ... I know something you don't. And what else is there ... it's an aura of danger ... of contempt ... just what is it that I can't quite get?

Haru snapped out of his reverie. 'You should see it when the fish are unloaded. There's not a spare pair of hands. It's all go. Yes … quite something … quite an operation.'

Once again, it's a bit like you're playing with us, Spencer thought.

Roxanne was oblivious to Spencer's concerns. 'I had no idea Haru of the magnitude of the operation here,' she said as she continued shooting. 'It's really very impressive.'

'Yes Miss Gething, Mr Tai has harnessed the bounty of the sea and is reaping the rewards.'

'He sounds like a commercial.' Spencer was bemused by Haru as he seemed to be spouting scripted slogans.

Spencer couldn't help but notice once again the extraordinary number of fit-looking young Japanese men trying to look like they were busy. There were men gardening. There were men idly talking in groups.

'It must be an expensive overhead all of these men doing little until the trawlers come in. How many are employed here? Their living quarters must be quite extensive?'

Was it his imagination, or was Haru annoyed by the questions?

'If you look over there on the horizon you can see one of our trawlers heading in now. You know,' he added proudly, 'We export to over ten different countries.'

'You didn't answer before Haru. How many men do you employ?' Spencer asked again. There was no mistaking it this time—the quick flash of anger on Haru's face.

'I really wouldn't know Mr Marlowe. You would have to ask our personnel manager.'

'This's quite an important question,' Spencer persisted. 'This is something the readers really want to know.' Spencer smiled his most engaging smile.

'Like I said, you would have to ask him.'

'Sure. And when could I talk to him? I imagine he has an office here on Molokai?'

'So sorry,' Haru said with finality. 'He's attending to some matters in California.'

CHAPTER FORTY-TWO

IN VINO VERITAS

That night the meal was spectacular. Spencer was a lover of Japanese food. This was undoubtedly the best he'd ever had.

The entree was miso soup with mussels. Followed by *chirashi* sushi, then a main course of miso glazed black cod, with bamboo shoots and wasabi.

'Mr Tai, I must compliment you on the cuisine, it's truly outstanding.' Spencer glanced at Roxanne who was clearly enjoying her meal.

'Yes, Mr Tai absolutely delightful,' Roxanne added, swallowing a mouthful of cod.

'I'll pass your compliments on to the chef.' Lee Tai smiled.

And then just when the idea of consuming more food was an impossibility, the waiters brought out a *yuzu* crème broulee.

'I trust, Miss Gething that you took some worthwhile photographs?'

'I won't know exactly until I see the proofs. But I think I can guarantee you'll like them and may I compliment you on your magnificent gardens?'

'Thank you, Miss Gething.' Lee Tai appeared genuinely delighted.

'I must say Mr Tai, I really had no idea of the size of your operation here. It must take up every minute of your day.' Spencer was hoping Tai would come out with something that didn't sound like a prepared script.

'Well Mr Marlowe I shouldn't complain. Business is good but sadly it takes up all of my time, leaving little opportunity for cultural pursuits.'

'*Ars longa vita brevis*,' he added with a smile.

Spencer thought for a second, scratching his head, he remembered his late father trying to hammer Latin into him. 'Ah yes—Art is long, life is short.'

'Very good Mr Marlowe, I fear I may have underestimated you.' Lee Tai clapped his hands, clearly delighted.

This could be the time to get political. 'What do you think Mr Tai of the chances of the US and Japan going to war?'

'Japan is a peace-loving nation. There's no way they could ever get embroiled in such a war,' said Lee Tai waving his hand dismissively.

Spencer almost choked on his dessert. *Is this guy for real? Peace-loving Japan. What about Nanking and …? I think I'd better keep my trap shut.*

Lee Tai was the perfect host telling snippets of his history and how the business started. No mention Spencer noticed, of the invisible Stan Kemp.

Lee Tai signalled the waiter to bring out the coffee. He reclined in his chair. 'I do hope Mr Marlowe that you've enough for a suitable story.' He paused to take a sip.

'In my culture we usually finish a meal with tea. But I'm afraid I've been Americanised. Now, where was I? Ah yes … as I've said you can see around me the fruits of many years of labours. When I started this enterprise many years ago, I was obviously younger and certainly thinner. But when one stops to smell the roses, one inevitably embraces the good things of life. The fine wine and of course the fine food to accompany it.'

Lee Tai continued his rags to riches story. Roxanne tried hard to stay awake.

Lee Tai laughed. 'I do believe Miss Gething is ready for bed. Please forgive me for rambling on. It is a rare luxury for me to have such delightful dinner guests. In the morning we'll have breakfast on the terrace and of course, if Miss Gething wants more pictures, or if there's anything more you want to know? But I believe we've covered just about everything. So, I will bid you good night.'

Lee Tai motioned to a servant. 'Hatsuo, would you take our guests to their rooms please.'

CHAPTER FORTY-THREE

THE HORSE AND THE CHEF

It had been a busy night at Lee's bar and chef Koki was cleaning up in the spacious well-equipped kitchen. It boasted two refrigerators, a *sake* storage chamber, and a large pantry. A portable charcoal burning stove stood in the middle of the room.

Koki had a badly swollen jaw, making it difficult to talk eat or swallow. This, he thought ruefully, had some benefits as he'd been trying to lose weight. He was tall and appeared to be all arms and legs, but lately he'd noticed the beginnings of a paunch.

The chef surveyed his little kingdom—his kitchen. He locked the door. Standing in the entrance he put on his cap, grabbed a packet of Camel cigarettes from his trouser pocket and lit it with his zippo lighter.

Another man hid in the shadows, noting the features of the chef illuminated in the brief light from the zippo. A smile of satisfaction fleetingly crossed his features.

The chef was Japanese-American and had absorbed every nuance of American culture. But he was profoundly patriotic towards the Japanese Empire. A country he'd never visited. Drawing greedily on the cigarette, he flicked the glowing stub into the night and headed out down the darkened drive to his car.

He turned in alarm when he heard the soft pad of feet behind him.

'How ya doin'?'

Startled, the chef saw the formidable sight of the man who had broken his jaw.

Horse was an unnerving sight at any time. Tall and muscular, with his bizarre wig. Horse was just plain scary. He was rarely angry. His very lack of menace seemed to make him more menacing.

'What … what … what do you want?'

Horse smiled disarmingly. 'Jest wanna go back to my joint, for a chat.'

'I can't. I have to go home. Have to get sleep. I gotta go. Honest.'

'Nah,' said Horse, still smiling. 'You really want to come with me, don't ya?' At the same time, he pushed the barrel of his Smith and Wesson firmly into the chef's paunch.

'Here's the keys. You drive.'

They climbed into Horse's Model A Ford pickup. A disreputable looking vehicle with a cracked windscreen and torn upholstery. Multicoloured, the duco looked like it had been applied with a broom. In short, a wreck.

'Look I don't know anything, please?' He looked ready to burst into tears.

Still smiling, Horse put the barrel of his gun up to his forehead and in a gentle voice, almost like a mother chastising a recalcitrant child. 'I'm not gunna arx you again. One more word and I'll will blow ya head off. Now drive.'

The chief was filled with foreboding. Something about Horse's gentle manner chilled him to the bone.

Horse chattered away happily about the chances of the Dodgers versus the Yankees at the world series. The virtues of Ford over Chevrolet. Anyone listening to the one-sided conversation could be forgiven for thinking that they were two old friends on a guys' night out.

'Turn up this road.' Horse directed the chef to drive up an unlit narrow track. They bounced and shuddered over rough limestone, deep into rain forest, dark and forbidding. Twenty minutes later they drove into a clearing. By now Koki was shaking with fear, convinced Horse was simply going to kill him.

Horse gave the chef a pat on the shoulder. 'Ok buddy, out ya get.'

In front of them was Horse's home, his castle, his shack. Constructed from timber and daub and nestled in the rain forest, it was simple, even humble, but with everything he needed. Surprisingly, apart from the odd instrument of death and mayhem, Horse's little piece of paradise was tastefully decorated, albeit with the odd poster of well-endowed ladies, photos of motor cars and heavyweight boxing champions.

There was also a locked gun safe on the wall, made of stout, polished timber with steel mesh doors. Just visible through the mesh was an array of handguns, a shotgun, even a Thompson sub-machine gun. Horse took his weapons seriously.

Claude Demmer was a man of incongruities. In the middle of his spacious living room was an entirely unexpected and magnificent vintage barber's chair. Horse's pride and joy. The circular iron base was bolted to the floor. The framework was black wrought iron. It had an extendable footrest. The seat, headrest and footrest were covered in cowhide dyed a lustrous crimson. Koki viewed the chair as a potential tool of torture, when in fact Horse had bought it on a whim, with no evil intentions in mind. He would recline on it while he listened to his phonograph records.

'Ain't she a beaut?' said Horse, full of bonhomie. 'Don't worry about a thing. You'll be real comfy.'

Horse's apparent concern for the chef's wellbeing was far scarier than curses and bloodthirsty threats. The chef was shaking. He feared losing control of his bowels. For the first time he'd met someone who scared him more than his boss. He stammered and whined, now crying, with the tears running down his face. 'I don't know anything please … please?'

A stream of liquid ran out of Koki's trousers. He had just noticed next to the barber's chair there was a coffee table with an assortment of tools: pliers, hammers, and a collection of knives. Horse had figured the very sight of these common household tools may get a reluctant tongue to wag.

'This is home,' Horse said proudly. 'Nobody can hear us out here.' This said in a manner which suggested that perhaps two old pals might be about to play a phonograph too loud.

'You're going to tell me all about Mr Tai, an' what he's doin' on Molokai.'

CHAPTER FORTY-FOUR

A STROLL IN THE MOONLIGHT

Spencer lay down fully clothed on the futon, the traditional Japanese bed set in a plain teak base.

The room was spacious. Tasteful in the Japanese fashion with tatami mats and *fusama* wooden ceilings. Stunning watercolours and murals of women in traditional dress adorned the shoji screens with their solid timber frames and translucent *washi* paper. The ceiling fan just managed to stir the oppressive heavy tropical air.

His mind went over and over the evening with Lee Tai. Their host was both courteous and friendly. It was as he'd expected. Lee Tai had spoken at length, but in reality, said little of interest. It was practically a prepared script. What was in the big shed that was such a secret?

Noiselessly, he slid open the shoji screen leading to Roxanne's room. His feet sank into the plush carpet, which seemed to be the only concession to Western decor. Now standing by the sleeping form of Roxanne, Spencer felt distinctly uncomfortable.

'Roxanne, wake up,' he whispered in her ear. Roxanne at first startled, smiled and pulled back the covers. Spencer chuckled. 'I want to check out the big shed. Do you want to come and get some photos?'

'Ok, but that's not what I thought you had in mind.' Roxanne groped in the darkness for her sandals and some suitable clothes. She yanked on some trousers and a light jacket.

'This better be Goddamn worth it … midnight stroll in the dark. I must be nuts.'

Silently they threaded their way along the dark passageway to the rear door. Spencer noticed the door when they were escorted to their room, figuring it could only lead to the outside. Nerves on edge, heightened senses made their imaginations soar. Was that a noise? Could they be watching? Sound, fear, and intuition are the factors which rule when light is absent. Spencer tried to think of some excuse should they come across a guard doing a nocturnal check, quickly realising any explanation would sound laughable.

Lurking in the back of his mind was that Lee Tai wasn't what he purported to be. Was it that Lee Tai was just too glib, too smooth by half? He felt irritated with himself when he thought of the enigma of Lee Tai. Was Tai the genial, eccentric host or was he something else entirely? Spencer had dismissed the idea of any connection between the ambush at Lee's bar and the subsequent altercation outside the Royal Hawaiian. Those events, he reasoned, were both spontaneous, decidedly unprofessional, and would in no way have been connected to Tai.

Still, there was an air of ruthlessness about Tai, something he couldn't quite put his finger on, but nevertheless it filled him with unease.

The big house was silent, apart from the sounds of the overhead fans softly whirring in the background.

The passageway was in complete darkness as they padded silently towards the door Spencer had noticed earlier.

Spencer slipped the simple latch and they stepped into the cool night. They found themselves in what Spencer was sure in the daylight was a spectacular garden.

Moonlight filtered down through the palms as they made their way through the garden, along a path meandering through clusters of orchids and bougainvillea vines. The sweet scent of rare species filled the air. As they crept along the cobble-stone path, they came across a small wooden bridge, its handrails intricately carved to resemble sharks with mouths open wide to swallow their prey.

Under the bridge a stream trickled through to a lily covered pond filled with carp and koi. The fish, sensitive to human footsteps, raced to the surface, their mouths open waiting, for titbits, their golden scales flashing as they jostled each other.

The path led to an open space where the foliage was sparse. They could see the canning factory, and beyond that, the shed.

Exposed and silhouetted by the moonlight, they moved hastily towards the harsh black outline of the steel shed. It was large, cold, and strangely forbidding.

'This wasn't built to just store garden tools and bloody fertiliser,' whispered Spencer.

The narrow beam of his penlight showed a solid wooden door. Would they be able to gain entrance? Spencer shone the light on the handle. There was no evidence of a lock.

'This is it,' he whispered. 'The point of no return.'

He gingerly turned the handle. With a squeak the door swung open.

This is a bit disappointing. The shed had an entrance, a narrow hall or vestibule, opening onto an office with desks, chairs, typewriters. In fact, exactly what one would expect to find in a substantial business operation. Spencer flashed his penlight around, observing drums of chemicals. Spencer and Roxanne examined the labels: barrels of red lead oxide, aluminium powder, a glass gallon-container of glycerine, a tub labelled, potassium permanganate. In another corner numerous drums of paint were stacked. Some had obviously been partially used. There were framed black and white photographs of Japanese ladies and small children displayed on a cluttered desk.

All very normal. You could even say, wholesome, Spencer decided. This night-time foray was beginning to look like a wild goose chase.

Further inspection showed a variety of equipment: ladders, a rack of tools attached to a wall, wrenches, hammers, and saws. In fact, everything that you would expect in a working factory.

'What's with all the chemicals?' Roxanne whispered, raising an eyebrow.

Spencer ran the pen light over the drums of chemicals again, trying to remember snippets from his high school chemistry lessons. 'All these products are really no more than what you'd expect to be around a place like this. Seriously, there's nothing sinister, they're chemicals which are available over the counter at any hardware store.'

'Expect where exactly? What purpose do they serve?' Roxanne frowned, gazing around at the hodgepodge of assorted chemicals.

'Red lead oxide is used for pigmentation in rust proofing. Aluminium powder is also used as pigmentation, added to paint, nothing suspicious.'

'What about the glycerine?' whispered Roxanne 'Don't they use it for making nitro glycerine?'

'Nice try,' said Spencer, 'but I don't think anyone now days would seriously use it. It's far too unstable. It's far easier to use dynamite or gelignite if you want to make something that goes bang. In any event there was only one gallon of it and it has perfectly normal uses medically for dry skin and here on the island I'm sure they would have a good reason to have it on hand.'

Not giving up, Roxanne ran a finger over a label. 'What

about this, it sounds suspicious.' She peered at a worn container with a faded label and read the words out loud.

'Unfortunately, not.' said Spencer 'It's also known as Condi's Crystals. It's used as a disinfectant I think.'

Roxanne scowled. 'Well, we've drawn a great big blank. Let's see what other secrets the shed holds and then we'd better head back to the big house.'

Spencer shone his light on another door he felt sure would lead to another section of the shed. The door opened easily, leading on to a narrow passage leading to yet another door.

'Let's have a gander in the next room, a quick look, then get out the hell out of here.'

This door opened to a cavernous area which stretched beyond the reach of the feeble penlight. Spencer shone the penlight around, gasping at the sight before them. There were white-painted walls and a polished concrete floor. Hundreds of crates and boxes, all stencilled with US Army insignia, were stacked six feet high along the walls. Some had been opened, displaying their contents.

'My God, there's enough munitions here to equip a small army,' whispered Spencer.

Moving hurriedly from crate to crate, they discovered containers filled with Garand rifles, Thompson sub-machine guns, grenades, handguns, as well as boxes and boxes of ammunition.

'Eureka! So, this is where Marty Farris's stolen ordnance disappeared to.'

'What on earth's going on?' Roxanne yelped. 'I've got to get photos of this.'

'The question is,' said Spencer, 'what on earth does Lee Tai want with all this?'

CHAPTER FORTY-FIVE

OH DEAR

Roxanne gasped as the shed flooded with light. Lee Tai stood at the doorway along with Haru, Riko and two others, all holding handguns trained resolutely in their direction.

'Mr Marlowe, Miss Gething, what a surprise.'

The smiles from the formerly attentive staff were conspicuously absent. Spencer's first thought was escape. But four pistols pointed at them quelled any such thoughts.

Spencer assessed the men in front of him. He figured Haru was the next in charge after Lee Tai, his muscular build and confident manner suggested he'd be a cool and disciplined fighter with formidable martial arts skills. Riko was probably next in line, no doubt efficient, but without the self-assured bearing of Haru.

The other two looked like basic foot soldiers. One of them, Spencer thought was a teenager with acne that made his skin look like bubbly paint. The other a stocky man in his early forties, stolid, unimaginative, but someone, Spencer imagined, who would obey any order. Spencer assumed that all the men in front of him would be fanatical and would unhesitatingly give their lives for their emperor. Certainly, none would have any qualms about executing him or Roxanne.

Lee Tai had dispensed with his voluminous robe and was

wearing the uniform of a Major in the Japanese Imperial Army: a tunic buttoned to the neck, red flashes on the collar, a khaki peaked hat with a red band and a gold star in the middle of it, khaki jodhpurs, black riding boots. A sword hung at his side.

His face was unreadable, or was it? For a brief moment Spencer thought he saw excitement, a gleam in his eye. Whatever he saw made him feel distinctly uncomfortable.

Spencer had the distinct impression Lee Tai had anticipated their nocturnal ramble. Had he deliberately dressed to impress, or dressed to kill? What was particularly alarming was the white armband with red script on his left arm. Spencer was fluent in both speaking and writing Japanese and the writing on Lee Tai's arm was not difficult to translate—Kempei Tai, the feared Japanese secret police.

Spencer gave an involuntary gasp. He realised what had been niggling him; the Kemp and Tai advertisements blasted across the airwaves, and on billboards. Clearly Lee Tai had a sense of humour.

'What shall we do with them sir,' Haru asked Lee Tai in Japanese.

'Patience, Sergeant. All in good time. Riko, get two chairs from the office, I want them both bound securely.'

'At once, sir.'

Riko returned, struggling under the weight of two sturdily constructed steel chairs.

Roxanne clung to Spencer, who looked on grim faced knowing they could be shot without hesitation.

'You won't get away with this you fat creep,' she sneered.

This was met by the usual giggle from Lee Tai, but Haru was a different matter. Still holding his automatic in a rock-steady hand, he stepped up to Roxanne, giving her a vicious backhander across the face, bringing blood to her lips.

Roxanne screamed, but instead of being cowed she spat in Haru's face.

'Enough Haru. Do as you're told and get the wire,' Lee Tai snapped.

Spencer was now very worried. What did they want with wire?

Haru stormed off to the storeroom, returning with lengths of wire which looked like straightened-out coat hangers. Spencer had the uncomfortable feeling that this was a practised manoeuvre. *These guys have a routine. They sure know what they're doing.*

Haru handed his automatic to Riko. 'Any move and shoot them.'

'Ok Sir?' Riko queried, glancing at Lee Tai for confirmation.

Lee Tai nodded, then adding cryptically, 'Shoot them only if you must, but remember they're special guests at lunch tomorrow.' Lee Tai glanced at his watch. 'Well, later today in fact.'

Haru smirked. 'Sit on the chairs, now! The both of you.'

Spencer gazed at each of the men and knew there was no chance of not complying.

Haru bound Spencer's arms and legs first, twisting the wire so it cut into the flesh, his face close to Spencer's.

'This is nothing compared to what we have in store for you,' he whispered.

He then methodically bound Spencer's legs separately, each wired to a chair leg. More wire was then used to tightly bind his body to the chair. *This is worse than a straitjacket.* The wire bound his chest so tightly it was difficult to breathe.

Spencer had to admit, as far as binding someone; this was as good as it gets. And he knew there was no way he could possibly get out of these restraints.

Roxanne seemed to have lost any regard for her personal

safety. As the wire bit cruelly into her arms and legs, her face contorted with rage.

'You bastards, you'll never get away with this. You'll damn well rot in jail forever if I don't kill you first.'

'Allow me to introduce myself,' Lee Tai announced, ignoring Roxanne's protests.' I am Major Nakamura of the Imperial Japanese Army's Kempei Tai.'

Spencer grimaced, wincing with pain. 'Kemp and Tai— Kempei Tai! I don't believe it. The Japanese Military Police? Here in Hawaii? For God's sake. Oh, I see—I get it.'

Spencer shook his head. 'Bloody hell, there is no Stan Kemp, is there? I really should've put two and two together. But seriously, a Japanese man using a Chinese name, wasn't that just a bit … questionable?'

Major Nakamura's giggle broke into a loud laughing spasm. 'My little joke Mr Marlowe. I've enjoyed playing with the stupid Americans. I knew to them one Asian race was the same as another.'

'Ok, I get the joke. But what's it all about? Why the guns? What possible reason is behind it all?'

'I can tell you both, because you're not going to be able to tell anyone. In a week's time, Sunday morning, the seventh of December, the glorious Japanese Navy Air Force is going to destroy the American Pacific Fleet in Pearl Harbor.'

'You're stark raving nuts,' Roxanne exploded.

'No, he's not,' warned Spencer.

'What makes you so sure?' Roxanne gave Spencer a curious glance.

Spencer didn't answer her. 'So, I still don't get it, why all the guns?' he asked.

'And I thought you were reasonably smart,' Nakamura chuckled.

'I have five hundred men here on Molokai. I have been

flying them in in small groups for months. When the air attack is finished my men and I will attack the Schofield Barracks on Oahu. The Americans are completely useless as fighting men. They believe Errol Flynn and John Wayne will save them.'

'You don't seriously think that with five hundred men, you can take over Hawaii?' gasped Spencer.

'No, of course not. But everything is coordinated. First the airstrike. Then my attack on the barracks and then ...' here Nakamura paused. 'And then later that day, the Japanese Imperial Forces will invade Oahu. Mr Marlowe, I thought you were smart,' he said again. 'This is a very well organised operation, I'm what the Americans call "a sleeper". We Japanese play the long game.'

Spencer thought furiously. This was not the ranting of a mad man; this was a well thought out credible plan. 'One thing puzzles me, Major?'

'What would that be?'

'If Japan is going to attack and invade Hawaii, why on earth would you bother to invite us over for the weekend and give us the big sell on your operation. It doesn't make sense ... oh and while I'm at it, I guess you were responsible for the so-called hit man who tried to stick a knife into me? And let's not forget the clowns at your bar who tried to carve up myself and my associate?'

Nakamura's smile broadened, 'Ah yes, the chef Koki and some others. Sadly, they were well meaning, but absolute amateurs.' He frowned. 'It would also appear the fighting abilities of yourself and that fool Claude Demmer were rather ... shall we say ... unexpected. My men were instructed to discourage any enquiries into my operation. Unfortunately, their zeal exceeded their abilities. You will be pleased to know they won't be punished for their failure.'

'Thank you Major, their welfare means quite a lot to me.' Spencer rolled his eyes.

'I assume that's a little of your American sarcasm, Mr Marlowe?'

'Australian, in fact.'

'Same dog, different fleas.' Nakamura smiled.

'Ah yes, but getting back to my man Hayata. I must confess he was one of mine. I was a little surprised. Failure simply didn't occur to me. He had dispensed with, oh, so many of my enemies. The very idea that a bumbling journalist could possibly be a problem …' Nakamura shook his head. 'What actually happened? He was a very experienced man.'

'Let's just say he wasn't up to the job.'

'Where is he now?'

Spencer shook his head. 'Cyanide.'

'Excellent,' beamed Nakamura. 'A very wise career move. He knew how I dealt with failure. Oh, and of course your question about the invasion … well … although there is little doubt the attack and invasion will go ahead, diplomacy is an interesting business. Even now, as we speak, our diplomats are trying to avert the invasion. The stupid war-mongering Americans have managed to block most of Japan's oil supplies. If they can be convinced to have a change of heart, the attack will be cancelled. In the event of a peaceful resolution, you and Miss Gething would have written your article for the *Chronicle* on Kemp and Tai, and all would have gone on as normal.'

'Tell me Major, was it your intention to dispose of us all along?'

Nakamura sighed. 'Actually, I had what you might call a change of heart. I thought an article in the *Chronicle* would be a positive, in case the invasion didn't go ahead. But I suspected that you and Miss Gething would do some midnight exploring, and then of course …' Nakamura shrugged. 'You might say, once you decided to poke your nose in where it didn't belong then all bets were off. So, Mr Marlowe, you really only have yourself to blame. If you'd been a good little journalist, you and Miss Gething would have had a good night's sleep, Riko would've taken you back to Oahu later this morning, and that would've been that.'

'How do you intend to explain our disappearance. We really do have friends in high places. They're going to be a little suspicious.'

'Oh no… you and Miss Gething will die in a boating accident. Ah yes, the boat explodes, and all lives are lost. And,' he tittered again, 'I have five hundred witnesses. Anyhow,' Nakamura said dismissively, 'All of that is, as they say, water under the bridge.'

'Mr Marlowe it's truly a shame, things have turned out the way they have. I suspect if these were different times, you and I would have many things in common. However,' and he shrugged, 'now, I'm sure you of all people know the meaning of the Latin word, *poena?*'

'Yes … it means penalty.' Spencer shuddered.

'And the penalty is?' Nakamura prompted.

'The penalty is pain.' Spencer replied dully.

Nakamura giggled. 'Ah, Mr Marlowe you will be sorely missed. Yes, poena means penalty- *that which must be paid.'* You and Miss Gething must pay the penalty for your midnight rambling.' Nakamura clambered to his feet.

'I'm going to bed. A most enjoyable day to look forward to tomorrow, well in fact, later on today.' he concluded, glancing at his watch. He turned to the older soldier, speaking in Japanese. 'Watch them well Kaito, and you may watch the spectacle.'

Spencer's blood ran cold.

'What do you think's going to happen to us?' Roxanne asked, in a trembling voice.

Spencer hoped they wouldn't be put to death. He could see no point in telling her of what was said.

CHAPTER FORTY-SIX

GIDDY-UP HORSE

'My God, this hurts,' groaned Spencer. He could taste saliva thickening in his throat as beads of sweat trickled down his brow. He wracked his brain, mentally exploring any possible avenue but the pain from his bindings was constant, making it difficult to focus and he could see no solution to their predicament. Spencer could just hear in the distance the faint sound of the surf, a small reminder of the world outside.

Kaito showed no sign of lapsing into sleep. The gun focussed on them didn't waver and he said nothing. Spencer figured he was a placid and unimaginative foot-soldier, who had fanaticism drilled into him from the earliest of age. He was sure Kaito would execute them without a qualm, or regret. The harsh electric light streamed down, accentuating the cruel features of their implacable guard.

Spencer turned to Roxanne, his face haggard. 'I'm sorry to have dragged you into this, I feel as if it's my fault.'

'When you came into my room, I wish your motivation had been good old-fashioned lust.' Roxanne managed a small smile.

Spencer tried to focus but the pain made rational thought difficult. The inevitability of death had a curious effect. Spencer reflected on his life. It was sad that no one would ever get to know about his fantastic story. This brave intelligent woman who had unquestioningly followed him into this world of intrigue and murder would die with him. The unfairness of it all hit home with a jolt. Spencer was not one generally who dwelt upon what might have been, but this time he regretted his pig-headed foolishness which meant not only his demise but also Roxanne's. What, he wondered, would be the outcome for Michiyo? Would he just disappear from her life forever? He continued to explore any idea of escape. He thought of appealing to Kaito in Japanese, perhaps weaving some fantastic story of intrigue to convince the sullen guard he was in fact, an undercover agent for Japan. A number of bizarre plans tumbled through Spencer's mind, but they were discarded as quickly as he thought of them.

The bindings continued to cut his circulation. Spencer had no idea how long it would take before it would have a permanent effect, but then he thought bitterly, what difference does it make, we'll still be dead? Spencer grudgingly acknowledged Nakamura's expertise and ability to organise an army, especially given he'd achieved this under the nose of the US Military.

The machine guns, revolvers and long rifles smelled of the gun grease they were packed in. Even the grenades and ammo seemed to have their own distinctive metallic odour. It was not lost upon him that this arsenal would be unleashed on the innocent people of Hawaii.

'I hate to be a defeatist Spencer but if we're going to be shot, I'm beginning to think I would rather they got it over with. This's excruciating.' Roxanne groaned.

Spencer didn't reply but deep inside he knew a simple bullet to the back of the head wasn't what the major had in mind.

For a brief moment he saw Kaito's head nod. Was he falling asleep?

What possible difference could it make? He could have a heart attack and we'd still be no closer to getting away.

With a jolt Kaito snapped out of his momentary lapse. Shifting his weight from side to side, he scratched the back of his head, flashing Spencer a half smile.

Spencer grimaced. It was the only show of emotion the bastard had shown all night.

Even Spencer's meditation techniques brought him little comfort from the relentless pressure of his bonds. He'd lost track of time in the floodlit shed. It could have been night or day.

A sound. His ears pricked. *What was that?*

Was it an animal scratching at the door, or perhaps a branch, maybe a palm frond had fallen across the door, the wind causing it to rustle? The sound stopped. Maybe he'd imagined it. Certainly, the impassive guard either hadn't heard it, or attached no importance to it. After a few minutes the sound started again, stopped, then started. *It's not a branch, it's got to be an animal, maybe?* This time Roxanne heard it. She shrugged, tilting her head quizzically, she glanced at Spencer. He shrugged his shoulders, practically the only movement his bindings would allow.

The sound became more insistent. But still, it would start, pause, then start again. Their guard eventually noticed. He stood up warily, his pistol still pointed in their direction. The sound stopped again. The guard gazed around the room. His eyebrows furrowed. He seemed unsure of what to do.

The noise started again. Kaito plodded to the door. Sending a menacing glance in Spencer and Roxanne's direction, he jerked open the door, peering outside.

Kaito was propelled back into the room. This was accompanied by a loud sickening crack of bone and muscle. Kaito slumped on the floor, a look of surprise imprinted on his unconscious features. Horse stepped into the room.

'Jeez boss,' he said, removing his brass knuckles. 'I leave you alone for a few minutes and you get yourselves into trouble.'

'Horse, you're a sight for sore eyes. Can you cut Roxanne free and then me?'

Producing pliers from the pockets of his coveralls, he snipped Roxanne's bonds and then Spencer's. Spencer tried to stand, only to fall. The pain was like needles that'd been dipped in alcohol. Roxanne cried out in agony, she struggled to her feet, then collapsed like a drunken sailor. Horse effortlessly picked her up, placing her gently back in the chair.

'Thanks Horse. My legs feel like jello.'

After massaging their hands and legs they were both able to stand, pitifully, awkwardly, like babies finding their feet for the first time.

Spencer made his way to the motionless Kaito, each step a herculean effort. Kneeling down, he felt for a pulse. Nothing! Dead. Looking closely at his damaged face, Spencer noticed blood had seeped out of his mouth, nose, eyes, and ears. The force of Horse's blow, enhanced by the brass knuckles, had been catastrophic.

'You sure you needed the hardware, Horse?' Spencer enquired, managing a smile.

'Well boss, you gotta be sure, don't you?' Horse replied with a grin.

'How on earth did you know how to find us?'

Horse gave a truncated version of his chat with the chef.

'I'm surprised you got him to talk,' Spencer queried.

'Well boss,' Horse confided. 'Remember I'm from Brooklyn. Anyway, he was a cream puff.'

CHAPTER FORTY-SEVEN

THE GETAWAY

'How did you get here?' Spencer quizzed. 'But make it quick.'

'Well, me an' Koki had a real nice chat. You know boss, he's a swell guy when you get to know him.' Horse chuckled.

'Horse, we're in a hurry. Just the details, huh? And who the hell is Koki?' Spencer had the feeling this could be the start of a saga.

'Koki's the chef. We had a chat. I figured you might be in trouble. After I convinced the guard to have a swim, I headed up the track and saw the light in the shed. I could make out Tai and two others heading back to the house and I figured …'

'Yeah, ok … gotcha.'

'I moored the *Jailbird* behind two of the trawlers and rowed the lifeboat to the jetty, Horse said proudly.

'Wasn't there a guard on the jetty?'

'Yeah boss, there was,' Horse agreed.

'What happened, is he dead?'

'No boss, as long as he's a quick learner he'll be ok.'

'What, exactly, did he have to learn?'

Horse's braying laugh echoed around the building.

'Well boss, so long as he learned to breathe underwater,

he'll be ok. Mind you,' Horse added, scratching his head, 'he may have been dead before he hit the drink.'

'Horse, keep it down, please. We don't need these guys turning up with guns, screaming banzai.' Spencer glared at Horse despairingly.

'Banzai?'

'Horse, we gotta go. It'll be dawn in a few hours. But first, we need to do something about all this.' Spencer waved a hand at the weaponry stacked neatly around them.

'Wow,' Horse whistled. 'Look at all them typewriters.'

'Typewriters?' Roxanne raised an eyebrow.

'Chicago typewriters.' Horse pointed to a crate of sub machine guns and started laughing.

'Mob vernacular.' Spencer winked at Roxanne.

'Any ideas? It's not difficult to set fire to all of this. But it will bring the guards. There's going to be a hell of a bang.' Roxanne turned to Spencer.

'If I remember right from my misspent schooldays, I think the answer is with those chemicals in the first office.' Spencer thought for a minute. 'Horse, help me, I still can't walk properly.'

Horse virtually carried Spencer into the office, he didn't seem to find the burden of transporting a large male almost singlehanded to be any sort of effort.

Spencer cursed as he tried to get his legs to do what he wanted them to do.

Leaning heavily on Horse, they shuffled into the office. Spencer inspected the chemicals, 'Yes, this'll work.' Spencer murmured with satisfaction. 'Horse, roll out a barrel of aluminium powder, a barrel of red-lead oxide, and grab that tub of Condi's Crystals. Bring them to where the weapons are, then come back for the glass jar of glycerine. Oh, and grab that cotton waste, we'll need it as well.'

Horse moved the chemicals and placed them next to the

crates of grenades. He scratched his head. 'I don't get it boss … I mean … it ain't dynamite. I mean … what about a fuse? Hey boss, you gotta have a fuse, and this stuff, you sure it's going to go bang. You feel alright boss? I know you lost your memory a while back, you sure everything's working up there?' He tapped the side of his head.

'Horse, please just do it? Ok?'

'Ok, Boy Wonder, what on earth are you up to?' asked Roxanne, who was as mystified as Horse.

Spencer laughed. 'I remember this from my schooldays because I made a bomb from all this stuff when I was a kid and accidently blew up the teachers' toilet block.' He smiled ruefully. 'And then I was expelled.'

'Ok,' Spencer declared. 'Horse, if you can empty half the barrel of red lead oxide and half the barrel of aluminium powder, then mix a barrel so it's almost full with the combination of red lead oxide and aluminium powder. Put a layer of Condi's Crystals on top.'

'Jeez boss, are you really sure this's gonna work, I never heard no one in Brooklyn or Chicago do this?' He shook his head. Obviously as far as Horse was concerned, his previous associates knew everything there was to know about explosives.

'Don't worry Horse, it'll work. Trust me. I'd like to help but … I just can't. Grab that barrel there.'

'This one boss?'

'Yeah Horse, the red lead oxide. Unscrew the lid, pour half the contents on to the floor. Don't worry about the bloody mess, ok?'

Horse heaved the barrel over, watching as the red powder spilled over the floor. 'You sure about this boss?' he asked again.

'Sure Horse, sure as eggs. Now, grab that barrel of aluminium powder, don't worry it's very light. Unscrew the lid and pour enough into the red lead barrel so it almost reaches the top.'

Horse unscrewed the lid, dropping it on to floor with a loud clang.

'Try and … ah … do it quietly, please Claude.'

'Sorry boss, and I hate Claude, it makes me sound like a Nancy Boy.'

'We can't have that, can we Horse? But please, quietly and quickly.'

Oh boy this's going to make one hell of a bang. Spencer gazed with satisfaction at the forty-four-gallon drum, now three-quarters filled.

'Looking good Horse. I think I spotted a shovel in the other room. Grab that and stir the mix.'

Horse bounded off. Grabbing the shovel, he started stirring the potent mixture.

'How's that boss?'

'Good enough, Horse, good enough. This next bit is important. See that cotton waste over there? Put some on top of the chemicals in the drum.' Spencer watched Horse crammed in a wad of cotton.' Now, wait for Roxanne and I to get going, then pour the whole gallon of the glycerine on top, screw the bloody lid on, then run like hell. I reckon it'll take at least ten minutes to soak through. When the glycerine gets to the crystals, it'll cause a reaction and the drum will go up with one almighty explosion. Roxanne and I'll get going to the jetty. Can you wait five minutes before you pour in the glycerine? Meanwhile, Roxanne and I'll only be able to move slowly so we'd better get going.'

Roxanne grabbed her camera and leant on Spencer. 'I'm sure as hell not leaving without this,' she muttered.

Slowly and painfully, they hobbled out of the shed.

'See you at the lifeboat Horse. Remember, five minutes.'

Stumbling and staggering, clinging on to each other, it

reminded Spencer of a schooldays three-legged race. Using will power alone, he had to throw his leg forward, remain upright, then throw the other leg forward.

'This is murder,' Roxanne grumbled, clinging on to Spencer.

'You can do it,' Spencer grimaced, 'and we have to be quick about it. When that lot goes up, it'll take us with it if we don't get the hell out of here.'

They didn't notice the figure standing in front of them.

'Well, what have we here?'

Barring their way was a smug Haru, attired in a traditional men's yukata.

Roxanne gasped, holding a hand to her mouth. She gazed imploringly at Spencer.

'Don't worry, I'm not going to kill you. The Major has other plans for you. But that doesn't mean I can't have some fun.'

Spencer saw that Haru had adopted a fighting stance.

Spencer tried to ready himself, cursing his legs which still felt like lead weights and wouldn't do what he ordered them to do. Roxanne leant against a tree.

Without warning, Haru unleashed the ferocious frontal kick. Ordinarily Spencer would have had little trouble blocking and retaliating, but he was as impotent as a baby. The blow stuck with devastating force. He fell heavily to the ground. Spencer could tell Haru was operating on half power and his intent wasn't to cripple or maim. But meanwhile it bloody well hurt.

Bruised and winded, Spencer managed to get on to all fours, but he was breathing heavily. Haru danced around executing karate parries and thrusts into the air around him, apparently in no hurry, waiting for Spencer to pull himself upright. Spencer could tell Haru knew he was going nowhere. Haru could draw the spectacle out for hours if he wished.

'Come on, stand up. Stand up,' he taunted.

As Spencer painfully drew himself upright, trying to will his unresponsive body to do as it was told, Haru let fly with a foot sweep. Spencer crashed to the ground again.

Once more, Spencer laboriously climbed to his feet. Haru appeared relaxed as he came in with two quick jabs to the solar plexus, the pain shot through Spencer like fire. Haru then made the mistake of going for a blow to the head. Spencer blocked it, landing a brutal elbow into Haru's face, drawing blood. Haru howled in frustration.

'My turn gaijin,' he snarled.

Unfortunately, in Spencer's weakened state his elbow to Haru's face had little effect. Haru prepared himself to administer the *ushiro geri* or back kick. Given Haru's rage Spencer braced himself for a particularly savage boot. Spencer had applied this tactic many times and well knew the power behind it.

As Haru whirled around, foot in the air, there was a soft plop. The front of his elegant yukata was covered in blood, blossoming in a circular pattern. Haru stared at his chest, momentarily not understanding. He pointed at Spencer. His mouth moved silently, a painful wheezing sound as he tried to form words. Blood poured from his mouth. He fell. Tried to crawl. He collapsed.

'Jeez boss, I really can't leave you for a minute,' Horse guffawed, his silenced automatic still pointing at the now deceased Haru.

'This is getting to be a habit,' Spencer winced, mumbling his words. 'We're both grateful. That guy enjoyed using me as a punching bag.'

'You ok boss? You don't look ok.'

'So long as I can lean on you, I'll get there.' Spencer managed a tight smile. 'We really have to move; I reckon we're still in the danger zone.'

Horse unceremoniously stepped over the body, holding his arms out so Spencer and Roxanne could hold on.

With the big man's help the jetty was now only a hundred yards away. The breaking dawn made them stand out, silhouetted against the sky as they slowly made their way to the lifeboat.

'How are you feeling?' Spencer groaned as he spoke, rubbing a hand on a still stubbornly weak wrist.

'I'm looking forward to just sitting and doing nothing.' Roxanne managed a brave smile although it was obvious from the occasional grunts the pain was still intense.

Spencer turned his head back towards the island scanning for movement. He knew just one vigilant guard would bring their escape undone. He could imagine Nakamura's wrath if they were captured. *I'm not sure Nakamura would be concerned about the death of Kaito, but Haru? That'd be a different matter.*

At last, the final stretch was within their grasp. Each side of the pathway was a riot of colour with multi coloured hibiscus. An open space lay in front of them, the beach and the jetty tantalisingly close. Spencer was on high alert for any sound or sight of Nakamura's men. Horse's presence was certainly comforting and he was a formidable opponent, but no match for Nakamura's men with their submachine guns, and their sheer weight of numbers, if they were alerted.

Perched at the end of the jetty Spencer observed a small wooden structure. A crudely made workman's hut. Or possibly a tool shed, Spencer thought. Fashioned from weathered timbers with a palm frond roof. Leaning against a wall Spencer could see a pair of crutches. Spencer glanced at Horse, pointing. 'Were those there when you arrived?'

'Dunno boss, it was dark. I was concentrating on the guard.'

Just then the door of the hut was flung open, a tall man with a leg in plaster hobbled out, a carbine slung across his shoulder. Spencer gasped, he recognised the man, Tora, who he'd immobilised with a knee strike when he and Roxanne helped a drunken Horse at The Royal Hawaiian.

Tora stared at them, momentarily puzzled, he grinned, exposing an assault of broken teeth. Swiftly unslinging the carbine, he chambered a round into the breech. The mechanical click of the mechanism sounded as clear as a bell in the tranquil morning air.

'I gotta try and plug him boss.'

'Leave this one to me,' Spencer whispered. 'You've no chance against the carbine. He'll pick us off one by one and there's nowhere to hide.'

'Keep coming gaijin pigs, keep coming.' He spoke quietly in Japanese, holding the carbine to his shoulder.

'Wish me luck.' Spencer turned to Roxanne.

Spencer daggered a finger at Tora, thundering in Japanese, 'Put that gun down this instant you fool.'

Spencer could see the confusion flash across Tora's face. A Caucasian speaking Japanese, and showing no fear?

Spencer winked at Horse, continuing in Japanese, 'We're meeting Riko-*san* and Haru-*san* here on the jetty. They'll be arriving shortly on the *Rising Sun* to take us on a tour. When Mr Tai hears you've pointed your weapon at us in this threatening manner, I shudder to think what he'll do to you.'

The colour drained from Tora's face. Struggling to find his voice, he whined, 'I'm sorry. I didn't understand. Please don't tell Haru-*san*.'

'I don't know what you're saying but keep it up,' Roxanne whispered.

Spencer forced his reluctant legs to propel him forward up to the now shaking Tora. 'And just where's the other guard. I suppose he's having a sleep in the hut, eh? You're both going to be in trouble. Both of you are meant to be coming on the *Rising Sun* to help out for the day.'

'I don't know where he is,' Tora babbled. 'He's meant to be here It's not my fault.'

'Put that damn gun down. You're a disgrace man.'

Tora turned, leaning his gun against the weathered timber boards of the shed. He was still apologising when Spencer defying the pain in his arms brought a karate chop down on Tora's neck. In spite of his poor circulation the edge of his hand was still as hard as ever.

As Tora slumped against the wall of the shed Horse sprang forward, grabbing the unfortunate guard by the shirtfront ready to rain further blows on him. He grinned, 'Jeez boss, you killed him. How 'bout that?'

Meanwhile Spencer leant against the wall of the shed hugging his arms, his face white and contorted. 'Oh my God, that bloody well hurt.'

Roxanne held a hand to her face, muttering something unintelligible.

Tora lay slumped across the wall of the shed. Roxanne felt for a pulse, there was nothing.

'Dead.' She nodded at Spencer.

'Whadya reckon boss, over the side?' Horse just stared dispassionately at the body.

Roxanne appeared to be in shock. She drew a deep breath as the body tumbled over the side of the jetty. 'Oh yeah. There he goes.' Roxanne held a hand to her chest.

'We gotta move Horse, but quick. Show us how good you are at rowing.' Spencer flashed him a quick grin.

'Don't you worry boss, my little row-boat's gonna just about fly. I tell you ole Lee Tai ain't gonna be a happy little slant eye, if your funny gunpowder does its stuff. It will work, won't it boss? It's been, what … I dunno, it's been twenty minutes maybe.' His forehead wrinkled.

Spencer was now concerned; he had no doubt about the

effectiveness of the crude bomb but … *Just how long will take for the glycerine to soak through? What if the ingredients are out of date, what if … Hell, it just has to work?*

'Don't you worry about a thing Horse; it's going to go up with a bloody big bang any minute now.'

Spencer looked down, relieved to see the small dinghy still moored just as Horse had left it.

Roxanne put a hand to her mouth. 'Look, there, in the water. Oh, my God!'

Floating face down was the other guard.

CHAPTER FORTY-EIGHT

A NEW DAY DAWNS

Horse pulled away from the jetty. With each powerful stroke of the oars, his muscles bulged under his shirt and the sweat poured down his face. For all of Horse's devil-may-care attitude, Spencer knew Horse would have been under no illusion about Nakamura, or what fate may have awaited them at his hands. Spencer and Roxanne sat hunched over in the dinghy, massaging their hands and feet.

'Spencer, how in hell, did you know that … that … guard … what was his name, Tora … didn't know that Nakamura or Lee Tai or whatever you want to call him, had captured us and was planning to execute us?'

Spencer had regained his equilibrium. The pain in his legs was now a dull throb. He chuckled. 'I didn't know for sure. But I figured as we'd only been caught last night Nakamura aka Lee Tai wouldn't have had a chance to tell his minions we were the enemy. In fact, being the all-omnipotent ruler, there was no particular reason to have told them anything. The first they would've known was when some of them got to witness our demise.'

'He was really going to kill us?' she whispered.

'Oh yeah.'

'One other thing?' Roxanne thought for a moment, holding a finger up.

'Shoot.'

'I would've thought that Tora would have been a little puzzled at the sight of Horse blithely strolling along the jetty with us?'

Spencer shook his head. 'Of course, the thought passed through my mind also. But remember there was never anybody on the island there without Nakamura's permission. And Tora had to make an instant decision. He saw the tall gaijin and the photographer lady who were both here as Nakamura's guests, and he would have assumed that Horse was here in one capacity or another. But overwhelmingly his fear of Nakamura and the brutal consequences of doing the wrong thing affected his better judgement.'

'I had no idea what you were saying to Tora, but whatever it was you actually had me convinced. You looked so God damned angry. Hell …what a performance.' Roxanne grinned as she massaged her legs.

'I'm starting to get sensation back,' Roxanne exclaimed, continuing to knead her limbs. All of a sudden, she threw her hands in the air. 'Damn and blast, I didn't get any pictures.'

Dawn sent shimmering rays over the placid sea. It wasn't lost upon Spencer this dawn could well have been their last. He shuddered, pondering on what sort of grisly death Nakamura had planned for them. Horse strained at the oars the gentle splash of his rhythmic strokes was strangely soothing. Free, free, Spencer's perverse sense of humour made him smile. He could even put up with being locked in a room with the verbally challenged Victor Smith.

Spencer silently reflected on their lucky escape. He had some idea their death was meant to be a particularly gruesome one.

'You, ok? Cat got your tongue?'

'Just another day in the life of action heroine Roxanne and her trusty camera.' Roxanne managed a brittle laugh.

Spencer kept scanning the island and the surrounding ocean for any activity. He knew if Nakamura learnt of their escape, he'd have every possible vessel pursuing them.

They could just make out the *Jailbird* moored behind a trawler when they heard the first explosion. A huge fireball rose above the shed. The shock waves rocked their tiny craft. Heat washed over them.

'Ouch,' Roxanne yelped, as hot cinders descended on her. Burning debris fell all around them, creating a maelstrom of lethal red-hot pieces of metal and junk. Shrapnel plummeted into the sea, sending plumes of hissing water into the air. A pervasive, overpowering odour of sulphur making made them cough and splutter uncontrollably.

Spencer gazed awestruck at the savage beauty in the stunning array of colours against the backdrop of the breaking dawn. This, he decided, looked like the work of a mad cosmic artist splashing wild hues into the universe. Then came another succession of blasts. Even more powerful than before. It looked like a pyrotechnic display, with sky rockets and penny bangers adding to the spectacle. The sounds of the exploding weaponry hurt their ears, as more and more violent explosions reverberated through the atmosphere.

'Well, whadya know about that?' Horse chuckled.

Spencer laughed out loud. The explosion seemed to act as a release for the tension of their last hours. Roxanne grabbed Spencer's hand; she was enthralled. 'Who's a clever boy then? This time I'm getting pictures.'

With the practised skills of the true professional Roxanne was getting photo after photo, all the time talking to herself. 'Good one, great. Yeah, that'll be a front page.' Her face a study in concentration, she shot through a roll of film in minutes.

If I offered to row her back to shore to get closer pics, she'd probably jump at it. Roxanne was in her element. As she continued shooting, the air was rent by another two massive explosions, followed by a series of loud cracks.

'That'll be the ammunition going up.' Spencer gazed in wonderment at the destruction brought about by a distant memory of a childhood prank with explosive chemicals. 'If only the headmaster could see me now.'

Men scurried around. They were too far away to hear voices. The scene was one of utter destruction and chaos; the shed had ceased to exist; palms had been levelled and spot fires had broken out in the vicinity. It seemed to Spencer that Nakamura, for all of his organizational skills, hadn't a plan for this sort of disaster.

Spencer peered into the half-light hoping for a glimpse of Nakamura, but no luck.

Spencer was braced against the guard rail, his hands gripped tighter than was necessary. The cataclysmic scene of violence unfolding in ever increasing explosions all in vibrant technicolour.

Any minute someone surely must look out to sea. Spencer was confident Nakamura would have a vessel armed and capable of a decent turn of speed. At this point they were far from being out of danger. He figured it wouldn't take Nakamura long to discover Spencer had something to do with the destruction and when Haru's body was found, he would certainly search the island and scour the sea.

The fire storm discovered yet more fodder for its voracious flames, there was another round of ear-splitting explosions. The massive amount of guns ammunition and grenades had foolishly been stored in the one place. Spencer thought with satisfaction, this would have to put an end to Nakamura's attack on Honolulu. But what of the attack on Pearl Harbor? Had history been rewritten? Would there now be no such attack?

With Horse's help, they clambered aboard the *Jailbird* and collapsed on the deck.

'Let her rip, Sunshine.' Spencer managed to sit up and give the big man a thumbs up.

Bouncing over the waves, the *Jailbird's* big diesels were on full power. Spencer and Roxanne were constantly scanning the ocean between them and Molokai, now rapidly receding on the horizon. Huge plumes of smoke continued to billow from the ruined shed. There were occasional blasts as more explosives succumbed to the rapacious blaze.

Spencer's limbs were finally gaining full function. It now seemed that a pursuit was unlikely. Reclining on the polished wooden slatted seat on the fly bridge he focused on Horse, braced at the wheel, seemingly without a care in the world. Spencer reflected on the vagaries of life. If not for Horse, both he and Roxanne would now be either dead or suffering some unimaginable torture at the hands of Nakamura or his helpers.

Studying Horse from behind, the wind stirring his ludicrous wig, Spencer's imagination went into overdrive. Horse the soldier? Spencer could imagine him charging an enemy machine gun nest, wiping it out, gleefully finishing off survivors with a swift thrust of his bayonet. He could envisage the President of the United States pinning the Congressional Medal of Honour on Horse's chest, shaking his hand, while Horse smiled, and said, 'Dey was cream puffs.'

Conversely, it was just as easy to imagine a different scenario; Horse being strapped into the electric chair for one of the many murders he had committed or would doubtless commit in the future. 'Pull the switch, cream puff.'

Horse had a spring in his step, whistling tunelessly as he left the helm briefly to grab a thermos of coffee.

'Say, boss you wanna go see the Warriors next game? I got tickets.'

Nothing fazes Horse, he's just killed three men. He could easily have been killed himself if things went wrong. Maybe it was just the release of tension, but Spencer couldn't help himself, he burst into laughter.

'You ok, boss?'

'Yep Horse, I'm fine. Couldn't be better. I'd love to go to the game.'

Spencer figured Horse's life had always been punctuated by skirmishes, gunfights, knife fights, and fist fights; in fact, peace harmony and calm would be as foreign to him as snow on Waikiki Beach.

'When we get back to Honolulu, I've got to get to Matt Spinetti and Walter Crabtree's office as quickly as possible.'

'Doan worry about a thing boss. I got my jalopy parked at the pier.'

Honolulu loomed large. Roxanne raised her arms above her head, yawning.

'Well, tough guy! We survived, didn't we? I could do with a shower, ugh… I think we could both do with a shower. A change of clothes wouldn't be a bad idea.'

'Oh no.' Roxanne wailed, her hand up to her face.

'What? Come on lady, out with it.'

'My damn clothes. I had some new shoes, hell… a new dress, makeup, and God knows what else. And it's all still on Molokai.'

'Would you like to go back for them? Molokai's a pretty quick trip.' Spencer laughed.

Roxanne rolled her eyes.

The *Jailbird's* big diesels roared as Horse edged the boat up to the wharf, his deft hands effortlessly manoeuvring the big craft into its mooring.

'Next time you want a photographer to come with you on a story…' she paused, briefly touching his arm. Spencer waited for the rest of the sentence, then eventually Roxanne pointed a finger, grinning. 'Make sure I'm invited; I don't think we're likely to come across another Major Nakamura. Do you know, these snaps should get on to the front page of the *New York Times*?'

Spencer laughed. What a remarkable woman. Having just escaped from a ghastly death she'd already moved on and was ready for the next adventure.

Spencer jumped onto the wharf, collapsing as his still weakened muscles gave way.

'Bloody hell, that hurt.' He closed his eyes and pulled a face as he climbed back on to unsteady feet.

Horse lifted Roxanne, gently placing her beside Spencer.

'Ok Horse, the jalopy, if you please? We're in one hell of a hurry.'

'This is it?' Spencer gazed in dismay at the beaten-up wreck that was Horse's Model A Ford pickup. 'You're kidding me, does it actually run?' *It's had more hits than Ed Sheeran.*

'Don't worry about a thing,' soothed Horse. 'Get in.'

Spencer opened the passenger door for Roxanne. He climbed in beside her, staring at the torn upholstery.

Horse squeezed into the driver's seat, punching the starter button. With a muted roar the Model A leaped forward, tearing up the bitumen, accelerating like a jumbo jet on full power.

Spencer clung onto the roof. His body flung side to side as the Jalopy screamed its way through the light traffic. Roxanne clung to the door frame, her eyes closed, muttering unintelligibly under her breath. Spencer thought it sounded suspiciously like prayers.

A tradesman with a wheelbarrow filled with tools screamed in horror as he saw the disreputable Model A bearing down on him. In desperation he flung the barrow forward where it overturned, spilling cans of paint, hammers nails and brushes onto the roadway.

Spencer turned and waved. 'Sorry,' he yelled, his words drowned out by the primal scream of the hotted-up Lincoln motor.

'My God,' yelled Roxanne. 'Slow down.'

Her hands were braced against the dash as the jalopy was accelerating at breakneck speed. It left the docks turning into Aiea Street.

'What on earth's under the bonnet?' Spencer yelled as the big v8 roared as contentedly as a racehorse at full gallop and ahead of the field. Horse hadn't slowed down as they tore along Vineyard Boulevarde. Pedestrians scattered. A US marine shook his fist, hurling abuse as the Model A rocketed past.

'Well boss, de original was a bit slow, so I had it fitted with a Lincoln V8. Good, ain't it?'

Spencer was in a hurry but doing these colossal speeds in a train wreck of a car made him wonder if they were going to survive Nakamura, only to be killed in Horse' s jalopy. The big V8 snarled like an enraged beast, as the Model A went round another corner defying gravity, rearing up on two wheels.

Horse was oblivious to the fortunately light traffic he'd so far had managed to avoid colliding with. Spencer closed his eyes as they screeched into Kalakaua Avenue and Horse pressed the pedal to the metal even harder. When Spencer opened his eyes, they were screaming down Punahoe Street. Graceful palms, plantations and fortunately zero traffic helped calm his frayed nerves.

Roxanne breathed a sigh of relief. 'Well, we haven't hit anything yet.' she yelled, managing a slight smile. 'You must admit the boy can drive.'

'Thank God, we're just about there.' Spencer pointed at the sign. 'Acacia Place.'

'Quite enjoyed that, actually.' Roxanne grinned.

'So boss, how do you like my old bucket of bolts?'

'It's … ah … quite impressive Horse. I'm not entirely sure it resembles the vehicle that rolled out of Henry's factory.'

'Who?'

'Ford … Henry Ford.'

'Oh yeah, him. Gotcha,' he chortled. 'Yeah boss, she's been bored out to two-sixty cubic inches. She's got a four-barrel down draft carby, high lift cam and extractors.'

'Oh,' said Spencer, not having the vaguest idea of what Horse was talking about.

Spencer had to admit it seemed as if Horse's skills weren't only fighting and shooting, his driving skills were pretty impressive.

'Where did you learn to drive like this?' he yelled.

'Well boss, when I worked for Luciano in Chicago, I had to pick up stuff in Canada and deliver it back to Lucky, an' de Feds always seemed to want to stop us and have a chat.'

'Stuff?'

'Yeah boss, stuff.'

Spencer smiled to himself. Horse, for whatever reason, didn't want to elaborate on his past. Spencer had read about the prohibition era. He figured Horse would've been in the thick of it, running illegal booze for the mob during the ill-fated prohibition decade.

Horse described some of his exploits, with one hand on the steering wheels as he expertly and nonchalantly hurled the car around bends.

Spencer could make out the offices of Spinetti and Crabtree. Horse still hadn't noticeably slowed down.

'I can see the jalopy has a lot of go, does it actually have much stop?'

Horse guffawed. 'Well boss, she don't stop that well, so long as ya give me a bit of warning, she'll be Jake.'

CHAPTER FORTY-NINE

MAKING PLANS

Spencer levered himself out of the jalopy, his legs shaking. He wondered whether the tremors were brought about by his ordeal on Molokai, or Horse's driving. Roxanne also climbed out, only to collapse on the ground as her legs gave way beneath her. Horse gently helped her to her feet.

'You, ok?'

Roxanne grabbed the bonnet of the model A, steadying herself. 'Yup, fine. Fine and dandy, thank you kind sir.'

Stella stared in horror at Roxanne and Spencer's haggard appearance as they entered the office.

'My God, what's happened? Are you ok?' Without waiting for an answer, she ushered them into Matt Spinetti's office.

Spinetti blanched, 'Have a seat, please!' He jumped up, placing three seats in front of his desk.

'We heard an explosion coming from Molokai, we figured you two,' and he grinned, 'or perhaps three, had something to do with it.' He jumped up, yelling, 'Crabs, get your ass in here.'

Walter bounded into the office. 'Spencer, Roxanne … Horse?'

Matt Spinetti cast his eyes over Roxanne and Spencer.

'You two look like hell. Tell us all about it.'

The pain, combined with lack of sleep, hit Spencer with

a jolt but he knew they had to tell the agents everything and quickly.

'Before I start, I think we're going to need some sustenance.' He glanced at Roxanne.

'Coffee, first.'

As if by magic, the door opened. Stella entered bearing a tray, 'Coffee?'

Horse immediately jumped up and bowed. 'They call me Horse,'

Spencer smiled at Horse's extravagant bow and obvious attraction to Stella. He grinned at Roxanne, who winked.

Horse certainly appeared to be immediately entranced by Stella, as he held out a massive paw. Stella smiled and blushed.

'Stella.' she replied holding on to Horse's hand for a little longer than socially correct.

Walter noticed the interaction and smiled. 'Stella, I suspect our guests may be hungry.' He glanced at Spencer.

'Yeah, I could eat a horse, if you'll pardon the expression.'

'Ok, if you're hungry it's taro burgers.' Stella bustled out of the room. Before long they heard the rattle of plates and cutlery from the kitchen. Tantalising odours made their mouths water in anticipation.

'Lunch time.' Stella wheeled in a wooden trolley laden with the taro burgers, their delicious tang exciting their taste buds, long overdue for sustenance. Nestled on the bottom tray of the trolley rested a wooden crate filled with ice cold bottles of Coca Cola.

As they demolished their burgers, washed down with the Coke, Spencer and Roxanne poured out their story to a grim-faced Walter and Matt. Walter took notes.

Walter and Matt conferred for a few minutes. 'Ok I think we've got it all, we're going to relay all this information to Washington. We're recommending immediate action. Lee Tai or Nakamura, or whatever his God damned name is, is going to feel the full force of the US military. You tell me he reckons our guys can't fight. A platoon of marines should sort the sonofabitch out fairly quickly.'

Matt glanced at his watch. 'We know you've had one hell of a time and you need sleep and recuperation. Do you think you need medical attention? You're both tottering like a pair of drunks. We can get a doctor here quick smart.'

'Speaking for myself, the bloody bindings hurt like hell, but already I can feel everything returning to normal.'

Roxanne grinned. 'I'm ready to jitterbug the night away.'

'We'll have armed marines guard you for the next few days, so go and get some sleep. We'll let you know what happens.'

CHAPTER FIFTY

A CAREER CHANGE?

Spencer slipped into his trunks and trod carefully to the beach opposite his shack, his legs still a little confused about their role. He waved at the armed marine guarding his front door as he went. The marine was certainly a reassuring sight. Spencer's eyes focussed on the face of Lee Tai, aka Major Nakamura, still prominent on the billboard.

Seeing this idyllic beach scene on this island paradise, it was almost impossible to believe that currently a large part of the world was engaged in a brutal war.

A nearby group of college students were relaxing, throwing back Budweisers as they belted out the Glen Miller hit song, "Chattanooga Choo Choo" in unison.

Spencer listened to the lyrics, laughing at the students' humour. "Pardon me Roy, is that the cat that chewed my new shoes?"

Spencer found himself tapping his feet. To him, the lyrics of this innocuous song seemed to capture the optimism of the United States and its "can do" attitude. Just hearing these students enthusiastically singing this song filled him with renewed optimism. These Americans really are unstoppable.

The enticing odour of the steaks they were cooking, the familiar smell of onions frying on their readymade barbeque; a stack of bricks with a hot plate laid across, all added to a scene of optimism. No tin-pot German dictator or insignificant Japanese emperor was going to interfere with their destiny.

Spencer's brush with death still played through his mind. Nakamura's plans now destroyed created more questions than answers for Spencer. With the invasion of Hawaii probably quashed, did this mean that history would be rewritten and there would be no attack on Pearl Harbor? Did it also mean the course of the Second World War had a different climax? Maybe America doesn't join the Allies in its fight against Japan and Germany.

These thoughts went round and round. Once again, he was frustrated in the extreme that there was nobody to confide in. Matt Spinetti and Walter Crabtree would be perfect sounding boards, but he knew once he unloaded his fantastic story he would be whisked away by the men in white coats and administered any variety of bizarre drugs, which would reduce him to a babbling lunatic.

Diving into the water, Spencer felt the tension of the previous days washing off him. He yelped in pain as the salt water stung his wounds.

The bruising and wire cuts into his flesh were starting to heal, even the sting of the salt water on his red raw lesions felt cathartic. The ocean was alive with surfers on their long boards. Spencer swam powerfully out beyond the breakers, grimacing as his muscles responded. With every kick and stroke, it felt as if the salt water was the elixir of life, washing away his pain.

Cursing the fact he had to go to work, Spencer reluctantly headed back to the shore. He towelled himself, his body glowing from the effect of sun and water. He cast an eye longingly again over the gentle surf he'd just left behind. *Hell. Why not? Bugger the* Chronicle *and bloody Vic. I reckon I've earned some more surf time.*

'Woo hoo,' Spencer yelled in exhilaration. The college guys

cheered. 'Go for it buddy.' With that Spencer sprinted back into the surf and swum strongly out beyond the breakers. *Good one, legs.* His relief to have functioning limbs was palpable. For a moment he felt as if he was back in Perth, as a kid revelling in the waves at Scarborough Beach. Reluctantly he thought with a smile, time waits for no man, but then perhaps it doesn't really apply in my case.

Spencer finally body surfed a wave to shore, revelling in the tang of the salt water.

He towelled himself and managed to jog back to his shack. Refreshed in body, but his mind in turmoil. Waiting in the driveway was the familiar grey Plymouth.

'What's the greeting?' Walter smiled. 'G'day, did I get that right?'

'I'll make you an honorary Australian,' Spencer quipped.

'We have news,' beamed an obviously happy Matt Spinetti.

They sat down in Spencer's kitchen and over coffee they told Spencer about the latest developments.

Walter nodded to Matt, opening his notebook. 'Washington totally accepts your story. As we speak the marines are on Molokai and the resistance apparently is minimal. There were a few fanatics who literally launched themselves at our marines armed only with knives, bayonets, and handguns. They were cut to pieces.'

'Suicide by marine,' Matt added with a thin smile.

'On a serious note, the State Department and the President believe although the planned invasion and attack on Pearl Harbor were going to happen next weekend, Sunday the seventh, they now believe the attack has been shelved. But they acknowledge Japan is still potentially a danger. They don't believe Japan would now mount such an attack as the militia force from within has been neutralised, thanks to you and your colleagues. The only downside to the operation so far, is no Nakamura. The *Rising Sun* has disappeared along with … what's his helper's name?'

'That would be Riko.'

'Also,' Walter added, 'we've seen nothing of that malevolent creep Haru. He's probably with them. They were his two most trusted lieutenants.'

'I'm afraid Horse rather killed Haru.' Spencer laughed, almost choking on his coffee.

'I think I owe Horse an apology for the unkind things I've said about him in the past,' Walter acknowledged ruefully.

Spencer took a sip of his coffee, pondering for a moment before speaking. 'You owe a very big thanks to Claude Demmer. Without him, we'd be dead. From what I gathered not a very pleasant death.'

'There's going to be awards and a ceremony for you Horse and Miss Gething.' Matt assured him.

Walter then turned to Matt before speaking. 'I'm not entirely sure you want to know this, but …' He shrugged his shoulders. 'We had a man on the inside at Nakamura's mansion, he's disappeared, we've heard rumours he'd been tortured and …' he hesitated and nodded to Matt again.

Horrified, Spencer glanced at the two men. 'That's bloody terrible … awful … what was he … was he married? Did he have children?' Spencer shook his head and once again he gazed searchingly at Matt and Walter, realising just how close he and Roxanne had come to a brutal finish.

Matt too looked grim faced. 'Yes of course it's tragic, but … it's not quite what you might think. The guy in question was actually a particularly nasty piece of work. We'd previously arrested him for selling heroin to, would you believe—'

'This guy was a button man, selling smack to young fools,' Walter cut in. 'Some no more than school kids … so we sorta gave him an option. Work for us and take your chances, or go down for a ten stretch.'

Spencer had absolutely no idea what a button man was but he understood the evils of the heroin trade so he was inclined to take the view, sometimes you can't avoid collateral damage. But all the same, he felt whatever the operative's crimes were, he didn't deserve to die at the hands of Nakamura.

Clearly Matt and Walter were not exactly losing sleep over the death of their informant.

'Did you see the pool at the front of the mansion?' Matt spoke up.

'Yes, Roxanne wanted to go for a swim in it,' Spencer said.

'That pool had a shark in it, a massive white pointer. The pool was something else. It was kept at the right temperature for such a shark. No expense spared. Apparently, Nakamura's idea of an afternoon's entertainment was to have people he didn't like thrown into the pool so he could watch them being eaten alive. This we believe is what he had in store for you and Miss Gething.'

Spencer shuddered at the memory of being in the clutches of Nakamura and the realisation how close they came to an unimaginable death. Walter and Matt seemed happy to relax and listen to the details of Spencer and Roxanne's encounter with Nakamura.

'Tell us exactly how you managed to escape from the shed.' Matt drained his coffee.

When Spencer described how Horse had enticed the unfortunate Kaito to open the door, they both dissolved into a paroxysm of laughter. The death of Haru, shot by Horse with his silenced automatic, also garnered a smile.

'What we really want,' Matt looked at Walter for confirmation, 'is to get Nakamura under lock and key. But he seems to have vanished off the face of the earth. Sadly, with the *Rising Sun* stocked and fuelled he could be anywhere.'

'If captured, what would happen to him?'

Matt leaned back in his chair, interlocking his hands behind his head, and with a satisfied look. 'Oh yes … because he's a Hawaiian citizen, he would be hanged as a spy, and I can't tell you how much I want to catch the bastard.'

Walter stood up and gazed out of the window at the peaceful beach scene and then abruptly turned to Spencer.

'We have a proposition for you.' Walter seemed nervous as he turned from the window, glanced sideways at Matt, and cleared his throat.

'Let's hear it.' Spencer waited, smiling.

'How would you like to join our team? It would involve some training. It's an interesting job. With your knowledge of Japanese and your obvious street smarts we both think …'

Matt nodded his approval. 'You would be a natural. What do you say?'

Spencer was surprised, the way his trips to the past seemed to duck, dive, and weave in incomprehensible directions made him wonder if there was an unseen force pulling invisible strings.

'Your first job would be to try and track down Nakamura,' Walter continued, 'you'd have virtually unlimited resources. Well, do you need to think about it?'

'Well, I was getting a little tired of Victor Smith.'

The "Battle of Molokai" as it came to be known as, simply couldn't be contained. The explosions had resonated across Oahu. Spencer had the go ahead to write the story—well—most of it. Matt and Walter insisted on censoring small portions.

Victor Smith had been even more tongue-tied than usual but finally managed to spit out, 'Yes well … ' and then a serious round of buts, and ums, and ers. Spencer finally gleaned both he and Roxanne were going to receive a raise in salary.

CHAPTER FIFTY-ONE

NAKAMURA AND THE HORSE

Kaiaulu, the gentle trade wind caresses the Hawaiian Islands, a zephyr that is a balm to the soul. However, it was unlikely Major Nakamura paid attention to this or any other beauties of nature.

In the early hours of the morning the staff at Lee's had already gone home. Peace and quiet reigned. The only light was a small lamp burning in his office.

Nakamura knelt in front of his impressively large open safe. There was a stack of Japanese occupation currency printed and ready to go in anticipation of the conquest of Hawaii. There was also a considerable bundle of US currency with the likeness of one Benjamin Franklin.

With great haste he threw the US currency into a large canvas holdall and sifted through papers he was about to destroy. He knew his masters in Tokyo were an unforgiving lot. Nakamura was unhappy about leaving Hawaii, believing it was his destiny to be the omnipotent ruler of the Hawaiian Islands.

He mentally cursed his stupidity at not executing the Australian and the photographer when he'd had the chance. He had unfortunately relished the idea of seeing them ripped to pieces by the shark in his pool. Even now he licked his lips, and felt a stirring in his loins at the memory of those he'd thrown into the arena, as he liked to think of it.

An uncertain future awaited Major Nakamura in Japan. He wondered if with his large stack of US currency there might be another place where he could sit out the war in comfort and luxury. As these thoughts whirled through his mind, he heard a sound.

He spun around. Hovering in the doorway, all smiles and good humour, was Horse, a long barrelled automatic held rock-steady in his hand.

'How ya doin', Lee?' Horse's smile, as always, was warm and engaging.

Nakamura's face drained of colour. The sight alone of the bizarre figure of Horse with his ridiculous wig was enough to scare any man. To his credit, Nakamura quickly regained his composure. 'Ah, Mr Demmer,' he giggled, 'You gave me quite a start.'

In his safe was a loaded Japanese Nambu 7.9 mm pistol he realised was out of Horse's sight. If he could just distract this bizarre fool for a second. Nakamura felt his confidence returning. As he focussed again on the unusual apparition that was Horse, his smile broadened.

This man really was an idiot. Gun or no gun, he was no match for a major in the Kempe Tai.

'As you can see, I have a large amount of cash here, and,' he added with a smile. 'I'm happy to share it with you.'

'Gee that's real swell of ya.'

'So, would you mind putting down the gun?' He giggled again. 'It does make me nervous.'

'Nah.'

Nakamura decided to change tack. 'I would remind you, I'm a Hawaiian citizen and I'm unarmed.' Nakamura started to feel a little uneasy. There was something unnerving about this big man with his gun pointed unwaveringly at him.

'Unarmed? That just don't seem fair, do it?' Horse even managed to appear sympathetic.

Nakamura rose clumsily and sat on a chair behind his desk. He glanced longingly at the pistol which was now easily within his grasp. With that, Horse delved into his overalls, pulling out a shiny nickel-plated 0.38 revolver. He smiled as he threw it into Nakamura's expansive lap. 'Well,' he said the smile broadening. 'You're armed now, ain't ya?'

As Horse's gun dropped into his lap, he frowned, his head tipped to one side. 'Huh?' His eyes widened as he realised the implications. There was a soft belch from Horse's silenced 0.22 Colt. Simultaneously, a third eye appeared in the centre of Nakamura's forehead. His head fell back against his chair. Horse stood for a moment, glanced around the office, then continued stuffing the money into the holdall, whistling.

Horse gazed again at the scene before him; Nakamura's face aimed at the ceiling, a grotesque look of horror, open mouthed in a twisted grimace, eyes wide open.

Horse paused for a minute. *What to do next?* It'd been suggested by some that Horse was perhaps not the brightest globe in the hardware store. What Horse was good at was thinking under pressure. Possibly because the act of murder wasn't something that fazed him.

Smiling he took the 0.38 revolver he'd thrown into Nakamura's lap, placing it firmly in the now limp hand. Stepping back to admire his handiwork he quietly exited the office.

CHAPTER FIFTY-TWO

AUNT GLADYS

'We have news.' Walter Crabtree's excitement practically galloped along the telephone line.

Spencer pounded away on his vintage typewriter. The story of the encounter with Lee Tai, or Major Nakamura as he was now known, was being banged out laboriously on his cumbersome Underwood, ready for the next edition. The copy had to be submitted to government censors, but it was still the story of the year. Victor Smith was beside himself, proving to be something of a hindrance to getting the story completed.

'Well, er Spencer, well really I think that … yes what I really think is … er … yes er yes that, I think yes, I think that, that you will … that is … that is certainly be in for … be in for a raise.' He beamed owlishly.

'Wonderful Victor. Sorry, I have to take this call from agent Crabtree.'

'Spencer could you, Roxanne, and Horse get over to our office ASAP? Boy, do we have news.'

'We're going to Matt and Walter's office. I'm going to tell Horse. He's invited as well.' Spencer leant over Roxanne's cubicle.

'Horse,' Spencer bellowed across the department. 'Your presence is required by the United States Government.'

'You don't mean me boss?' Horse's face paled as he edged his way nervously into Spencer's office.

'You're the only Claude Demmer I know.'

Spencer smiled to himself, thinking that as a general rule Horse wanted to have as little to do with officialdom as possible.

'Jeez boss what's it all about?'

'Nothing to be alarmed about, Slugger. They love you. It's all kisses and hugs, I'm sure. Follow me troops,' Spencer crooked a finger at Horse and Roxanne.

'Hang on just a minute,' Roxanne cried out as she gathered her bag and camera. 'what's the hurry, is everything ok?'

Victor Smith held up an admonishing finger as they exited the front door. 'Look I … what I mean is …' Victor was ignored as they headed out to the street. Rita smiled and waved, mouthing silently, 'Good luck Spencer dear.'

Spencer strode up to his Ford. 'I'll admit it's a bit mysterious but I think it's good news.' He leaned over opening the car door, pulling the passenger seat forward, motioning Horse to sit in the back.

'I gotta surprise boss, have a look at this.' Horse shut the door of Spencer's Ford and winked at Roxanne.

Parked next to Spencer's car was a new Cadillac four door convertible.

Spencer and Roxanne gawked at each other in stunned amazement.

'Horse!' she exclaimed, 'it's magnificent. Is it really yours?'

'You betcha.'

Roxanne walked around the car, running her fingers lovingly over the gleaming black duco.

Spencer knew the sleek and stylish Detroit product was the pinnacle of American automotive engineering. It was far more impressive than the other vehicles from his century. Elegant in black, with matching black soft top, it was dazzling.

'It's got a radio,' Horse proudly announced.

'How good is this, Spencer?' Roxanne thrust her hand through the open window, stroking the soft leather upholstery.

The rear passenger door opened with a gentle click. Roxanne and Spencer piled into the back seat, feeling like royalty as they reclined on the broad expanse of luxurious cowhide. Spencer reflected that even in the 1940s new cars still smelt like new cars.

Grinning from ear to ear and with the radio softly playing the latest Glen Miller tune, "Moonlight Serenade". Horse eased the column shift into first gear. As he released the clutch, the big sedan glided majestically onto the boulevard.

'Ok Horse, and there's no hurry.' The memory of the hair-raising trip in the jalopy was still fresh in Spencer's mind.

'Yeah, boss. It's gotta 346 cubic inch V8, it's a series 62.' Horse went on to describe gearbox's, brakes, diffs, and all manner of things mechanical. Spencer smiled politely and made appropriate appreciative noises.

The big Cadillac swept silently up to the door of Seismic Photography. Walter leant on the brick pillar of the dusty porch impatiently awaiting their arrival, coffee in one hand and a cigarette in the other.

'Your car?' Walter glared at Horse. He didn't seem to share Spencer's and Roxanne's enthusiasm for Horse's newest toy.

'Anyway, come in, come in.' Walter quickly recovered his good humour.

Walter ushered them into his office, where Matt Spinetti was waiting. 'Horse has a new Caddy.' Walter announced.

'Really? And how were you able to afford that, Horse?'

'Can we leave it for just a moment, what's the news?' Spencer snapped.

'We've found Nakamura. He's dead.' Walter stubbed out his cigarette. 'The staff at Lee's place discovered his body this morning.'

'A single gunshot wound to the head,' Matt confirmed.

'Suicide?' Roxanne queried.

'Well,' Matt continued, 'this is where it gets interesting. Shot between the eyes. Personally, I've never seen anyone commit suicide like that.' Matt gave Horse a probing stare, eyes narrowing. 'What about you Horse, you've been around, you ever see that before?' Matt stared hard at Horse. 'Well Horse, unusual wouldn't you say … BUDDY?'

'I've always said dese Japs are pretty clever.' Horse smiled like a cherub.

'I'll say they're clever.' Matt glared at Horse; his voice now raised. 'Nakamura was holding a 0.38 and he was shot with a 0.22. How clever was that?'

Horse shrugged, staring out of the window, blank faced. 'Peachey day again ain't it?'

'Now here's another strange thing. Nakamura was found with his safe open and a bundle of Japanese occupation currency. Clearly the invasion of Hawaii was a done deal. But here's the odd thing, there was no US currency. You'd think with all the takings from the bar there'd be quite a stash wouldn't you … Horse?'

Horse pondered, and after a minute he raised a finger.

'I know,' he announced. 'Someone broke in and stole the loot.'

'Really? And you turn up with a new Caddy. What do you reckon Horse, would you say that was … just a bit of a coincidence perhaps?'

Horse gave his best 'who me?' look. 'An ole aunt from New Jersey sent me the lettuce.'

'You seriously expect us to believe that?' snarled Walter.

Spencer watched, bemused. *If I didn't know Horse better, even I'd believe him. He should be selling used cars.*

'Aunt Gladys sent me a letter with the moolah. Aunt Gladys

was a school teacher,' he proudly announced. 'She was the only one in the family with any book learning.'

'Now, there's a surprise,' Matt sneered.

'She sent me a letter with the cash.'

'Of course, you no longer have the letter? 'Walter suggested.

'Right here.' Horse fished through his overall pockets, then with much aplomb handed over the missive.

Walter started to read the letter and within seconds was doubled over with laughter, He handed the offending piece of paper to Matt.

> *Dere Claude,*
> *i am poorly the doc ses i got canser so im sending*
> *you munny before i croak.*
> *Yore luving aunt glad.*

Matt handed it on to Spencer, who chuckled and gave it back to Horse. 'School teacher huh?'

'Yeah' said Horse proudly. 'She used ta even read books.'

Matt and Walter were speechless.

CHAPTER FIFTY-THREE

HORSE BREATHES A SIGH OF RELIEF

'Saturday night at seven. Horse as well?'

Walter had rung Spencer. They were all invited to a cookout at Walter's house situated on the beach overlooking Diamond Head.

'May I come in?' Roxanne stood in the doorway of Spencer's cubicle; her brow puckered.

She leant against the door jamb, cigarette in hand. Spencer thought Roxanne looked stunning in her high-waisted trousers with the full legs and cuffs. The fawn trousers with a dark blue shirt seemed to compliment her girl-next-door appearance. Spencer gazed fondly at her. It looked like she'd put her face up to the sky and received a rainbow of freckles.

Roxanne's courage, her *joie de vivre*, and her irrepressible humour all contributed to the growing attraction which Spencer felt. This was playing havoc with his emotions. He knew that with Roxanne it would have to be all or nothing. He mentally cursed the bizarre predicament he was in. No matter how hard he tried, he couldn't see a way of resolving the situation.

Do I explain things? Guess what Roxanne, I'm a time traveller from another century. And then the likely response … Oh really! I'm so glad you shared that with me. It explains everything. Now we can get married and live happily ever after.

Roxanne on the other hand was all business. 'Is Horse off the hook?' she asked bluntly.

Spencer laughed, motioning to one of his office chairs. 'Have a seat, enter the inner sanctum,' he said in a stage whisper. 'Walter and Matt believe absolutely that Horse went to Lee's. Shot him and took whatever cash there was.'

'Wow!' Roxanne sat with a stunned expression. 'It certainly would explain the Cadillac, and … Oh my God! What about that preposterous letter?'

Spencer pushed back his chair, resting his feet on his desk, admiring his latest acquisition, a pair of black and white Oxford shoes matched beautifully he thought with his grey lightly checked trousers.

'But my lovely, there's more to tell.' He waved a forefinger in the air, like a stage ventriloquist about to reveal the mysteries of the universe.

'Stop it, this instant. For God's sake, tell me what's going on. It can't be that bad or you wouldn't be smiling.' Roxanne laughed.

'Well … here goes. Matt and Walter have been kicking this around for some time now. I imagine Horse has been feeling a bit nervous waiting for the knock on the door. But they—'

'They?' Roxanne interrupted.

'Yeah well, they—meaning Matt and Walter and their boss or bosses—know bloody well Horse shot Nakamura and stupidly tried to stage it as a suicide. He then took the loot. Whatever the loot was. Certainly, enough to buy the Caddy. But … and here's the good bit, they figure that a dead Nakamura isn't such a bad thing. It puts an end to what might have been a serious diplomatic incident, and things with Japan are a bit ticklish at the moment. Apparently, Washington now believes

Japan has put the idea of attacking and invading Hawaii on ice. Meanwhile the US is going to pull out all stops in building up the capability of their armed forces.'

'What about Nakamura? How do they explain away a spare corpse?'

'These guys have some serious clout. Nakamura's death is officially a suicide. In fact, I'm just writing up the story now for tomorrow's edition.'

Roxanne grinned. 'So, Horse is off the hook and keeps the loot?'

'Got it in one.'

'And you, me and Horse have been invited to a cookout at Walter's house on Saturday Night.'

'Do you realise what Saturday night is?' Roxanne frowned.

Spencer took his feet off the desk, leaning forward his hands steepled under his chin.

'Yes, Saturday the sixth, the night before the supposed Japanese attack.'

Spencer had almost convinced himself Matt and Walter were right. Surely after what had transpired there was no way the Japanese would now mount their attack on Pearl Harbor, or would they?

CHAPTER FIFTY-FOUR

SATURDAY THE SIXTH OF DECEMBER 1941

Spencer and Roxanne surveyed the scene at Walter's Christmas party. Spencer had arrived in his Ford just as Roxanne was paying the cab driver. Fairy lights were strung across palms and shrubs. The sounds of merriment rang through the air. People were arriving, calling out to other revellers. A record player was belting out swing tunes as couples gyrated across the makeshift dance floor, erected on the crisp green lawn.

'This is noisy. How about we go up there?' He pointed to the balcony on the first floor. 'I can't hear myself think.' Spencer leaned closer to Roxanne.

Roxanne was subdued as they climbed the stairs, Spencer glanced at the ocean the surface rising and falling with rhythmic ease.

The balcony had coloured lights and Christmas decorations, and a barrel cut in half and filled with Budweisers on ice. Spencer grabbed two bottles, snapping the lids off and handing one to Roxanne.

'Well, Miss Gething?'

Roxanne smiled at his formal address.

'I never said, but I thought you were terrific when Nakamura captured us.'

'To use one of your Australianisms, I think I was bloody stupid,' Roxanne replied with a frown. 'Spitting in that creep Haru's face, wasn't the smartest idea.'

As they stood on the balcony, they observed Horse's black Cadillac silently enter the property.

'Look at that?' Roxanne whispered. 'Horse isn't alone.'

An uncharacteristically well-groomed Horse, resplendent in an eye-wateringly bright Hawaiian shirt and a pair of narrow-waisted wide-leg fawn linen trousers and two-tone chocolate and white saddle-shoes, was opening the door of his Cadillac with a flourish.

'Well, well, Horse and Stella, who would've guessed?' Roxanne murmured 'If it wasn't for that silly wig, he'd look like a movie star.

Out stepped Stella. She immediately linked her arm through Horse's.

Spencer and Roxanne both smiled at this unlikely turn of events.

'I hope Stella enjoys boxing,' Spencer joked.

Walter bounded through the door, full of energy and Christmas cheer.

'Spencer, Roxanne, there you are. So glad you made it. Beer's in the icebox, steaks on the barbeque and we have music to dance to.' He disappeared, off to meet and greet guests.

Roxanne was quiet as she leaned against the balcony, soaking up the view of the ocean.

'Who would've thought?' she said quietly. 'Even Horse seems to have found someone.'

Spencer didn't reply. They stood for what seemed an eternity, just taking in the view.

Roxanne suddenly giggled. 'I don't believe it. Stella has

Horse's weapon in her hand and seems to be stroking it.' She then realised what she had said and blushed furiously.

'What on earth,' Spencer amazed at what he'd heard.

Horse and Stella had exchanged pistols each admiring the other's weapon.

Roxanne was still embarrassed at her choice of words and was laughing out loud as was Spencer.

The balcony was decorated with Christmas lights, a decorated tree and oddly for Hawaii, Walter had managed to find mistletoe which he had strung up crisscrossing the balcony.

Roxanne grabbed Spencer's hand and dragged him to the centre of the room.

'What on earth are you doing?' he protested, laughing.

'Spencer Marlowe. You're standing squarely under mistletoe. It's Christmas, and … I love you very much.' With that, she threw her arms around his neck kissing him hard. Spencer felt himself responding. His emotions in a turmoil as he hungrily returned the kiss. He gently moved away, not knowing what to say or do. His feelings for this beautiful woman were intense, his emotional state was being torn apart. The uncertainty of his existence in 1941 Hawaii. The guilt he now felt, thinking he'd betrayed Michiyo.

'Sorry, maybe I shouldn't have done that. I've got to go to the bathroom.' Roxanne mumbled, fleeing with tears in her eyes.

Pacing up and down the balcony Spencer was miserable. For someone who prided himself on being decisive and clear thinking, he was a mess. If only, if only he could explain. This was so unfair and so bloody hopeless.

Standing disconsolately against the timber balustrade, oblivious to the laughter and gaiety downstairs, Spencer gazed at all of the happy people. The barbeque was in full swing with endless quantities of burgers, steaks, and chicken wings, being cooked with military precision by a beer-swigging Walter Crabtree. There was noise and Christmas carols. In fact, everything that made for a celebration.

A group of revellers burst into a spontaneous rendition of Silent Night. Spencer had never felt less like celebrating in his life, as he gloomily surveyed the scene, oblivious even to the calming effect of the mighty Pacific Ocean.

He had no idea how long he'd stood there, but he realised he was not alone; a subdued Roxanne stood next to him. She placed a hand on his arm. She laughed; a laugh tinged with bitterness. 'Don't worry I'm not going to try and seduce you. 'Roxanne turned and faced him.

'I don't understand what's going on, my instincts,' she paused to wipe tears from her eyes. 'My instincts tell me that you feel for me as I do for you. A kiss like that can't be faked. For some reason you're not telling me the truth. You use as an excuse your Japanese girlfriend or fiancé, or whatever she is. As an excuse for there being no us. But you never mention her. You've made no serious effort to be reunited with her. It's been a year since you were released from the lock up. In that time have you made any effort at all to communicate with her. Or her with you?'

Spencer was silent. He couldn't think of a plausible response.

Roxanne turned away from him and for a second gazed down at the happy revellers below. "You Always Hurt the One You Love" could be heard drifting across the palm dotted garden.

'How ironic is that. The song says it all, don't you think?'

Roxanne then changed the subject. 'Just look at that! Stella and Horse are really getting to know each other.'

Spencer's hands were on the handrail as he took in the scene below. Horse and Stella were dancing cheek to cheek on the portable dance floor.

'Lucky Stella,' Roxanne murmured once again with that

slight edge of bitterness. Roxanne turned once again to Spencer. 'When was the last time you received a letter from your … *intended?*' There was a pointed emphasis on intended.

Spencer was silent, in a quandary, not knowing what to say.

'I believe there's something you're simply not telling me. You really need to know that I love you and I trust you, and whatever dark secret there is, you can tell me.' Roxanne came close, touching his hand.

Spencer had an overwhelming desire to pour out the whole unbelievable story.

If ever there was someone, I could trust it's Roxanne. But still he held his tongue.

He remembered the difficulty he had with Michiyo who'd never been able to completely accept his story. Spencer stood there looking a picture of misery.

Walter appeared on the balcony behind them, a Budweiser in his hand. 'Hey, you two party poopers, come and join the gang downstairs. And Spencer, that offer we made to you about joining Matt and I in our business …' he added a sly smile. 'It still stands, even though Nakamura has committed suicide.' He then pointed an accusatory finger at Horse who was attempting a not very professional jitterbug. He shook his head. 'We know Horse is a crook. But we could probably use him on a contract basis as well. Anyway, sleep on it and let us know, ok. I gotta get back to my cooking.' With that he bounded off down the stairs singing lustily.

'Offer? This's the first I've heard,' she said coolly. Roxanne gazed at Spencer the question hanging in the air.

'After we escaped from Molokai Matt and Walter asked me to join them at,' he frowned. 'At Seismic Photography. Do you realise I don't even know the actual name of the government department they work for?

'Are you going to accept?' Roxanne raised an eyebrow.

'With all that's happened I must admit I haven't had much of a chance to think about it. What do you think?'

Roxanne once again turned to the view of the couples on the dance floor.

'Those photos I took of the armaments exploding on Molokai reached the attention of the editor of the *New York Times*. They've offered me a job. In New York.'

This was a development Spencer hadn't considered. He saw before him the beautiful face of Roxanne streaked with tears.

'I guess … what you're saying is …'

'I can't go on like this. Working with you day to day. It's just making me … unhappy. The only thing that can work for me is getting the hell out of Hawaii. And this is my opportunity.'

Roxanne stood, now noticeably keeping her distance from him. She was not the sort of person to dissolve into a torrent of tears. It seemed to Spencer that she was struggling to come to terms with an unpalatable reality. But he knew that with her strength of character, she would move on. She would get over him and ultimately, she would thrive. She was a fighter, a survivor. But at this moment the thought of losing her was simply overwhelming, it was unthinkable.

Spencer stood with his hands on the balcony rails. He had been aware of his growing attraction to Roxanne. Foolishly, he had thought it could be contained. Trying not to dwell upon things, he had figured life as he had come to know it, would just go on. Life would be work, the beach, fishing, in fact everything normal people did. Of course, he wasn't entirely sure exactly what normal people did in 1941. Clearly, they didn't spend time on the internet. Life was in so many ways extraordinarily slow. He was still grappling with the concept that in many cases the only contact was by letter, or expensive and unreliable international phone calls.

The world that Spencer knew, where world affairs, tragedies, natural disasters were beamed around the world in milliseconds, was a lifetime away. He now realised nothing ever stayed the same and that the time had come for a decision. He realised that in this world, the only person who meant anything to him was Roxanne, and the thought of that anchor of stability not being a part of his future, whatever that future was, he found inconceivable. To add to his misery was the feeling he had in some way betrayed Michiyo. He turned to Roxanne and put his hands on her shoulders.

'It's time for me to go. You can't begin to imagine how difficult this is for me. Can we leave it for tonight? I'll call you tomorrow … and try to explain things.'

It felt a little as if a weight had been lifted off his shoulders. The decision no matter what the consequences had been made. Tomorrow he would tell Roxanne everything. If she ridiculed him and decided he was a lunatic, then so be it. He also realised he would have to explain that just as he had mysteriously arrived, it was entirely possible that one day, he would leave in exactly the same way.

For a moment Roxanne was silent, digesting what he'd said. She held his hand, 'You're going to tell me everything? All about your past life, your fiancé, everything?'

Spencer nodded.

'Oh, my God.' Roxanne chuckled. 'I do hope you're not going to tell me you're an axe murderer.'

'Tomorrow, ok?' Spencer leaned over and gave her a chaste kiss on the cheek.

Spencer said his goodbyes. Stella and Horse were in a passionate embrace behind a date palm, so he decided not to interrupt them. He climbed into his convertible and pressed the self-starter. The sound of the side valve V8, burbling musically always seemed to lift his spirits. *It sure as hell sounds better than modern cars.*

For the first time that he could remember, he felt at peace with the world. He concluded that sometimes you simply had to compromise. He had no idea what Roxanne's response was going to be to his story. His underlying problem was not knowing how long he'd be trapped in this time warp for— another day? A month? A year? Fifty years?

The enormity of what the new day would bring was now filling him with anguish. He realised he'd be crossing a line once he told Roxanne all. Spencer loved Michiyo absolutely and had believed he could never betray her—but where on Earth did you turn to get advice on this situation?

For the first time he started thinking about a future. Had the world changed from the century he came from? Would America go to war? What lay in the future for Australia, if the bombing of Pearl Harbor never happened? Should he accept the job with Matt and Walter? Did it mean that after a courtship, Roxanne and he would be married? Would they have children? Spencer's thoughts spun around his head in a whirlwind of confusion. No matter how hard he tried to move on, Michiyo's face appeared before him.

Be realistic, you'll never see her again. Live for the moment, this is what you have, this is real.

He drove on through the peaceful tropical night, smiling as he thought about Roxanne and their kiss. A kiss that had changed everything. A kiss which promised so much more. Rather guiltily he remembered an old saying, ... some love is fire, some love is rust. But the finest, cleanest love is lust.

Spencer's emotions continued to swirl around inside him. Roxanne's tear-streaked face appeared and then the features of Michiyo superimposed over them, and he again was wracked with guilt.

Spencer drove up his rutted rough coral driveway, *I'll have to tidy this place up, I guess.*

Clothed in the anonymity of the night, the six Japanese aircraft carriers (harbingers of death and destruction) steamed towards Honolulu, each sinister bulk cutting through the black ocean.

CHAPTER FIFTY-FIVE

THE WORLD TURNS

Unlocking his door, he turned on the lights and gazed fondly around his simple beach shack with new affection. Feeling pleasantly tired, he dwelt again on Matt and Walter's assurances the attack on Pearl Harbor was now not going to happen.

It seems as if history really had been changed.

In spite of his tiredness Spencer couldn't help again dwelling on the outcome of world events. Once again, he was starting to feel engulfed by the possibilities of the world he now wondered if he was destined to remain in. The euphoria he'd felt on deciding to tell all to Roxanne was replaced with a sense of foreboding as he realised he was in a world of uncertainty. Uncertainty he'd unwittingly added to.

But maybe, just maybe, this is where he was meant to be. Spencer was convinced he had a lot to offer. He envisaged a life with Roxanne, children. Walter and Matt's job offer was intriguing and exciting. Life in Hawaii, even with the drawbacks of the lack of technology, was certainly pleasurable. So what if there were no smart phones or computers, no flat screen TVs? In fact, no TV at all.

Spencer realised the trappings of wealth, were just that. Trappings! Here we have the glorious ocean and all of the pleasures that go with it. We have wonderful culinary delights; the cottage is comfortable, big enough for two. He smiled at the thought of the trusty V8 Ford waiting to be started, the growl of its power plant. Not a BMW with air-con and power steering, but it still gets you where you want to go. These myriad confusing thoughts rampaged through his subconscious. Time for sleep. Still Michiyo's features kept appearing before him.

Things will be clearer in the morning he told himself. Spencer pulled off his clothes and collapsed onto his bed. His thoughts flashed to Trilby Lim as the young brave but terrified woman, and then as the older lady whose life was ebbing away. His keen sense of regret that he wasn't able to tell her the whole fantastic story.

His last thoughts before the blackness of sleep overwhelmed him was the memory of the evil, giggling Nakamura. Horse's gleaming Cadillac. The sly Wayne Kitchener. Roxanne with a tear-streaked face, and then nothing.

***

'Wake up darling. Today you're getting married.'

Spencer glanced at his Rolex; it was four minutes past seven in the morning. He closed his eyes, muttering, 'I'm back, I'm really back.'

'Have you been away?' Michiyo stroked his cheek, she looked troubled.

'Yes.' His voice cracked as he held back tears, 'But I'm here now.'

Spencer's emotions ran through him like an out-of-control rollercoaster. A sense of loss. Roxanne obliterated as if she had never existed. Shame at knowing how close he came to betraying Michiyo. But conquering all, being reunited. He knew that the grief and loss he felt would take time to heal, and the healing process had to be a solitary one. But then he was used to being unable to explain.

Michiyo smiled adding, 'I can't believe that we've chosen the anniversary of the attack on Pearl Harbor for our wedding day.'

THE END

BOOK THREE

MANHATTAN STING

CHAPTER ONE

WELCOME TO THE JUNGLE

T subway from Queens to Manhattan was crowded. A sea of humanity, dense, and motley. A man sat hunched in a corner seat, leaning back against the chromed metal-panelled partition. He drifted in and out of consciousness, stirring occasionally with a start, then floating back into sleep.

This didn't particularly arouse the interest of the other passengers. This was New York, and in the Big Apple, you didn't display too much interest in other people.

A brief moment of consciousness. Spencer Marlowe glanced around at the collection of subway passengers. The gaudy and the gorgeous. The officious, the timorous, the sophisticated, and the bemused.

Where am I?

With a hiss and a clank of brakes, the subway train ground to a halt. The denizens of New York alighted, shuffling to the doors that opened wide, spilling onto the waiting platform.

Spencer followed the teeming throng, looking for inspiration. He found himself surrounded by walls of grey. Grey above. Grey below. Grey faces. A tunnel of black. Yesterday's news, cigarette packets, candy wrappers, overflowing trash cans. He winced at the rancid odour of stale urine, unwashed bodies. A suspicious look, a sideways glance. Were the faces of the city staring?

Where are the mobile phones? Everybody has a mobile. No, please? It can't be.

Spencer clambered up the subway stairs, his sense of foreboding increasing with every step. A light, drizzling rain greeted him as he emerged onto the sidewalk. Unaccustomed to the light, he squinted at the sign—Canal Street Subway Station.

Clad in well-worn tan Oxford shoes, pleated trousers in a nut-brown, check shirt, a chocolate-coloured leather bomber jacket, creased and faded, Spencer peered in disbelief at his image reflected in the mirror of a furniture shop display. Taking shelter under an awning for protection from the now-clearing intermittent drops, he noticed a police officer studying him, navy blue shirt and tie. Law enforcement with a sixth sense for crime and criminality.

Time to move on, I guess.

Spencer shuddered as he waited for the dream to end, inhabiting a twilight zone where sight, sound and smell existed in an ethereal nightmare. His survival instincts told him to move along … play the game … *It's not going to last. We're going out for breakfast. Michiyo said she wants to see Grand Central Station. I'd like to walk across the bridge to Brooklyn. There's just so much to see.*

But still the dream persisted like a nagging toothache that hammers away constantly, reminding you that all's not well. Aimlessly strolling along Canal Street, Spencer turned right into Broadway. The welcoming bright lights of a shop advertising Rolex watches grabbed his attention. Green with a golden crown, the word "Rolex" stretched diagonally across the advertising banner. He glanced at his wrist. No watch. *I had a Rolex.*

A moment of triumph as a sliver of memory returned to him. *It was gold … and stainless steel, nice. A present. Someone important gave it to me.*

ACKNOWLEDGEMENTS

The Hawaiian Intervention is the second installment in the Spencer Marlowe adventure series.

As always, I would like to thank my beautiful wife, Jenny. Had I not had the benefit of her enduring patience and literary skills, these (and no doubt further stories) wouldn't have seen the light of day.

Janet from Red Room Editing, with her extraordinary talents, turned amateurish scribbles into something readable. Her invaluable mentoring over many Zoom sessions would have tested the patience of a saint.

I think it only fair to mention the original inspiration for Spencer Marlowe and the guys who triggered this late-in-life flurry of writing.

For the past three decades a small group of motorcycle buddies and I had ridden Harley Davidsons and other makes of motorcycles across a number of countries: Australia, India, Thailand, Sumatra and beautiful Bali.

We would hire motorcycles and a guide and circumnavigate the island. Many Bintangs would be consumed, and tall tales would become taller with each passing year.

While sitting by the pool at our favorite hotel, the Yulia Beach at Kuta, Bali, I had a brainwave. Why not write a book and incorporate my lunatic motorcycle friends, thinly disguised of course? So, *Spencer's War* came to pass. I had so much fun writing the story I thought, hang on, I'll do another. And so *The Hawaiian Intervention* was born.

Why Hawaii? As it happens, Jenny and I were married in 2006 on a beautiful Hawaiian beach, just as Spencer and

Michiyo had planned in *The Hawaiian Intervention*.

The motorcycle buddies only receive an oblique mention in the second novel, but they do deserve the credit for the initial inspiration. For those readers who know these nefarious friends of mine, they will recognize the similarities, the downright lies, and the not-so-subtle poetic licence.

So, in alphabetic order we have Phil 'The Doc' Beinart, whose medical skills saved at least one life in years gone by.

Along came, Wayne 'never complain' Ginbey. Wayne survived unscathed from those halcyon days of riding Harleys at suicidal speeds through Perth's Darling Range, and wisely decided to retire while his luck held out.

Wayne's brother, Keith 'do you need help with that bottle?' Ginbey, rode with us for many years. Keith periodically fell off his motorbike, fortunately without doing any permanent damage.

Peter 'Popeye' Collings, whose mechanical talents often saved the day, was indispensable when emergency repairs were required. His respect and love for the indigenous people of Australia was certainly inspiring.

'The Toad', Ian Lenane was there through thick and thin. An argumentative little bastard with a heart of gold, he certainly stood tall amongst his peers.

Dave 'The Spook' Bidstrup. What can I say about Biddy? A talented auto electrician who got us out of trouble more than once.

A more recent blow-in, Dave 'Betty' Weadley, was a football tragic with a keen interest in literature.

Martyn Farrand who joined the group, foolishly believed British motorcycles could keep up with Harley Davidsons. Oh boy, was he wrong. After many years he saw the error of his ways and bought a real bike.

George 'The Framer' Demmer was another keen rider. George's plan was to own the largest collection of motorcycles in the Southern Hemisphere. At last count he was close to achieving his objective.

Alan 'The Killer' Lambert is renowned for his placid nature. Shy and sensitive Alan was certainly diverse in his interests and hobbies. His collection of vintage Victorian walking sticks was most impressive.

ABOUT THE AUTHOR

Over recent years Kelvin has developed a late-in-life passion for writing and is the author of *Spencer's War*, *The Hawaiian Intervention*, and co-author of the musical autobiography, *Oh How We Rocked*. He lives in Dianella, Western Australia and is currently working on sequels in the Spencer Marlowe series, as well as a crime noir novel *The King of San Francisco*, with a co-author.

Follow Kelvin on Facebook